# COSMOPOLIS

Published in the United States by Cleis Press Inc., P.O. Box 8933, Pittsburgh, Pennsylvania 15221, and P.O. Box 14684, San Francisco, California 94114.

Printed in the United States.
Cover and text design: Cecilia Brunazzi
Cover illustration: Ward Schumaker
Typesetting: CaliCo Graphics
Logo art: Juana Alicia

First Edition.
10 9 8 7 6 5 4 3 2 1

Grateful acknowledgment is made to the following for permission to reprint previously published material: "Fud-u-u-a!" by Miriam Tlali originally appeared in *Soweto Stories*, Pandora Press, London, 1989; reprinted by permission of the author. "Leaving Home" by Rosie Scott originally appeared in *Queen of Love*, Penguin Australia and New Zealand, 1989; reprinted by permission of the publisher. "The Women's Baths" by Ulfat al-Idlibi is reprinted by permission of Three Continents Press, 1901 Pennsylvania Avenue NW, Washington DC 20006. Copyright © 1988 by Michel Azrak and M.J.I. Young. "A View on Spain" copyright © 1990 by Simone Fattal. "Rootlessness" copyright © 1990 by Eilis Ni Dhuibhne.

Library of Congress Cataloging-in-Publication Data
Cosmopolis : urban stories by women / edited & with an introduction by
    Ines Rieder. — 1st ed.
        p.   cm.
    ISBN: 0-939416-36-0 : $24.95. — ISBN: 0-939416-37-9 (pbk.) : $9.95
    1. Fiction—Women authors. 2. Women—Fiction. 3. City and town
life—Fiction. 4. Fiction—20th century. I. Rieder, Ines, 1954 - .

PN6120.92.W65C67   1990
808.83″9321732″082—dc20                                                    90-32596
                                                                              CIP

# COSMOPOLIS
## Urban Stories by Women

### edited by Ines Rieder

CLEIS
PRESS
PITTSBURGH•SAN FRANCISCO

I would like to take this opportunity to thank my families on both sides of the Atlantic as well as my friends who have made it possible for me not only to work on *Cosmopolis* but also to lead a cosmopolitan life. I can live on and move back and forth between different continents only because their homes are always open to me.

Most of all I want to thank Marlene, who has been my soundboard, advisor and critic all along. Felice Newman and Frédérique Delacoste from Cleis Press have given me the best support publishers can give, and Laura Lynn Brown has been a patient copy editor. I also want to mention all those who have been actively looking for material, who have helped solve translation and editing problems and who discussed ideas with me: Alison Read, Amy Christiansen, Cecilia Brunazzi, Emiko Terasawa, Eric LeRouge, Jill Hannum, Laskshmi Kannan, Micha Warde, Patricia Sieber, Shanta Gokhale, Silvia Artacho, Takamori Kazueko. I would also like to thank Barbara Wilson from Seal Press, Urvashi Butalia from Kali Press, and the women from Attic Press, Dublin, and Orlanda Frauenverlag, Berlin, for putting me in contact with a number of writers. A special thanks to the publishing houses which gave me reprinting permissions.

Throughout the book foreign words are not italicized. Whenever their meaning is clear in the context, they are left untranslated; otherwise a translation is provided within the text. Personally, I'm not very fond of footnotes and I thought that it would be in the spirit of a cosmopolitan collection to neither highlight nor eliminate expressions which are frequently used in other cultures. For the same reason, British spelling has been retained for stories from cities where British rather than American spelling is the standard for written English.

# Contents

# CITIES ON THE EDGE

# CITIES TIED TO THE PAST

# Tales of Many Cities

Ever since I can remember I have been fond of traveling, curious to venture out and get a taste of something new. As a teenager with virtually no money in my pockets, but with a sleeping bag and an address book filled with names of people whom I didn't know, I took off to discover the old European cities. I did lots of hitch-hiking then; it was much cheaper than taking the train, and you did see things differently from a car window. I watched the landscape with fascination, but I never stopped long enough to enjoy life in the country—the goal was to reach the city, any city.

Having grown up in Vienna, one of the old European capitals, I took city life for granted. Hurrying along through crowds of people, inhaling car pollution, listening to the squeaking noise of streetcars passing by, going to the theater several times a week, and spending hours in cafés—all this seemed to be the most natural thing in the world. I enjoyed the city's anonymity, going places without being recognized and sitting among people without having any social obligations. I moved as easily through Vienna as I later moved through Paris, Rome and New York. The speed might vary, the people might talk to each other in different languages, but in the end, it didn't matter. Urbanity has its own rhythm, and city patterns have their own rhyme.

On my first and only visit to India I began to question all my notions about city life. There cities had lost all coherence; like a dress whose seams were bursting, I found the cities of India beyond human control. It was 1978, and I asked myself if this was what our future would be like. In the early eighties, I stayed in Cairo, Mexico City and Istanbul, and those visits left me with the same uneasy, almost bewildered sensation which I had experienced in Bombay and Calcutta.

But then I was only a tourist. The real trial did not come until 1984 when I moved to São Paulo, Brazil. After a few months, I knew for sure that this wasn't a city to grow old in. Later I wondered if there was any city left in this world in which I would like to be in my old age.

Is it a consolation to know that millions live in similar circumstances? The same pollution and around-the-clock ear-pierc-

7

ing noise of construction crews. The same loss of all notions of space and dignity. The same overpriced food, whose origin is unknown and whose flavor has been made indistinguishable by chemicals. The same frenzy, speed, lack of time, the same alienation and loneliness.

Nevertheless, we are drawn to the big cities, and we seem to have left behind small towns and villages forever. Almost everything desired by human beings living in post-industrial societies can be found in cities. Jobs, entertainment, easy access to all means of communication. Those of us who have grown up in big cities, or who have moved to them, are too attached to their ever-changing melody and cannot fathom returning to the monotony of the country.

Very much to the dislike of people in big cities everywhere, cities are in constant flux. It's not only the houses or the streets which change, but also the people who walk those streets and who live in those houses. Cities need migrants to stay afloat and to grow. But the "natives" (themselves the children of migrants) often reject these newcomers, since they have been made to believe they own their cities. People move to the city for opportunities, most of which are of course never realized. And the examples of the few who have made it are quickly turned into fiction, which in turn perpetuates the dreams which motivate all those ready to come.

Who owns the cities? I often tend to think the owners are a nameless, faceless, anonymous mass, whose most visible representatives seem to be politicians, bureaucrats, street people and the police. Women are offered few opportunities, either for self-realization or happiness. Under these circumstances it's not surprising that some of the women whom you will meet in this book are crushed by the cities they live in, others are perplexed or bewildered, and only a few are looking for alternatives.

Cities are as old as history itself. And every city likes to make believe that it is the center of the world. In a certain sense, a true city has to be a center, created of its own universe.

Historically, the majority of people have lived in the country. Prior to 1800 few cities had more than a million residents. In 1800, only two and a half percent of the world's population lived in urban areas. By 1900, there were ten cities with more than a million people. In 1970 the United Nations claimed that already twenty-eight percent of the world's population lived in urban places, which by UN standards are places with more than twenty thousand inhabitants.

By 2000, the UN predicts half the world's population will live in cities—including up to seventy-five percent of Latin Americans. São Paulo and Mexico City will each have over twenty-four million inhabitants. New York will seem small by comparison.

When I seriously began to look for contributions to *Cosmopolis*, I had all these things on my mind. I wanted to collect writings which reflect our lives in the cities, stories appealing to our fantasy that would let us forget the day-in day-out conditions that make us sad or incite us to get up and do something when something can be done. I wanted to show life in some of these mega-cities to give readers a glimpse of the future, which is already the present for women living in Bombay, São Paulo, Mexico City. I wanted to present the great metropoles of the age of industrialization and capitals of centuries-old traditions such as Rome, London or Vienna. I envisioned narratives about Damascus, supposedly one of the oldest continuously inhabited cities in the world, San Francisco, one of the most popular, and Soweto, in the news as the symbol of resistance to apartheid since its 1976 riots.

I was lucky to receive stories from these cities and many others. It wasn't easy to find all of them and it was even more difficult to sort through them and make a selection. Until the very end I had hoped for manuscripts from Rio, Buenos Aires, Lagos and Moscow—for various reasons they never materialized. I also had thought that I would get to see a larger number of stories from smaller, but equally famous cities.

Since women are often the perceived outsiders, city heroines created by women writers are often strangers who have entered a world which is not theirs. They may be lonely and alienated. In "Strangers in Paradise," the first section of *Cosmopolis*, the stories range from Rosanna Fiocchetto's fantasy of Rome as a world leader in urban disintegration to Fae Myenne Ng's San Francisco tale of survival in a story whose characters share no common language, not even the language of the country in which they live.

Even those women who have grown roots in a city, because they were born there or have lived there for a long time, experience personal alienation, often combined with the growing pains of the city. In "Urban Growing Pains" we see how women respond to this estrangement in whatever way they can. In Berta Hiriart's Mexico City, an elderly woman arms herself against the demolition team which comes to take her house. Maria-Antònia Oliver's

Barcelona represents one woman's inner world, a love song to a city.

"Cities on the Edge" gathers stories of the political turbulence of our time. Here we see how political circumstances force women to action. In some cases, like Micha Warde's Beirut, women are reduced to verbal condemnation, because armed conflicts carried out by men limit women's possibilities for action. In Lydia Schend's Berlin, two women walk the streets to spit and wipe and rub out the graffiti of fascists. In Caitlin Richard's Washington D.C., a television-drugged woman tallies a month of murders.

Finally, we have "Cities Tied to the Past," the tranquil aftermath. Here we have the timelessness of rituals, as in Ulfat al-Idlibi's account of the women's baths of Damascus. And Elizabeth Wilson's description of a hot summer day in London, once the center of a powerful empire. Now, with the empire gone, people have to adapt to a new post-imperial way of life.

Current political events in Eastern Europe made it difficult to complete this project. I was prepared for a quiet fall 1989—after all, a rather uneventful decade was coming to an end. I knew that changes were on the agenda, but I had thought that it would be another three or four years before the so-called Iron Curtain would come down. The opening of the Berlin Wall, the new government in Prague, the founding of a Party for the Homeless in Hungary—all these events came long after the stories in *Cosmopolis* had been written.

I don't think I would have approached this anthology any differently, except for including more Eastern European stories, but when it came down to working on the final editing, I was torn between my work and sitting in cafés, reading all the available newspapers. At first I could not believe that the world I had grown up in was no longer the same. Over the weeks I have gotten used to the idea, and a brief stay in Prague in December, right at the time of the presidential elections, allowed me to see with my own eyes that the old order is being dismantled.

As a city person, I'm excited about all these events. How women will fare in all this is quite impossible to predict. By presenting these global tales, I hope to inspire women not only to look out their windows, or to peek into their neighbors' yards, but to open their doors and step out into the streets of their cities.

Ines Rieder
Vienna
February 1990

# STRANGERS IN PARADISE

# ROME
ROSANNA FIOCCHETTO

*According to Rosanna Fiocchetto, the main activities of the Romans are: "to move for various reasons from one end of the city to the other in their cars since it's impossible to use the inefficient public transport system; to go shopping; and to drive around for hours searching for a parking space. Once in a while some organization calls a meeting on traffic problems, but these meetings never take place because the conference papers and the participants arrive too late due to traffic congestion."*

*To have a car of her own is essential for a woman living in Rome. "While sitting in a traffic jam—and I spend many hours this way—I write. In my car, I elaborate strategies, have discussions with friends, make up with my lover, eat a snack. . . I always keep paper and pen, as well as a small library, in my car. During the Soccer World Championship this summer, traffic will come to a total standstill; then I will write an entire book while sitting on my four wheels."*

*Rosanna Fiocchetto was born in Rome in 1948 and has lived there all her life. She works at Rome's women's bookstore; founded Estero, the lesbian publishing house; is co-president of the Centro Femminista Separatista di Roma, Rome's autonomous women's center, and the Italian Lesbian Association. She has published many essays, nonfiction books and poems.*

12

# The Day Rome Went Crazy

Suddenly Rome went crazy. One never begins a sentence with an adverb, but Rome really did go crazy suddenly.

There had been some almost imperceptible warning signals. Hardly anyone had noticed. But nobody could have guessed what would happen later on. Only I had some suspicions; I felt the wind of folly on my back and had an irresistible desire to laugh, jump up, and do somersaults. This was without doubt strange, since I am usually serious and very sad. But other disconcerting things occurred, a sort of revolt of the objects.

It started with the clocks: Friday, May 17th, at eight in the morning, they all stopped for a minute at the same time. Then their hands jumped an hour ahead, after which they went back to functioning regularly. This abnormal behavior by pendulums, timers, alarm clocks, cuckoos and even sundials provoked chain reactions all day: school children, believing they had awakened too late, rushed to school, crossing the streets so fast that twenty were run over and killed by cars. Traffic was paralyzed by people who hurried to work, surprised by time's sudden flight. Countless people had terrible arguments due to a nonexistent delay; altogether chaos ruled until everybody understood that, mysteriously, a whole hour had been stolen. Since it was too difficult to convince everyone to set back their clocks, the authorities gave up and decided to close the matter.

Thus the first wave of folly passed without official repercussions. But then it was the phones' turn: whoever tried to make a call was connected with an unknown party. Calling was like playing roulette: one hit on the right number only by luck. The puzzle

13

drove technicians crazy all day. They hypothesized about sabotage or a magnetic storm which could have disturbed the circuits; they considered every possibility, but the phenomenon continued. Finally, exhausted, they postponed working on the problem until the next day.

That night, a gigantic colorful rainbow appeared in the sky, visible from all the neighborhoods of the city: for half an hour one could hear thousands of people "oohing" about the marvel of the century; then it silently disappeared, dissolving in stupendous fireworks.

And then, at dawn, the first fires of folly began to light. The fountains in all the squares began to boil, exhaling heavenly pink fumes surrounded by azure light; then transparent soap bubbles began to gush out of the fountains, bursting with a ringing sound when they came into contact with the air.

In the university's main auditorium, gloomy Professor Ercole Muratore suddenly used his deep baritone to sing his daily Latin lessons. Nobody could stop him, neither during his lesson, nor during the following hours. After a few weeks, the professors who could not stand opera were forced to hand in their resignations to avoid nervous breakdowns.

Suddenly the white, pharaonic monument of Vittorio Emanuele II in Piazza Venezia was transformed into a gigantic Smith-Corona typewriter, whose keys struck on their own. Paper, a hundred meters wide, was inserted in the typewriter's thick roller. Neat letters in elegant italic type were printed on it, clearly visible from far away. Under the eyes of the horrified passers-by, an invisible author composed line after line of odd poetry and sonnets. Unseen hands then pulled out the finished sheet, rolled it into a ball, threw it up in the air, and made it disappear among the clouds.

The Colosseum was filled to the brim with earth and turned into an enormous flower vase. On the ruin's slopes a primitive and rare vegetation of unusual proportions began to sprout: red tulips high as trees; feline carnivorous Brazilian plants with a sinister and bloodthirsty look but also with splendid and hypnotic colors; Tuberoses, amaryllis, fuchsias, begonias, tiger lilies, violet irises, swaying lilacs, bright edelweiss, monstrous snapdragons, pale narcissus and shameless poppies. Their intense and hypnotic smell stunned the curious who had approached to admire them. People were intoxicated and infected with a wild desire to dance. The old blooming amphitheater was surrounded by couples dancing whirling waltzes, or by single people who, possessed by a silent melody, pirouetted, jumped into the air, joined with others in a happy jig, and pretended to dance the steps of a sensual tango or gave themselves up to a frantic can-can.

Meanwhile, similar reports arrived from abroad: the folly which had let loose in Rome, caput mundi, seemed to have infected the whole planet.

In Paris, an imposing flock of birds from all continents thronged the Eiffel Tower. Birds of prey, migratory birds, waders, diving birds and galliformes glided to their destination after their long flights, resting happily on the tower's iron structure. Small, astute hummingbirds came trilling; then charming, shivering birds-of-paradise arrived from the tropics. Next, bewildered by the heat, the penguins arrived; and blinking their dazed eyes, the night birds. The stormy petrel approached, bringing along clouds pregnant with rain; the solemn eagle intimidated many of the smaller birds. The swallows shot off like white arrows, occupying the top of the tower; the magpie took a place under the arch, bowed by the weight of stolen jewels lugged in its beak. The albatross and the seagull carried a salty sea-smell; the lyrebird, the toucan, the ibis, the heron and the golden pheasant were especially admired because they arrived in such an elegant line. At the end came a throng of finches, sparrows, robins, goldfinches, bullfinches, titmice and canaries, while the parrots with their loud voices directed landing operations.

The Tower was swarming with feathers, colorful tails, magnificent wings and tufts of down. Many built nests and sat on eggs; others scratched about or pecked each other affectionately. Most of the birds, excited by this extraordinary encounter, chattered nonstop, each in its own language, flapping their wings, squawking, chirping, cooing, hissing, peeping, croaking, trilling, warbling. The Eiffel Tower disappeared under this tide of birds, and seemed to move and fly about. There was terrible confusion until all the birds, as if obeying an enigmatic command, began to sing together, striking up the Internationale.

In Moscow, the fifteenth-century towers of the Kremlin melted slowly like burning candles. The ground of Red Square turned pea-green within a second, provoking an urgent meeting of the Supreme Soviet to decide a name change. Next, river traffic had to be interrupted due to a similar unexplainable phenomenon. From the Baltic Sea, the White Sea, the Caspian Sea, the Black

Sea and the Sea of Azov the most diverse kinds of fish, from cod to sturgeon, from eels to sharks, all converged in the Don, by swimming upstream in the canals. They darted and swam in orderly lines according to their size: minnows, anchovies, carp, tuna, mullets, sardines, mackerel, tench and dolphins, without deigning to look at one another, while occasionally sticking their heads out of the water as if to look at the scenery. After reaching the capital they made a brusque about-face, concluded their outing, and went back to where they had come from. No one understood what their goal was, because fish are singularly devoid of expression.

The White House in Washington turned bright red. All CIA and FBI agents were mobilized to find those responsible for what was defined as an international provocation by the Soviet-Cuban secret services. But even the best informed sources could not solve the mystery. The President of the United States ordered the building bleached white to eradicate the infamous color. A squadron of one hundred bleaching specialists worked day and night for a week, trying numerous types of solvents, but they didn't succeed in even brightening up the red. The new red epidermis stubbornly resisted every attempt to do away with it. In the end, everybody had to resign themselves to the harsh reality: it was indelible. The President had only two options: to move someplace else, or to accept the current situation and change the wallpaper to match the rest of the residence. He wavered for a long time between these alternatives, incapable of making a choice because of the sudden shock; finally, after having spent many sleepless nights, eight kilos lighter and prey to an uncontrollable nervous tic, he preferred to resign.

Besides, the country had become ungovernable. This political and economic crisis was in fact provoked by a curious metamorphosis: the gold bars kept in Fort Knox had all been transformed into milk chocolate. This had caused a violent disturbance on the stock market, surpassing the famous and violent crash of 1929. To make the situation worse, all the computers malfunctioned simultaneously: they refused to transmit stored data. To show symbolically that they had renounced memorization, their screens obsessively showed only one old film, "Queen Christina" with Greta Garbo.

A new Great Depression hit the United States, and consequently the entire world, causing a massive return to barter economy. The instability was so great that people no longer trusted money. Almost everyone hid it away hoping for better times, and new value relations were established in the streets, as in the great oriental bazaars: for an egg-laying hen one could have a television set; a book was exchanged for a pack of cigarettes. On top of that, the military hierarchy had disintegrated and overnight the Pentagon had become a Triangle, a transformation which was claimed as a victory for the women's movement.

Considering the dire situation, it might have been easy for any nation to start a blitzkrieg, profiting from its adversaries' disarray, and take over world power. But all countries had their own fish to fry: the governments still in power were so busy stemming the tides of collective craziness that they had no time to nourish war ambitions.

In Wolfsburg, Germany, the workers at the big Volkswagen factory refused to go on producing cars, trucks and tractors; they began to produce tricycles on the assembly lines.

Gangs of nomadic clowns, until recently faultless government employees or incorruptible bankers, were traveling all over Europe performing terrible jokes and spraying whomever they met with water pistols. Hundreds of people dressed as Superman were determined to help people who did not need them, with their nonexistent superpowers.

The recently founded UAC, Union of Autonomous Children, born from the ashes of UNICEF, organized an imposing marathon on roller-skates from the Alps to the Pyramids, and about ninety percent of the kids capable of peeing on their own ran away from home to join in.

The Pope decided to give his wealth to the people; but, even stranger, nobody was willing to accept it. Adult males, thanks to a sudden development of their mammary glands, began to nurse the newly born, and formed thousands of collectives to demand the opening of baby-parking in all work places. Women, on the other hand, gazed into each other's eyes and fell in love, as if swept away by a love epidemic: many who met in supermarkets were seized by a sudden coup de foudre, and ran away together, leaving their shopping carts behind. Countless political parties were formed, and their platforms included the most varied objectives, from liberating bees from forced honey production to recycling phone booths, useless by now, into single-unit discotheques.

Thus, slowly but surely, everybody got used to living in an

unsystematic system, in convulsive change, unpredictable and illogical. To be secure meant to be sure of nothing. Today nobody remembers the day on which the world went crazy, because folly has a short memory. But I remember that on that day in Rome, when it all began, the first and only ones to happily welcome the upsetting of normal life were lesbians.

*Translated from Italian by Ines Rieder and Cecilia Brunazzi*

# TANGIER
SIMONE FATTAL

*Tangier is truly the model of an international city. It was first a Phoenician trading post, then an Arab city, and finally under Spanish occupation until 1923, when it was officially declared an international city, governed by Britain, France, Spain, Portugal, Italy, Belgium, The Netherlands, Sweden, and, later, the United States. In 1956 Tangier was integrated into the newly recognized kingdom of Morocco. Because of its special status as an international city, it became the refuge and often the home of many expatriates.*

*Simone Fattal was born in Damascus, where she spent her childhood. In 1967 she settled in Beirut. She studied philosophy in Lebanon and France, and spent the next ten years painting. She moved to the United States in 1980 and founded The Post Apollo Press, a literary feminist publisher. She translates literature into English from French and Arabic. In recent years, she has spent time in Tangier.*

# A View on Spain

I entered the Rembrandt Hotel. A lot of people were in the hall. I recognized an old friend from Beirut; although she had put on a lot of weight, the smile and gestures were unmistakably hers.

"Hello, Mouna," I said. "What a surprise to see you here in Tangier!"

"It's unbearable and intolerable here," she cried. "We arrived this morning from the States, spending a night on the plane, and then we had to wait an hour at the airport for a bus. Since eight o'clock this morning we have been in this lobby waiting for our rooms!"

It was about noon.

"Wow," I said, "how come? This is terrible indeed."

"Well, I don't really know what's going on. They told me at the desk that they have to wait for the manager, and that the manager is asleep and that nobody is to wake her up."

"What brought you here?"

"I have been invited with this group of professors from the U.S. to attend the Asilah Summer Festival. Do you know about it?"

The Asilah Summer Festival started a few years ago in the little town of Asilah, an hour south of Tangier. It had expanded from a small festival just for artists and musicians into a more ambitious one, and this year they had added professors to participate in the intellectual and political debates.

"Yes, I know about the Festival. I'll be going there too. I'm spending the summer in Tangier, and I'll be there."

We were interrupted by a sudden bustle. We saw the porter rush up to a young woman of startling beauty who was descending the stairs. Her long black hair was coming down over her shoulders. We couldn't believe our eyes. Was she the manager that nobody had dared to wake up? Mouna said, "I imagined her to be a formidable, authoritarian, older woman. But she looks so young, so rested and well. . ."

At last the rooms were assigned to the party from the States. They left and for a while the lobby was empty.

I had come from my own hotel to the Rembrandt to have lunch on the terrace. The view from there was superb. I also liked the fact that the Rembrandt reproductions, which must have adorned the hotel's walls since its opening, were still there. The Rembrandt was probably built in the late twenties or early thirties. It had belonged, I was told, to an American fellow. He must have had a special predilection for the Dutch painter. The pictures presented a tremendous contrast to the glaring light of the outside world.

I looked at the dark portraits. I always stayed longer in front of Lucretia's portrait, whose original I had seen at New York's Metropolitan Museum. Lucretia, wearing a white glowing satin dress, is looking straight at the viewer. Her eyes express the ultimate wonder at the injustice of the world. Her innocence has been abused. She has been betrayed and she is forced to commit suicide. She is dying and still holding the dagger that she used. A few drops of blood are dripping. The first time I saw this painting I nearly fainted. Nowhere had I seen more despair and questioning than in the eyes of that young woman. To have found it in this unlikely place made me shudder every time I saw it.

I could never stand her stare too long, so I hurried to the terrace to look out on the water and the faint blue line opposite the bay.

It was a beautiful day and one could see very clearly quite far. I tried to imagine the life of the hotel's first owner. Was he a painter himself? Could there be a further connection between the inner world of the Dutch master and this landscape? Could one find an unsuspected affinity between Rembrandt's fascination with innocence and guilt and this city, associated so much with sin and primeval life?

The sea was azure blue. I could hear a few cries. I had expected Tangier to be more like Beirut, a city with a lot of noise. But there was little traffic. The afternoons were quiet and the mornings were moderately busy. I had come from the bank where I had gone to change some money. I had seen a rather elegant, very thin man in his fifties waiting in line. He was tanned and wearing shorts. Nervously he had come up to the clerk, holding a golden credit card in his hand.

"Sir," he said in French,"I need fifty thousand dirhams, the same as last week. Is it OK?"

"Of course," replied the clerk readily.

"Then I will be back for them in half an hour." He disappeared.

I wondered how this man could spend the equivalent of five thousand dollars a week in cash here in Tangier. On what? Drugs, young men, orgies? But all these can be had for so little. I felt uneasy, confronted with something I didn't quite want to understand or think about.

And so I had crossed to the Rembrandt Hotel. I was sipping my wine, lost in the contemplation of the sea, when a couple came to sit at the table next to mine. I recognized the beautiful hotel manager. Her companion was a handsome middle-aged American man. He could have been cast in a Hollywood movie, if Hollywood were still making the romantic films we have been brought up on. In those films the hero goes to Tangier looking for adventure.

"How beautiful it is," he said. "This bay is so big!"

"This is not the bay," she laughed. "The bay is only there, to the right. What you are seeing on the other side is Spain!"

"Spain!" he exclaimed.

"Yes," she said, "Spain! I have a view on Spain, right from the window of my room."

He took her hand and kissed it, and they were lost in each other's eyes.

"I hope we will look at that view together," he said, still holding her hand. They lowered their voices and I stopped listening to their conversation. I was leaving anyway.

At the hotel's entrance I met Mohammad Chukri, the writer, and we went to have a cup of coffee.

"How is Paul Bowles these days?" I asked.

"He is very ill. He no longer receives people the way he used to. Only an hour a day, between six and seven in the evening. It has been his destiny," he added, "to live here. It was Gertrude Stein who told him to go to Tangier. That was in Paris in 1931. He came and stayed."

"Yes indeed, his destiny."

"It is as if he was from here," he went on. "There are three storytellers who go to Paul Bowles and tell him their stories. He listens to them and then he writes it all down. As for me, it is entirely different: I write my own stories and I write them in classical Arabic."

"And how does Paul Bowles understand their language?"

I looked at Mohammad. Behind the pale and aging chronicler of Tangier, I saw the young boy he must have been, prey to the foreign men who come here because youths are so handsome and so poor. In this culture, it isn't shameful for a young boy to lose his virginity, especially if he can bring home some money to the family.

"Remember Mahmoud Darwich, the Palestinian poet, when he came to the Asilah Festival a few years ago? He complained about the hotel, the food, the organization? Wasn't that funny?"

"Yes, but thousands attended his poetry reading."

I wondered why Mohammad Chukri had not been invited to the Asilah Festival along with so many writers from the Arab world. He trembled at my question; suddenly he reminded me of the Frenchman at the bank, shaking in the same way. But where one could see an uneasiness and a devious gaze in the Frenchman's eyes, Mohammad's eyes were clear and looked straight into mine.

"There are an awful lot of bookstores in Tangier," I said. "It's a pleasure to see that."

"Yes," he said, "people are reading more and more about religion."

"I understand. I would too if I lived here."

We strolled around town and walked down the little alleys. Passagio Di Alphonse XIII. I enjoyed reading the street names; they still had their original signs, going back to the days before Tangier was reunited with Morocco. Because of the varying architecture I could study history as I walked along. There was the Spanish rococo theater with ornate balconies and wrought-iron fences. There were the Italian-looking villas that one sees around the Mediterranean—in Alexandria, Beirut or even Damascus and Istanbul. There were the stairs leading to the souk lined with shops, hidden behind encumbered doors.

The town must have been so lovely in the old days. But now a lot of buildings were in decay. We entered through a huge wooden sculptured door which led to a warehouse. At one point, it must have been a very important khan. The inner courtyard under the huge dome was still empty; modern shops had opened along the sides, replacing the bags delivered by caravans. But was that a real change? In fact, this is why I love Tangier. I can feel that the city has a very private life, but at the same time it has always been cosmopolitan. It has a traditional ritualistic Islamic way, as if there is no past but a continuous present.

As I was leaving the souk, I involuntarily bumped into a woman. I turned around to excuse myself and I was stunned by the extreme horror she expressed. Her eyes were fixed on me from behind her veil, which covered her whole face with the exception of her eyes. Nobody has ever stared at me with so much majesty and dignity. She did her utmost to convey—without words—her outrage. I had transgressed her space, and maybe her world, and she was turning this incident into a confrontation. She was offended, and she was telling me so with her whole being. There was no pardon for it, no matter how many excuses I uttered over and over again.

I was back at the door of the Rembrandt, where I saw the group from the States boarding the bus to Asilah. I decided to join them.

I have always enjoyed the hour-long ride to Asilah, and I especially liked the moment when, at a certain curve of the road, the ocean appears. Each time I would think of Tarek Ben Yazid. I had the impression that he also had come to that spot by the ocean, and that the ocean had stopped his horse. The Arab conqueror, who had come all the way from Homs, had then turned his horse's bridle to the right and gone up the coast to cross the mountain which leads to Spain and bears his name. (Gibraltar, of Arabic origin, is the contraction of two words: Djebel, mountain and Tarek, the conqueror's first name.)

When we arrived in Asilah, to my surprise and shock I saw huge blocks of concrete aligned on the jetty by the thousands. They looked like the work of a conceptual artist.

"What on earth is that?" I cried.

"They are building a port," someone answered. "But don't worry, it's going to be a fishermen's port."

"A fishermen's port, indeed! Who are they fooling? Asilah has a fishermen's port. They don't need to build a jetty of that magnitude just for Asilah's fishermen! They must be building a port for big boats, big yachts. Possibly for the tourists' yachts that the cultural festival is supposed to be luring to these shores."

That evening, while I was having dinner at the restaurant with my good friend Farid, I felt dejected, in spite of the evening's loveliness. The people of Asilah and of the country around it were walking up and down the Corniche. What will become of them if Asilah turns into a haven for tourists? Will they end up being the servants of these strangers or will they be pushed back, somewhere inland, leaving the shore to the exclusive benefit of foreign money?

Farid, a sculptor who regularly spends his summers in Asilah, was also apprehensive.

"The port is being built by Romanians. They got the contract since they had offered the best and cheapest conditions. They have come here with everything they would need during their stay. The other night I saw a fisherman with a big grouper. I congratulated him on his catch, but he told me that a Romanian had caught it and had sold it to him. The Romanians even brought the food they would need while working here."

We were sitting under the vine of the moorish café. I could just picture the signs all along the jetty glowing and beeping: "The Cheapest Lobster," "The Cheapest Prawns," "The Cheapest Moonlight by the Bay". . .

"Farid," I said, "why don't we die now very quickly?"

"Are you afraid to die later?" he asked, and added, "Maybe you should write a story about this place."

Later on he asked me, "Why don't we go to Larrache and visit Jean Genet's tomb?"

Larrache is a city further down the coast, and I had heard a lot about its beautiful architecture. We decided to go there later in the week.

I returned to Tangier late that night. I took a cab. The wind had started to blow and a few young men were walking up and down the streets. As we turned a corner, I felt taken back to Beirut, right around the Lord's Hotel, next to my house. The place had the same lights, the same feeling of being close to the beach. I recalled running on the cold sand and swimming, swimming in the dark sea.

A few days later, I went back to the Rembrandt for lunch. A tremendous agitation greeted me in the hall. Many people were streaming in from the streets. This time my friend was not there. I asked a young man, "What is going on?"

"The manager, the manager, look!"

I pushed my way in and there in the middle of the hall, under Lucretia's portrait, was the young woman, lying on the floor.

Nobody had questioned her absence, as she was so often late coming down from her room. She had been brought back from the beach, where she apparently had spent the night. She had been stabbed; a dagger was found in her hand, just like in the portrait above her head. But this time, they were looking for a murderer.

# PARIS
## Sophia O'Neill

*Walking in Paris, one sees the old aristocracy, the
memories of revolutions, the lives of artists who left their
imprints on the real and imagined landscapes of the city.
The past is ever present in the streets of Paris.*

*After World War II, Paris became the largest
metropolitan area on the European continent; the city
still draws large numbers of people from all over the
world—workers searching for employment, artists for a
nurturing environment, refugees for a safe place, in this
city which was the first to come up with a human rights
charter, proclaiming "liberty, equality, fraternity" for all.*

*Sophia O'Neill was born on August 2, 1965 in
St.-Germain-en-Laye, a Parisian suburb, the daughter of
a French father and an English mother. She attended the
Lycee International, and received her Baccalaureate from
Notre Dame, Paris. She then left for London University
where she received her MA in International Journalism
in 1987. She worked for BBC/Channel 2, producing two
documentaries, and did research at the British Film
Institute. She returned to Paris in 1988 and
died on December 28, 1989.*

# Not So Alone in Paris

For a moment I think Elle, who is standing at the counter of this dingy café, is exhausted and drifting into sleep. But her eyes only close momentarily to savour her red wine. Maybe she is immersed in the images I picture clustering in her mind. Although I think she has mentally left rue Chanzy, she can still hear the few voices around her. The café is calm, and nobody is smoking at the moment. But the bitter smell of the cold cigarette stubs in the ashtrays lingers on. Elle's heavy camera bag rests at her feet.

She is a photographer. She mostly takes pictures of actresses and actors, helping them to get work. She prepares their professional portfolios, constantly working with stereotypes. I think she is aware that she awakens certain desires in producers' eyes when they take a look at her photographs. As a result, does she dislike herself?

Sometimes I imagine in her a violent desire to show some of them what they really look like. Generally it's the young, overconfident male actor who believes that he might charm her. With women it is often the opposite. If women could be made to feel happier about the way they look and more innovative about possible roles to act in, then they might—even momentarily—think differently about themselves.

She lives in her studio to cut costs. Sometimes she rents it out to Jean-Pierre, who does pack shots for medical products and cosmetics. Mostly he seems lighthearted and satisfied with his work. Elle could not understand why, until it dawned on her that his life is filled with options. Hers is a day-to-day struggle, learning to live with disappointments. He is intoxicated by the city, which has taught him that his duty is to make conquests, while she has to figure out how to present herself. We both have wondered what would happen if women stopped wearing make-up, stopped being polite and pleasant, stopped smiling.

Her personal distress pushes her to take pictures of some of the contradictions in our culture—particularly the ones that leave women bereft and living on the edge: unemployment, poverty, prostitution. She has been photographing women almost everywhere in Paris since 1981, the year the socialist government took office. At that time she was offered a small grant to start her own project, but it has not been renewed. However, Elle is determined to create an archive of women's pictures. The last hundreds of shots reveal the increasing disparities and a growing sense of insecurity throughout the city. Her street photographs show the presence of police everywhere in Paris, and she has recently made a series on the Guardian Angels in the Metro.

The eyes of some of the people she has photographed will remain with me forever. She touches something deep and troubling within our society: beyond our rituals, our work, our games, there is a loneliness, a desperation, an alienation. Her own, but others' too. She never photographs institutions, "because they swallow up women." She pictures women's weary hands, the wealth of witchlike aristocrats, the worn stilettos of a thirteen-year-old in the game. . .

Her work was exhibited in a small gallery in the Marais—the area between Beaubourg and the Bastille. This neighbourhood was left to the people after the revolution. Until about fifteen years ago, they lived ten to a room in squalid streets, without service. Now the yuppies have moved in and renovated the houses. Mansions, concealed behind heavy ornate doors, in narrow and sometimes cobbled streets, have become museums, libraries, salons de thé, antique shops and designer clothes stores. Elle thinks that the Marais is charming, but rarely appreciates the people who come to comment on her work. She is convinced she can take good pictures only of those she loves. Yet this dimension is never picked up in the commercial equations she has to figure out with gallery owners.

Colette and the literary women of the Left Bank must have worked this way at the beginning of the century. After all, Colette had reached a certain independence and self-fulfillment by leaving the man who had entrapped her in marriage. Writing had been her means of liberation. It is Colette that Elle brings to mind as she sips her red wine and gently tilts her head.

There is something disturbing about Elle's lingering presence at the counter. It is rare to see a woman drinking cheap wine. She drinks with her eyes open this time, and I see the green waters of the Seine, gently polishing the paved stones, reflected in them. For a moment a dreadful thought pierces my mind: I hope she would never end up alone and drunk under one of the charming Paris bridges, another "failed" woman artist. No, she wouldn't. I recognise the signs of the community she belongs to, almost a uniform: cropped blond hair, two earrings in her left ear, a jean jacket, a white T-shirt, the Levis. She has an inner landscape that I'm allowed to enter because I also carry part of it inside me. I know we will survive, despite the fears and the social pressures that bully us and try to tame our wilder sides. Cities guarded by governments and ruled by money will not force us to cower under their power.

We exchange glances, acknowledging each other's presence. She sees me looking at her, as I write down a few more lines. She does not move. She must know that I am recreating her in my mind. The question for me is whether to describe her as she is or as I wish her to be. If I sensed for a moment that I was inconveniencing her, I would leave. But she sips on.

I imagine Elle in the salons of the Entre-Deux-Guerres. Colette knew many of the women who attended them—what conversations Elle would have had with them. They were baronesses, canonesses, cousins of Czars, illegitimate daughters of grand dukes. They were protected by their social rank; they lived outside the limits of the law. They cross-dressed to flout male authority and often lived together, without causing any moral outrage, because their society did not—as ours still does not—recognise women's desire for each other.

Colette envisioned a female community where women could develop their creativity and exorcise the demanding, aggressive, repressive attitudes present in their relationships with men. Older women supported younger, less experienced and less secure women. They were tender and affectionate with each other. They kept accounts, journals, diaries and commentaries on daily life, revealing huge gaps between their exterior gentility and their private passion, frustrations and unacknowledged creativity. Many of the writing women of the Left Bank also set up bookshops and publishing houses and met at artistic gatherings which they advertised in their publications.

Nothing like this happens nowadays. The Women's Center used to be alive with debates and meetings in the early seventies, but women no longer get together to show each other their work or to talk about strategies to transform society and make it a better place for women to live in. Economic survival has forced so many of them to accept jobs that don't lead anywhere, and they are left with little time to organise anything else, let alone see much of their friends.

I'd bet Elle dreams of the day she will no longer have to photograph actors and actresses. By then, she will have made it on the backs of others—in her case, those who were suffering. Then she will also be a big name, perpetuating a celebrity she despises. She has promised herself that she will put more time aside to try to bring women together—maybe set up an exhibition by women photographers about female aesthetics. She doesn't like this title, but it would suit the current cultural climate, which is overintellectual. Integrity is a luxury of financially independent women.

I wonder whether Elle is really happy, or whether she simply knows how to appreciate the quality of certain moments. She had just been walking through the Tuileries gardens. The morning was bright. The trees trembled in the sharp blue light. The beauty of some of the marble muses, goddesses, and the classical priestesses had uplifted her. The quantity of female figures, nesting in the curves of buildings and dotted around monuments, was reassuring, although she knew full well that statues only inspire the feelings sculptors want others to have. Even executed with a high degree of naturalism, they remain ideals, private dreams transformed into public statements, a projection of a certain romanticism. Or, as Baudelaire wrote, "monuments are the archives of universal life," the silent legend of history written by men, for men and glorifying men in their various conquests. . . and within which women's lives, women's deeds and participation in human affairs remain neglected and undervalued.

Sometimes I wonder why Elle stays in a city that presents her with such a version of the past, tells her lies, and forces her to be equally economic with her truth. But the capital of France is the only place that offers her any possibility of acting on her love for women. It also encourages a certain necessary experimenting: the assertion of her individuality. I can picture her living in a hut on one of the still-deserted Normandy beaches, facing the immensity of the sea. Such a life, though escapist, would be healthier, less stressful, less expensive.

Elle does not fear loneliness. She would be accustomed to it by now if she had not met someone to share her life with. But she would miss walking down rue Jacob where Colette used to live with her cat, Kiki-la-Doucette. Those of us who have read descriptions of it never pass by without imagining the one hundred and seventy-five thousand pieces of lozenge-shaped, multicoloured confetti that had been glued all over the doors, the cornices, the columns, the closet shelves and large areas of the walls by the tenant with odd interior decorating tastes who had lived there before.

The terraces with basket-woven seats; small coffee cups; red, white and blue ashtrays under awnings with flowery lettering announcing the café's name; the newspaper kiosks; the dark blue plaques of Paris' twenty arrondissements; even the dirty smell of the Metro, where Elle hides behind a book so as not to be accosted—all are part of her interior landscape. One day she might decide to leave it all behind, but until now, she has been unable to go away for very long, or very far.

Paris by night is another reason to stay. As she isn't much of a sleeper, Elle often walks through the animated quarters until she feels weary, getting glimpses and echoes from the underworld where people dance to salsa, and Latin rhythms, jazz and African beats are progressively harmonised in mixed bands. Elle's studio is fairly central, so she hasn't far to go to hit the noise and bright lights. Cafés stay open until five in the morning. . . if she feels threatened she will find refuge in one of them; however, she carries a small can of mace in her pocket, just in case.

To relax and enjoy herself Elle sometimes visits a barge on the Seine very near the Eiffel Tower. Once a month the Chaland barge is transformed into a dance hall. Women of all walks of life come to exchange glances, smiles and feelings. Skirts are all lengths and textures, although leather is very much in fashion. Legs are dressed in jeans, be they tight, shapeless, faded or creased down the front. Haircuts vary from Amazonian style to coloured locks on a shaved scalp. Here women dance, exchange a few words: "oh, excusez moi. . . tiens . . . bonsoir," caress each other inadvertently. I have walked among them, watching, passing, sharing.

Upstairs it is a little quieter: you can have a long chat while sipping a gin and tonic or a kir, looking out onto the waters and the city's lights slowly sinking within them. I remember Elle, because someone gave me a free pass to one of her shows and pointed her out to me one evening I was there. I recall that special sense of happiness, of belonging, having a space of our own. There was inevitably an air of distress in some of the women's eyes, but this was not the back street that women without money or connections are often relegated to. At night the barge comes to life; we women are no longer vulnerable; we don't want to hide. We can smile, happiness in our eyes, even for a few hours, because we can dream.

A couple enters the café in rue Chanzy. The bartender stops knitting. She turns the radio down and looks across to me as if to apologise. I know she has been watching us and probably realises that the voice of a woman singing in some distant studio, blotting out the rest of the world, offers us some sort of security. She rinses a few glasses and repeats the words she must have said at least fifty times today.

"The weather's nice," she says.

"I'm thirsty," says the male half of the couple.

"First signs of the summer. . ."

"I'll have a glass of red wine, thank you."

I decide it is time to go. But Elle seems to be ordering again. As I reach the counter to pay for my Perrier, her espresso is served. The sugar is at my end of the counter. I hand her two neatly wrapped cubes. She drops one into her little cup of strong black coffee and puts the other one to her lips. As we both hear the sound of her teeth crushing the white crystals, we look at each other with all the affection we can put into that language. . . and I leave her the words I have been scribbling for the last hour, before heading back to work.

# AUCKLAND
ROSIE SCOTT

*The Maoris, who settled Auckland eight hundred years ago, called it Tamaki Makau Rau, the spouse of a thousand lovers. Auckland has a population of nearly a million, many of whom are indigenous Maoris, thus making Auckland the largest Polynesian city in the world. Due to its two spectacular natural harbors, Auckland has become New Zealand's main port. Rather than focus on the neat, established city population who live in comfortable houses far removed from the city's underclass, Rosie Scott's Auckland is filled with those people who have been forgotten, left behind, or never made it.*

*Rosie Scott was born in Wellington in 1948. After completing degrees in English and drama, she traveled, working in journalism, publishing, theater and social work. She has lived in numerous cities, but usually returns to Auckland. She is now writing full time in Brisbane, Australia.*

*Rosie Scott has published in* Rolling Stone, Metro *and other magazines. Her novel* Glory Days *was published by Penguin, and is available in the United States from Seal Press.*

33

# Leaving Home

It is the relentlessness of Auckland which amazes her at first. The noises, stink, bad air assault her continually; it is like being caught up in an evil-smelling machine. It is also immediately apparent to her that the house fronts separating city people from the menacing streets are only a game of make-believe, the magic ring that children draw around their huts. They must know, she thinks, that all the terrible forces lurking out there could easily break down the eggshell-thin doors and burst inside, that they are no defence. Like their own strange kitchen, for instance, with its high ceilings and the matchwood walls which some past inhabitant has stripped down, leaving a rough, dust-weeping shell. She wonders seriously how any of them can be safe in there. The poisonous air seeps through the cracks; the inane honking of the city is in their ears day and night; outside there are people with hearts of stone who want to destroy her and her children. Locking the door each night is only an act of faith, like making the sign of the cross. There are still windows to smash in with muffled bricks, people disguised as meter-men, survey-takers or even priests, evil troubled people who can enter her house at will and damage her without compunction.

She suspects she is not adjusting. She finds it almost impossibly painful to recall the humming countryside she has left, with its silences and privacy, their front door always innocently open.

The children say, "Why do we have to live in this dumb place?"

The littlest one has just come from watching the mentally retarded people up the road. They sometimes fight in the street, grimacing like big trolls. She says she saw them throwing bits of wood into the road.

34

"They were real angry. They was snorting like bears," she says and shuts her mouth again, her eyes grave as she thinks it all over.

"Yes, and Val kept standing in front of them and staring," says the biggest.

She watches them, appalled, her children catapulted into this extraordinary world. It is as if their own life inside this fragile wooden house is beginning to duplicate the city rocking away out there. The children run in and out leaving a trail of clothes, sandals, scrunched-up pieces of paper, their knickers, cups and plates, orange peel. Their hair becomes dirty in minutes; they always look grubby; they have shrieking fights up and down the street. Since they've come to Auckland even their cuddles are violent; they launch into her like butting animals, faces crimson, their bodies as hard and unyielding as goats. They are frightened and excited and unsettled at the same time. For instance, they already know the territory better than she does because they have to survive in a world she is not part of. They bring new shy kids home all the time; they run off to unknown destinations and come home filthy, with mean mouths and shining eyes.

"Shut the door," she calls as they gallop in and out of the passage.

She is sitting in the kitchen with a city friend, Juliet, who never answers her when she speaks, just lets her words hang in the air.

"The trouble is everything pongs in the city; have you noticed?" she is saying to Juliet. "Well, not everything, I suppose. The vinegar factory down the road, it's like wine gone off. Dog poo, fumes, pollution—you can't escape it. Even the flowers. All I have in the garden are onion flowers. Have you smelt onion flowers in the very early morning? And then I realised the other day that there is a whole generation of millions of people who will live and die with the sound of traffic in their ears all their waking hours. And the smell."

She doesn't like this friend whose children behave well, and who looks around the house in a superior way. She pretends that her own daughters are exemplary and that she herself is smooth as silk.

"More coffee?" she asks.

Outside one of her children calls out in an ugly voice, "Shut your face, bastard!"

"They're tired," she says quickly, avoiding Juliet's eye, pouring coffee with her tattered old country hands. "Absolutely exhausted. We're still not used to the noise of the city. None of us is sleeping."

She looks out the window trying to appear unconcerned and her eye is caught by two Tongan schoolboys walking along the street, one pushing two bikes, the other strumming his guitar. It is the beginning of the holidays; they look hopeful, soft, as they talk about their burgeoning life. The innocent music goes on up the road and she is comforted.

"Juliet, my friend," she says, "are you going to say something? Or just sit silently not liking my kitchen?"

"Oh, Regan," says her husband tenderly when he gets home. "Why don't you just talk to people you like?"

"The children were nightmarish as well," she says and they make a face at each other. "I kept my end up, though. I never flinched."

"Any mail?" he asks, pouring out a beer for them in his companionable way.

"Juliet acts as if she can't believe I occupy a legitimate position in the universe because I'm so uncool. I'm such a yokel," she says. "It's a look of disbelief, basically."

"Ah, a bill," he says. "Thank God, I thought they'd forgotten us."

"So why are we friends?" Regan says, going over to look out the window pensively. "I've fought against it, believe me."

Later on they all go for a walk to the park, the girls running back and forth to make sure their parents know the way. She and her husband walk like lovers out of habit, holding hands and looking inquisitively at the subtropical lushness around the gracious wooden villas. They stand and watch some Samoan adolescents play volleyball on the court at the edge of the park. Every night in summer the kids gather, and play gracefully, almost in silence except for bursts of laughter. The sounds of the game are muted in the dusk, the thud of the ball on the asphalt, their laughter, a snatch of bantering conversation, the scuff of quick feet as they run.

She has seen the same group before. It was on a Saturday morning, and they were sitting together, their shoulders touching, under the pohutukawa tree in the middle of the playing fields. They were singing a song of support to their team, and the electrifying three-part harmony was like a river of pure sound.

She watches them playing with an ache of loneliness; their closeness and the joy they take in each other's company suddenly make her homesick for everything she left behind. She wants fiercely to belong to a place again, and a group of people; she wants to be cushioned against the cruelties of the city by that familiar kind of accepting love. She feels as if she is swollen with a longing that will never be satisfied, and that she will never feel safe again.

"Shall we go?" her husband says, giving her his kind arm. They walk towards the children, who are calling to each other like birds on the other side of the park.

That night Val dresses herself as a princess in a long skirt and tattered cardboard crown from the dress-up box. She hugs her doll very tightly. Regan can't help noticing that the weight of the crown is resting lightly on her daughter's small ears, making them bend out awkwardly from under her hair. The sight of them makes her weak with love. The girls have just had a bath and they look pink and dreamy, like big beautiful dolls. They are sitting motionless watching "Ready to Roll" on TV. It is a clip of three musicians capering on powerful apelike legs, hammering at their guitars menacingly. Their hair is frizzed out, blood-tinged from the smoke pouring out onto the stage; they are like zombies prancing among the clouds of red smoke. The children watch them intently, unblinking.

She says to her husband, her eyes fixed, disturbed, on the screen, "I feel I have to justify my whole life for her. She's the kind of person who decides how we all have to live."

"What are you talking about?"

"Juliet. The city."

"God almighty," he says, "aren't you being excessive about this?"

"Probably," she says absent-mindedly, "but then it's an excessive situation, I reckon. Because don't you remember the country? No one, but no one ever looking you up and down critically? And never having to lock a door, not being scared of evil?"

"I remember," he says. "We've only been gone a month."

She goes and sits on his knees and smooths his hair with the ease of long practice.

"I'm glad at least you're still here, but . . ." she says lovingly.

"That's nice, Regan. You too. It's just a matter of adjusting, I suppose."

"Adjusting to what? A pathological state?"

"What do you mean, pathological?" he says. "It's just a normal bloody city."

"Is it?" she says. "I like it so much when you're being a little shining beacon lighting up the way for us all."

She goes to lean out the window. Most weekend nights there is an edge of violence to the noise, abuse up and down the road, things being smashed, parents giving terrible unforgivable hidings to their children, men fighting in the street. There is a strident brassy hum to the place. Souped-up cars howl round the roads in the darkness; women scream; there is a feeling of pain and danger in the air which turns her blood cold.

Tonight there is only a bike revving up for what has seemed hours, a child wailing, and, far away in the distance, a Sally Army band thumping sweetly. She notices that the lone tree in their garden is coming into full leaf.

"I've never liked heavy metal," she says, leaning against the sill. "Except for Led Zeppelin in small doses." Her husband comes up behind her and rests his body against the length of her back. She can hear his calm breathing.

"You want a beer?" he says, but neither of them makes a move. They just stand there dreamily, looking out the window, resting lightly against one another, balancing in the dark.

## NEW YORK
### MARY RUTKOVSKY-RUSKIN

*Four hundred years ago, native Americans lost
the island of Manhattan to the New World land-grab of the
Europeans. By the twentieth century, that island of green
pastures was considered the world's center of power,
wealth, and "progress." Since it was the port of entry for
many European immigrants to the United States, New York
became home to large numbers of different peoples and
cultures, each settling in their own neighborhoods.
The European immigration was stopped in the twenties; in
the forties, Black Americans leaving the rural south for
the industrial north poured into the city; and in the fifties,
large numbers of Caribbean and Latin American immigrants
flocked in. During the last decade, New York once again
became a trendsetter, this time as "home" to a
rapidly increasing number of homeless.*

*Mary Rutkovsky-Ruskin's current work in progress is* Let
Them Eat Tuna Fish, *a collection of interrelated stories
about seven women living in a single occupancy hotel
in New York. She moved to New York five years ago, after
living in Boston, Istanbul and Paris. She wrote
"Land of the Free" after returning home from
a small village in Greece.*

39

# Land of the Free,
# Home of the Brave

Re-entry into the Land of the Free: of what are we free? Microwave ovens and body building machines seduce us: "Have me, take me," they hiss and murmur, "plug me in," and we acquiesce because we are enchanted, entranced, drugged. We consume to feel less empty: Give me a new washing machine, another car, a country house.

In an airport cafeteria: "Shopping's cheaper than a psychiatrist," the lady behind the cash register says to her co-worker with a smile as empty as my stomach.

"Yes!" the co-worker replies. "Have you seen those cute magnet-things for the refrigerator? There's one that has a teddy bear climbing out of a shopping bag that says, 'Born to shop.'"

Both women laugh and a curly white receipt is tossed in my direction. "That'll be $3.25, Miss."

Re-entry and the bus driver at JFK angrily yells at a Dutch couple, "The first stop! Yours is the first stop! I've already told you twice!" As the delicate man and woman sit down, I turn and with a laugh say, "Welcome to New York!"

They try to smile; he clutches a Hyatt Regency brochure in his hand, which must be wet with sweat. "Airport bus drivers," I continue, "are so busy. . ." and the couple nod energetically; they want to believe me. "Where are you going?" I ask. He hands me the brochure. Interesting answer, I think to myself. No words required, only a pictograph, a photograph of a big steel and glass building, an international symbol for clean sheets, separate bath, crisp curtains and a bedspread in a familiar pattern. "The Hyatt, yes, it's the first stop," I reassure them, making eye contact with the woman.

The bus begins to move. It crawls past cement structures—airport architecture, so modern, so ugly, so cold—and then through a neighborhood, not old, not new but something in between, a community of boxes, places where clerks, secretaries and civil servants can go at night to eat, make love, sleep, shit. There is gray everywhere, in the sky especially, and everyone moves fast to get somewhere where they aren't. The next thing I know, the bus driver announces Grand Central Station and I step off the bus, grab my suitcase, flag a cab, slip in and lean back in the seat; red light: stop.

I watch the Dutch couple; they are talking to the bus driver again. In pantomime, he angrily jabs his finger in an easterly direction, angry in his knowledge; the Hyatt is just around the corner. He doesn't understand the pictures in the Dutch couple's heads, put there by the movie and television industry—visions of murderers and rapists lurking around every corner, ready to pounce at any minute, day or night. Images of a city of light, but on the screen, mostly dark. Sometimes a goddess, most times a monster. The New York of money and lust, ups and downs, rich and poor, a city containing everything human and inhuman, the divine, the gross, the ecstatic, the base—everything accommodated within this monolithic, panting organism, a huge twenty-four-hour deli-of-life. I think, "Is this home?" Home. Green, the light turns green.

I become conscious of the cab driver; he's Korean and I talk to him because I need to talk after so many hours of ping-ponging home. He's suspicious of my idle chatter, paranoid that I'm asking questions about his country: he knows and I know that the average New Yorker isn't curious about Korea. In accusatory tones, people say, "The Koreans are buying up all of New York!" "They're prejudiced and violent!" In my neighborhood Korean market, grandmother, mother, father, brothers and sisters all work together—they're always working, and is that anything to be angry at these people for?

Near Gramercy Park, the cab driver asks me where I was born, and when I say Connecticut, the conversation ends. A left on Seventh Street, a right on First Avenue and I'm out of the cab, on the street, my block. Is this home? A pedestrian yells at a man in a car, "You can't park here, there's no double parking allowed!" and I wonder why everyone's so angry in the Land of the Free, Home of the Brave. Too many months on a quiet island in the Aegean have not prepared me for this.

I put my bags on the filthy sidewalk in front of my door, next to the Ukrainian market where a matronly, kind old woman sells fresh butter and dried, strung mushrooms that hang from the ceiling. I like the mushrooms, the way they dangle; they remind me of Hawaiian leis. The Poles, Ukrainians and Russians of the neighborhood are so old; their children, their lives, have moved to the suburbs where there are trees and plenty of neighbors to compete with. Who can buy the most in the shortest amount of time?

My keys: didn't I put them in my boots, way back when, so long ago? My fingers touch the cold metal and I hear a jangle, a familiar memory-sound. I find the red key, marked for immediate entry, and I'm in the hallway. Is this home?

A hallway painted a pumpkin color, guaranteed to discourage potential thieves, excepting junkies because there's a time when priorities change and color means nothing because to live means to have veins of liquid fire; soar, forget, be consumed by the search.

Graffiti: an upside-down martini glass and the words, "The World is Drunk." Black etchings above the mailboxes, gibber-jabber or some ancient, cryptic hieroglyphics, indecipherable by a non-primitive like myself. Up, up, up to the fourth floor and *click*, the lock releases itself and whoosh the door swings open. Dry warmth smoothes over my face—steam heat. The old people next door love it; I hate it for what it does to my skin.

I put down my bags and look around. Is this home? There is the slim resemblance of a life I lived five months ago, after redecoration by Suzanne: purple curtains, a black cat mask, cookbooks, empty picture frames, a silver-sequined mask, a sewing machine, mirrors. Books everywhere.

I walk through the apartment slowly: who was this woman who lived here, slept in that bed, sat at that desk, read those books? I stare at my bed and wonder who's been sleeping in my bed? Who's been eating my porridge? I stroll into the once beautiful, once peaceful front room, now designated Suzanne's bedroom, and I wonder what it will be like to live with the Queen of Clutter.

She calls them chatkas, a yiddish word for knickknacks. The next few months should be interesting. Almost every day she will come home with an object. What is this need to collect something every day of the week? The need to remember? The desire to believe that this isn't for nothing, that life isn't just a random accumulation of Mondays, Tuesdays, Wednesdays and Thursdays?

42

Mary Rutkovsky-Ruskin

One night it will be old buns from the Jewish bakery that the baker was throwing away; another night, a Chagall book from a forty-percent-off Going-Out-of-Business-Can't-Be-Beat-Sale; spools of wire in rainbow colors; an old album cover, "The Harder They Come"; a photograph of two black boys at Rockaway Beach; a stolen subway sign that reads, "Forced Entry: Never force anything between subway car doors to keep them from closing." How much more can this room hold—have floors ever been known to collapse from the weight of memories?

I walk back into the kitchen. The apartment is silent and warm and I don't want to unpack; it will take days to do so, to admit that I am here and not there, where life was simple. There, where the silence was so complete one could hear the inner hum and vibration churning within the body. There, where it seemed easier to glimpse other forms of existence, higher than old worn-out habits.

The city hums beyond the windows, a mixture of electric fans, cars and heating units, all in unison. Is this what Ann-Margret felt like in that movie, when she traveled through a human body? Her voyage through the veins within the arms and legs must have been safe, but I wonder about the heart; did she journey through the heart? Its beat must have been a deafening sound, its spasm an earthquake for such a tiny being like her.

Suddenly the lock clicks and it's Suzanne. She screams to see me just sitting there. We hug and suddenly I realize that I desperately need someone to talk to, someone to give my words to after so many hours of talking to flying strangers. "Are you hungry? Restaurant? Bar?" she asks and yes, I remember there are a million and one distractions within a four-block radius. We run down the stairs, trot along the sidewalk and scream and wake the walking dead on the street, dressed in black, mourning for a lost planet or perhaps a lost self. The Moderns in Black. They look at us without expression; they have seen it all. Perceptions jaded and dulled by overindulgence or perhaps underindulgence of clean air, life, breathing.

Re-entry: days later, the Amtrak train carries me under the city through a dark, dark tunnel toward a land called Connecticut and suddenly I am surging into the light. I'm above ground; white light exposes a garbage-strewn earth. Cloud-spattered skies are displayed above, a backdrop to this scene of desperation, and the famous Swingline Stapler sign looks drained and old; a fifty-year-old woman caught without her make-up on in the truth of daylight.

43

The train enters Connecticut, where there are trees and a variation on the theme of The Land of the Free, Home of the Brave, oom-pah-pah, oom-pah-pah. Where the suburban shopping malls are full of people wearing pastel-colored sports clothes this season: lime green, pretty pink and pale blue is all that can be seen from horizon to horizon.

Re-entry into a nation running wild on the belief of their bestness, a melting pot where democracy now brings us the Marriott Hotel Creations Salad Bar where Italian, Mexican *and* Chinese foods can be mixed and matched: all new, certainly improved inter-cultural comestibles. "Be creative!" the poster says in bold, cheerful letters. It is imperative to be creative in the Land of the Free.

The waitress, mistress of the tables, smiles blankly, blinks brightly as she flits from crowded table to crowded table. "I *never* expected it to be *this* busy," she squeals in delight and I wonder what she's really feeling; her dress is circled with perspiration the size of cantaloupes.

So stuff your tortilla with pasta, put chile on your baked potato. Slip a piece of watermelon into your chow mein, and slap a dollop of sour cream in your vegetable soup. Go ahead, be courageous, be creative, be free.

Re-entry and I lean back against the plastic banquette, look around and wonder, is this home?

# MADRID
## KATE RISSE

*Compared to many other cities on the Iberian peninsula,
Madrid, which was merely a small Moorish fort during
the Middle Ages, has a very short history. Madrid was
never considered as gay as some Andalusian cities, or as
fashionable as Barcelona, and during Franco's lifetime,
Madrid seemed a rather contained, almost backward
capital by European standards. But as Spain's capital for
more than four hundred years, Madrid has accumulated
incredible amounts of wealth. In the eighties—along with
economic and social changes, brought by the socialist
government—Madrid's image changed, and people from
all over Europe are now flocking to the city to admire
its art, engage in its nightlife, and shop in
trendy stores and in what is considered one of
Europe's best flea markets.*

*Kate Risse has studied and worked in Madrid. She has
traveled throughout Spain but is most attracted to the
hustle and bustle of Madrid. She has worked as a Spanish
translator and counselor in a women's health clinic.
Currently, she works for* Partisan Review.

# The Stone Owl

The French windows that kept my room cool and dark in the summer's unbearable heat were latched shut. I dragged myself towards them. First I unlatched the painted wooden shutters and folded them back carefully. Then, after a good deal of effort, the heavy iron bolt lifted and I opened the doors, allowing the light and warm air to enter my room.

In the plaza below, street sweepers in blue suits shuffled along the cobblestones and swept rhythmically back and forth. They swept around fountains and under benches, picking up cigarette butts and scraps of paper, tossing them into brown sacks draped over their shoulders. I wondered whether these men had families to go home to, whether they had children in school and wives that made them coffee and packed them lunches. One gardener, a stout Madrileño, weeded a bed of tulips that were planted in perfect rows. The red petals were full and flawless against the grey city.

I took a sponge bath and let the cold water run down my back and over my breasts, and sprinkled myself with rose water I had bought in Cuenca. The lights were off in the house, and this enhanced the illusion that I was in a dark, cool cave underground. But the humidity was already seeping in through the cracks in the plaster and old windows in the apartment.

I dressed comfortably, but modestly, as I always did when I went out alone in the city. My light blue cotton dress and leather sandals were suitable for the hot weather. By dressing simply I could avoid the disdain of old widows dressed in black stockings and black suits who perched on their apartment stoops like old crows and shook their heads at young people. The gap between ages was so clear. "Cara dura," or "what nerve," they would sometimes respond in a whisper, their wrinkled lips quivering.

I left my house for the old section of the city. It was a habit every Sunday morning to walk through the crowded marketplace behind the Plaza Mayor. As I emerged from the metro into the old barrio of Madrid, I exhaled slowly, leaving behind the stale air that smelled faintly of urine and cigarettes. The cobblestones and the sides of buildings were grey. Even when the sun came out, the narrow streets remained dark and cool, sheltered from sunlight.

I was early, as usual, so I stopped at the bar on the corner for a cup of cafe con leche while the vendors set up their carts.

I was the only woman in the cantina, but I wasn't afraid as long as I wasn't alone, as long as there were other voices. My elbow rested on the smooth mahogany bar, and I watched the old men who sat smoking cigars. Beneath my feet lay dirty used napkins, cigarette butts, and shrimp shells that had not been swept up from the day before. Sometimes the old men stared at me without any inhibition, their bloodshot eyes bulging from sockets that seemed to fold neatly into their withered dark skin.

But on that Sunday in August the old men didn't look up when I entered the obscure, cramped room with its low ceilings and crudely carved furniture. I liked it that way. I was able to think clearly about my art students at the university, and what I needed for my kitchen and what kind of bargains I might find at the market. Sometimes I imagined myself finding an old oil painting by a great Spanish master, like a crucifixion by Murillo. But all the paintings I had ever found at the market were modern and weren't worth a duro.

At the bar, alone, I felt comfortable enough to order a second cup of coffee and a warm tortilla as I sat listening to the low rumbling chatter of the old men.

Outside on the street a young couple with a small child hailed a taxi, and two young women dressed in suits, and probably heading for church, passed the bar and stared through the window. They were my age. As they laughed they reached out and held hands. Their hands came together and swung in time with their pace. I hoped they could not see me hidden, sitting alone in the corner of the bar.

An old woman stood on the curb with a cart filled with gladioli, orchids, roses, and pink carnations. I thought of how I would love to buy flowers for someone.

The old woman hailed customers in her aggressive way, thrusting bouquets into their faces. A scarlet scarf covered most of her head, leaving room for a small tuft of silver hair that fell across her forehead. Her weak eyes were tucked into her broad face, and she was missing front teeth. But her smile was amiable enough to stop customers. As her arms gestured in exaggerated sweeping motions, I tried to read her lips, but I could not figure out what she was saying. A young couple stopped to buy roses. Each had a hand slipped into the other's pocket like they were Siamese twins joined at the hip. When the girl reached for the bunch of roses it was as though she resented having to let go of her lover; she quickly stuck her hand back into his pocket, gripping the flowers with her free hand. I reached for my leather purse and left the bar and headed towards the market.

A young girl glared at me at the top of the wide street where the market starts. I could see her out of the corner of my eye, standing still and staring. There were booths set up in the streets and on the sidewalk, although the best bargains could be found in the permanent stores that lined the street, many of them filled with antique jewelry and watches, old iron work, and various moldings.

As a child I used to walk these streets with my parents, shopping for antique furniture for our apartment near the Plaza de Santa Anna. We bought chairs and bureaus and a green velvet couch for almost nothing. Since both of my parents had died I had all the furniture I needed and probably couldn't afford any of these prices. Besides, I was after the junk and the decorative trinkets.

In the market I moved from cart to cart and each time I tried on a scarf or a pair of earrings the young girl was by my side, questioning me about my blond hair, my funny accent, or my gold watch.

"Alemán," I said, trying to explain that I was of German descent.

Her dress was the first thing that caught my attention. It was too small; the tightness around the arms suggested that she had already grown out of it. She carried a cardboard box filled with figurines which at first she seemed to be peddling. I did not get a close look in the box since she guarded it under her left arm, but I saw that they were crudely carved stone animals.

"Your hair is a strange color," she said in her Spanish, so filled with slang I could barely understand her. "It's pretty, though," she said, as she reached up and raked her fingers through it.

At first her forwardness startled me, but then she seemed so innocent that I didn't mind. She was talkative and took an interest in me, like my students did, as if I could offer her something, and she began to draw it out of me. I was candid with her and said what I felt.

Her bony fingers moved towards my watch and across the watch face. Her hands were dirty and calloused; although she was only about fourteen, they looked more like the hands of an old woman. She eyed my leather purse and felt it with the palm of her hand.

"I have a purse just like that at home," she said, rubbing the smooth leather.

I thought of walking away and excusing myself, but I couldn't. Her large brown eyes and black eyelashes pulled me towards her. I wanted to know where she lived and why she was following me. Her voice was delicate and almost brittle. The Spanish she spoke was musical, like a song she was singing to me.

"What are you called?" she said, uninhibited.

"Anna," I said, "and you?" I could hear her hands nervously stirring the stone animals in the box.

"Maribel Luz," she said.

She accompanied me through the market. Her long legs kept up with me, although I was a foot taller than she and ten years older. When she asked me to hold the box so that she could twist her shiny black hair up into a knot on top of her head, I glanced at the figurines and saw that they were made of soapstone.

We drifted through the crowd from one booth to the next, testing scented oils and trying on jewelry and sandals. Her friendly open attitude made me forget my rigidness and my solitude. In an antique storefront I spotted an orange and white ivory cameo.

"I can't go in that store with you," said Maribel, keeping clear of the door. She pointed to the box of animals she carried, indicating that she couldn't be seen peddling goods in another store, and I didn't question her. She quickly moved away from the store as I stood in front of the window admiring the painted tin boxes and porcelain dolls with lace dresses.

"I'll meet you down there on the corner," she said, and she leaped away.

I bought the pin for myself, put it in my purse, and went to meet Maribel on the corner. The sun was out and the beams of light uncovered the dust in the street. Dogs, with skin stretched tightly over their rib cages, picked in the garbage or napped in the shade beneath booths. A girl who resembled Maribel in age approached us with a tray of pastries. Maribel chose a chocolate Pepito and we split it.

I began to feel the weight of bodies against me. It was the same suffocating feeling I always have when I am among strangers. I slithered by tourists, students, old men, and bandits who were trying to steal or make a deal. As we neared the clothing section we were forced to move against more bodies, excusing ourselves in a fit of laughter.

"Don't lose me, Anna." She tugged at my dress and I needed to feel that pressure, that pull. I plowed through the crowd as if she were steering me. And when she let go of my dress I got wary and quickly swung myself around, hoping we hadn't lost each other.

Her mocking expressions made me laugh and made me forget the intruders around us. She made fun of a lot of the items being sold, as if she had been among the same jewelry and leather sandals all her life. She couldn't try on a painted barrette without rolling her eyes and tossing it back on the table. And when I questioned the vendors about their goods, she shook her head and pulled me along to the next table.

Her small hand felt cold and limp in mine. But when our fingers touched I felt united with another person. She seemed sincere and comfortable with me. I pulled her along through the crowd and as we held hands I was reminded of the two young women I had seen earlier, whose friendship and trust were locked into that grip.

"Anna," said Maribel, looking at me and putting her face close to mine. "I want to take you to my favorite booth."

Heaps of brightly dyed clothes lay in piles on tables. My favorite carts were the ones strewn with students' handmade uncommon designs, like baggy balloon pants, and long cotton shirts. Maribel held up a simple pink cotton skirt to her waist and swung her narrow hips back and forth like a small brass bell. I bought myself a belt. And because I hadn't shopped with anyone in so long, on the spur of the moment, I bought Maribel the skirt. In return, she reached into the cardboard box she carried and pulled out a stone bird that looked something like an owl with a big head and round bulging eyes.

"It reminds me of you," she said, looking up at me. "It's my favorite animal." She held my wrist and placed the figure in the palm of my hand. The owl was smooth, and warm, and roughly carved.

"It's beautiful," I said, and hastily put it into the pocket of my dress.

A row of Indian shirts in blue, red, and yellow patterns were draped over a table. The blue and black pattern was conspicuous, and quickly caught my attention. It was pulled from a rack and handed to me. The shirt flapped slowly in the light breeze that hailed the afternoon. I slipped my pocketbook over my shoulder and placed it on the table. The warped mirror made me look too wide. At the slightest shake of the head, the designer was by my side with a thick plastic belt that she wrapped around my waist.

"It looks majestic," she said, pulling out the tufts of fabric from beneath the belt so that it puffed up more and made me look like a balloon.

I turned around to ask Maribel her opinion, but she was gone. So was my purse with the cameo and all my money. I thought maybe she had borrowed it to buy us a drink, so I waited in the heat in a blue bloated shirt among women pressing me to buy clothes.

I thought I saw her in the crowd but it was only the girl who had sold us the chocolate pastry.

All of the varied sounds in the market became one solid noise, a buzzing in my ear like the mosquito you can't find at night. The motion of people scurrying around made it difficult to breathe and I thought of my apartment, dark and quiet and cool. If I could just sift myself through the mass to the beginning of the market I could make it home.

I peeled the shirt from my back and threw it down on the table and as I quickly looked both ways, left and right, I could feel the weight of the heavy stone owl in my pocket as it flapped against my thigh.

## SAN FRANCISCO
### FAE MYENNE NG

*San Francisco, the city so well known for its natural beauty, its earthquakes, and its large lesbian and gay community, is also home to one of the largest Chinese communities outside China. For a long time, San Francisco's Chinatown appeared to be a closed, insular world. The Chinese exclusion laws (by which the United States limited Chinese immigration) created a bachelor society of oldtimers in Chinatown. For these oldtimers, transcontinental marriage was the only available option. Men came to the United States, worked until they had saved enough money, returned to China to marry, and eventually found their way back alone. When the immigration laws changed after World War II, many families were reunited. In "Last Night," a Chinese couple is presented in the autumn of their lives. San Francisco is a city of great cultural diversity, where many different groups have learned to live together, speaking the common language of their humanity.*

*Fae Myenne Ng is a native San Franciscan. Her short fiction has appeared in many publications, including* Pushcart Press XII: Best of the Small Presses *and* Introduction to Literature *(Holt, Rinehart and Winston, Inc. 1991), and* The One You Call Sister: New Women's Fiction *(Cleis Press 1989).* The First Dead Man and Others, *her collection of stories about oldtimers of San Francisco's Chinatown, received the 1988 San Francisco Foundation's Joseph Henry Jackson Award.*

# Last Night

When Hang Fong Toy finally awakens, she can't tell if the rhythmic pounding is one of her headaches or just the water pipes banging again. She looks around the room, listening. The street light falls through the Venetian blinds; the slanting lines make the room seem larger.

You Thin Toy sleeps curled toward the wall, a brush stroke on the wide bed. He's a retired merchant marine and has sailed the world. Now he spends afternoons at Portsmouth Square, playing chess and telling stories about himself as a young man. "Like a seagull," he says, "I went everywhere, saw everything."

His old-timer friends like to tease him. "So, why do you sit around the Square now?"

"Curiosity," he says. "I want to see how you fleabags have been living."

You Thin knows all the terms for docking a ship; Hang Fong can name the parts and seams of a dress the way a doctor can name bones.

Hang Fong sews in a garment shop. She's only been outside Chinatown for official business: immigration, unemployment and social security. When the children were young, they took her to Market Street, the Emporium and J.C. Penney's, but now, without translators, she's not an adventuress.

There was a time when her desire to return to China was a sensation in her belly, like hunger. Now she only dreams of it, almost tasting those dishes she loved as a young girl. Sometimes she says to You Thin before falling asleep, maybe a visit, eh?

After raising their children, Chinatown has become their world.

They feel lucky to have an apartment on Salmon Alley. Louie's Grocery is around the corner on Taylor, and Hang Fong's sewing shop is just down the block. Their apartment is well situated in the back of the alley, far from the traffic fumes of Pacific Avenue.

Hang Fong and You Thin like their landlord, an old Italian lady, and her mute son so much that they have given them Chinese names. Fay-Poah, Manager Lady, and Ah-Boy, Mute-Son. Manager Lady wears printed pastel dresses that Hang Fong, a sewing lady, admires very much. Ah-Boy, a big man with a milky smell, works as a porter at the Oasis Club, but during the day he works around the building. When Hang Fong hears his broom on the stairs or the garbage cans rattling in the airshaft, she feels safe. It's good to have a strong man like Ah-Boy nearby. She tells You Thin, Ah-Boy is a good son, and You Thin nods. He likes to think that the anchor tattoo on Ah-Boy's arm makes them comrades of sorts.

Hang Fong thinks maybe Manager Lady left her window open. But then the sound becomes erratic and sharp. Hang Fong gets up, leans toward the wall. You Thin lets out a long breath.

Hang Fong presses her ear against the wall, listening. Her eyes are wide open. Suddenly she rushes toward her sleeping husband and shakes him. "Get up! Get up! It's the Manager Lady, she's in trouble!"

You Thin stretches out and props himself up on one elbow. He rubs his eyes, trying to wake up. The banging comes again, and the old couple stare at each other. Outside, a car screeches to an urgent stop. They listen to the faint bubbly hum of the fish tank in the other room, and then hear the rumbling icebox motor shut off with a final click. You Thin and Hang Fong look at each other; the silence feels big.

The pounding comes again. Once. Twice.

"Something's wrong! Manager Lady is trying to tell us that!" Hang Fong throws off her covers. In one motion, her legs whip out and her slippers make a swishing noise as she moves across the room. The overhead fluorescent light flickers and snaps and then is quiet. The room is bright, glaring.

You Thin squints, reaches over, and raps sharply, one-two-three on the wall.

A sound knocks back in return.

Hang Fong slaps the wall with her open palm; the sound is flat and dull. She presses palm and cheek into the wall, and shouts,

"Manager, Manager, are you all right? Nothing's wrong, is there?"

"SSHHH!!!" You Thin yanks her away. "Don't talk loud like that, she don't know what you say, maybe she thinks that you yell at her."

You Thin is out of bed, pacing. Hang Fong sits; she pulls her sweater closer around her neck. The sleeves hang limply at her sides.

"Let's see. . . wait a minute, where's Ah-Boy?"

"It's Tuesday; he's got the night shift."

"Oh. Tuesday. Right."

Last week, when You Thin was at Manager Lady's paying the rent, he looked out her kitchen window while waiting for her to come back with the receipt. He saw a Chinese pot beneath a pile of chipped plates. So the next day he returned with a blue vase, its floral pattern similar to many of Manager Lady's dresses.

"I see?" he asked, pointing out the window.

Manager Lady opened her mouth wide, as her hand fluttered toward the window.

"Oh. Si, si," she said.

You Thin pulled the window open. He moved the cream-colored plates and lifted the pot for Manager Lady to see. She nodded, cradling the blue vase to her bosom.

With both hands, You Thin carried the pot back across the hall. Under the running faucet, Hang Fong scrubbed hard. Red, green and yellow, the palace ladies and plum blossoms came clean. You Thin scraped away the last of the dirt with a toothpick. The characters came clear. Good Luck and Long Life. You Thin and Hang Fong laughed, feeling lucky.

"Worth a lot of money, in time," You Thin said.

"Something to pass on to the children," Hang Fong added.

You Thin told everyone on the Square that the pot belonged to a hard-working old-timer who died alone. Hang Fong said that it was a good omen that they were chosen to house this valuable object. "It's very old," she told her sewing-lady friends.

"So, should we call the Rescue Car?" Hang Fong asks.

You Thin looks out the window, distracted. He shakes his head. "Even if they get here in two minutes, best we could do is stand in front of the door with our mouths open."

Hang Fong knows that he wants to climb the fire escape and get inside Manager Lady's apartment. It's risky, she thinks. You

Thin isn't a young man and his step isn't always steady. She won't say anything, because the long years of marriage have taught her one thing: he likes his way.

"Well, what do we do?" Hang Fong asks. On the fire escape, a pigeon sleeps, its beak in its chest feathers. Hang Fong watches it. She hears the big engines of the garbage trucks churning up the hill. Foghorns sound in the distance, like help on the way.

You Thin asks, "Well, you think I could make that big step across to their fire escape?"

Hang Fong shrugs her shoulders. "Don't know; how do you feel?"

You Thin raises the window, looks out and snaps back in. Before Hang Fong can speak, he's run to the bathroom and clattered his way out carrying the long wooden board they use as a shelf over the bathtub.

"This is how. . ." He slaps the board. "This will reach from our fire escape to theirs. You hold this end, just in case, and the rest I can do."

Hang Fong grips hard, but she keeps a harder eye on him. Inside, she repeats over and over, "Be careful. . . be safe. . . be careful. . . be safe. . ." You Thin is a brave man, she thinks; You Thin is a good man.

One leg, then the other, and he is over there. He peers through the window, knocks, and then tries to lift it open. Shut tight. He has to pull hard, two, three times before it comes open.

You Thin feels along the wall for the light switch. All along the way, he speaks to Manager Lady, softly, in Chinese, "You're all right, nothing's wrong, don't be frightened. . ." You Thin believes in the power of the voice: a well-meaning word spoken in the face of ill fortune can turn luck around.

Manager Lady is a wide figure on the floor. Everything around her speaks of her age: the faded covers, the cluttered nightstand, the bottles of lotions and pills. You Thin takes her hands; he's happy hers are warm.

Hang Fong knocks in quick, urgent raps, and You Thin opens the door for her. She moves quickly through the entryway, kneels and takes Manager Lady's head onto her lap, whispering, "Don't be scared, don't be scared." Manager Lady's eyes open. She says something in Italian; the long vowels reach forth and hang heavy in the air. Hang Fong and You Thin look at each other. They understand.

You Thin says, "I go. Go to get Ah-Boy."

"You know where it is then?"
"Uh, let me think. . . where Lee's Rice Shop used to be?"
"No! Across from Chong's Imports."
"Yes, right, I know, I know."

The air outside is sharp. The street lamps cast an orange glow to the empty alley. You Thin moves quickly through Salmon Alley. But when he turns onto Pacific, he rests a moment. The long road before him is marked with globes of light. He runs his hand along the walls for support. On the steep hill, his legs feel strangely heavy when they land on the pavement and oddly light when they bounce off. He chants to himself, "Hurry. Important. Faster."

When he reaches Powell, he leans against the fire hydrant for a moment, glad that he's halfway there. He can see Broadway; it's still brightly lit. He's breathing hard by the time he gets to The Oasis. This late, it's been long closed. You Thin stands outside, banging on the big wooden doors and rapping on the windows. He cups his hands to the barred window, trying to see in. But with the glare from the street lamps, it's like looking into a mirror.

He takes a deep breath. "Ah-Boy, AAHHH-Boy-AAAHH!. . ."

Silence. Then the sound of flapping slippers, and Ah-Boy opens the door, mop in hand.

You Thin throws his arms about, waving toward Pacific. He slaps the restaurant wall, shouting, "Mah-mah. Be sick. Be sick."

Ah-Boy opens his mouth; his head jerks back and forth, but there is no sound. He lets his broom fall with a clatter. The heavy door slams shut.

Ah-Boy is a big man and You Thin can't keep up for long. At Pacific, You Thin waves him on.

You Thin watches for a moment as Ah-Boy moves up the hill. Yes, he nods, Ah-Boy is a good son.

When You Thin gets to the apartment, Ah-Boy is sitting on the floor with his mother's head on his lap, her gray hair loosened from its bun. She is speaking to Ah-Boy in a low voice.

You Thin and Hang Fong stand under the door frame, watching. "Just like last year," Hang Fong says, "just like Old Jue."

On the phone You Thin speaks loud. He pronounces the syllables as if each sound were a single character. "Numbah Two. Sah-moon Alley. Old Lady. Sick. You be the come. Now, sabei? I stand by downdaire, sabei? Numbah Two, Sah-moon Alley."

Hang Fong stands next to him, listening hard. She whispers something to him.

You Thin raises his head, and speaks even louder. "One minute. You know, Old Lady, she be. . . uh, uh. . . Old Lady she be come from Italy. You sabei? Lady not from China."

At the Square the next day, You Thin challenges the Newspaper Man to a chess game. You Thin plays with one leg raised on the cement stool. "My Car over your lousy paper Gun, and you're eaten." The Newspaper Man's children fold The Chinese Times on the next table. Lame-Leg Fong tries to tell You Thin which pieces to move. The #15 Kearney bus inches down Clay, its brakes squeaking and hissing. Cars honk.

You Thin tells his story about last night in between chess moves. He describes the distance between Salmon Alley and Broadway. His running motions make his blue sleeves go vlop-vlop in the wind. He repeats all the English words he used, tries to use the ones he'd heard, and makes all the faces Ah-Boy made. He walks the line on the ground to show what he did in midair. Little boys run by on their way to the water fountain.

Hang Fong tells the story without looking up. The ladies listen with rounded backs and moving hands. Sheets of fabric run from the machines to the floor. Clumps of thread knot around the chair legs; spools of color ripple above the ladies' bent heads. The overlock machines click; the steam irons hiss. Some ladies sing along with the drum and gong beat of the Cantonese opera playing on the radio. A voice booms over the intercom system, "LAST CHANCE TO HAND IN THOSE TICKETS, RIGHT NOW!" No one looks up. Some ladies cluck their tongues and roll their eyes. Others shake their heads and curse under their breath.

Many of the sewing ladies want to hear Hang Fong's story, but missing a sentence here or there, they can't follow the drama. Is it a story or is it real? The women become heavy-footed; the needles stamp urgent stitches into the fabric. Trousers fly over the work tables; the colorful mounds of clothing clutter the floor.

Eventually the grumble of the machines drowns out the story. A young girl runs in to ask her mother for money as the fish peddler arrives, singing out her catch in a breath as long as thread.

# URBAN GROWING PAINS

# MEXICO CITY
## BERTA HIRIART

*In 1950, the year Berta Hiriart was born, Mexico City was still fairly spacious, with large green areas. Within a few years, however, the word "smog" entered the vocabulary, and many of the city's archaeological sites were destroyed as pedestrian roads were converted into avenues. Berta recalls visiting the outskirts of the city to watch the construction of projects that would house a hundred twenty thousand people.*

*In October 1968, when the students were massacred at the Tlatelolco housing project, Berta Hiriart was eighteen. "This event had a lasting impact on me and my generation. . . my head was filled with the liberating ideas of the sixties: the anti-authoritarian slogans, the criticism of the family, the Beatles, and later, feminism."*

*Currently, Berta works for Fempress, the Latin American information agency, produces plays for theatre and radio, and writes journalism and fiction. "I'm still living in Mexico City, now the world's most populated, and even though it has a hellish appearance, it still holds some marvels in its heart."*

# Maestra Arellano

The place where the eagle screams
and where it opens its wings;
the place where it eats,
and where fish fly.
This will be Mexico Tenochtitlan
and many things are going to happen.
      Mexicayotl Chronicle

Today's paper carried the news: Maestra Arellano died in a shoot-out with the police. Several times I read the dry paragraphs describing her last days, in the hope that this was a mistake. It might be another Maestra Arellano, not ours from the neighborhood of Tacubaya. But all the information given corresponded to her, and when I thought about it more calmly, only she could be the leading character of this story. A worker who had spoken to the victim shortly before the incident said at the end of his testimony, "God, what an old lady! I didn't believe she was serious."

For thirty years Maestra Arellano was an indispensable person in the neighborhood. Without children, and with a husband employed by the national railroads, she had an enviable position for a woman of those times. Besides teaching, she had her own activities, which she wouldn't change for anything in the world, such as drinking a refreshment in the café right around the corner in the late afternoon. Yet she always had time for us.

If a child needed help studying arithmetic, the Maestra came with an abacus and multiplication tables. If someone got a prescription for an injection because of chest pains, increasingly common in the city, the Maestra came with her sterilized syringes which she kept in a silver box. If there was a wedding or a fifteenth birthday, the Maestra came. If someone died, the Maestra came. If there was a case of alcoholism or drugs, or the possibility of a miscarriage, or if there was a flood, or lack of hope, Maestra Arellano was always there.

I was lucky to have her as my teacher when I studied for my entrance exam to high school. Every Tuesday at four o'clock sharp she came, her hair done in the style of Marga Lopéz, dressed in her tight skirt and wearing her high heels. She spent a few moments with my mother, to inquire about the family or to talk about some radio broadcast, and then she sat down with me in the kitchen. While drinking lemonade, she explained the mysteries of the alphabet, the Etruscans, the life of the bees, the atoms and negative numbers.

Now I believe that I owe entirely to her the little which I retained from the sea of information accumulated during all these years in school. I also owe to her the good judgment that now and then—though not as frequently as I'd like—helps me in difficult moments. When I think that I'm going to explode, the image of the Maestra after her husband's funeral comes to my mind. "Let me cry for him," she pleaded with the neighbors who were trying to calm her. And she shut herself in to cry for him for an entire year, and at the end she reemerged with her usual disposition.

The world, however, did not know how to return her generosity. When the Maestra was ready to return to her former daily life, without pessimism or commiserating attitudes, the neighborhood was no longer the same. In reality it had started to change years before, along with the rest of the city, but so gradually that it went unnoticed. The Maestra was able to see the evidence of the transformation only because she had gained some distance during the time of her mourning.

The notion that everything old has to be destroyed in order to let in the new was applied not only to urbanism, but to everything else as well. The market was flooded with computers of all sizes and price-ranges. Kids were no longer learning the basic rules of counting, since it was much more attractive to spend hours playing with these new machines than to practice multiplication tables. Computers displaced the abacus, and AIDS sent the little silver box with the syringes to the garbage. There was no more demand for the Maestra, as if she herself had been covered with the dust of time and therefore was no longer of interest to anyone. There were no more weddings—now couples met and separated easily— nor any fifteenth birthday celebrations—the young considered them absolutely ridiculous. There were, in fact, no celebrations; people were broke because of the crisis.

All of a sudden she was confronted with a changed city in which she had lost her place. She made various attempts to maintain some community connections, but slowly she closed herself again into her house, from which she had tried to come out with such grace, not only because she was no longer needed by the neighbors, but also because she had nowhere to go. The café on the corner had disappeared, replaced by a luxurious shopping center, which had nothing to offer for the small income of a retired Maestra.

The park where she used to walk on Sundays lost its calm because it was now surrounded by thoroughfares, and she stopped going when all the birds began to drop dead due to the heavy concentration of lead in the air. She even had to give up the custom of visiting her only remaining friend Isabel, because she could no longer recognize the streets whose names, dimensions and directions had changed, and she got lost. Twice she tried to overcome this disorientation, but she wasn't able to get to Satellite City, where Isabel lived, and she returned exhausted from so much coming and going and risking her life. Every time she tried to cross the thoroughfare, she had the sensation that one of the thousands of cars, converted into a racing car, would run her over at any moment.

Her old house in Tacubaya had become a refuge, the only likable place in an increasing hostile world. However, she kept her good spirits, and rather than feeling nostalgic, she dedicated herself to cultivating various hydroponics. She cut branches of any climbing plant which came her way, spread them in water, and observed the results. Those which grew roots started new cultures. Within a few months the house turned into a garden and pretty much replaced the lost park.

At that time, I had already long been gone from home, but I kept myself informed about the Maestra through my Mama, who saw her from time to time. However, the earthquakes of 1985 encouraged my family, like so many others, to decide to move to the province. This situation added to the frantic rhythm of my own life, and caused me to lose sight of the Maestra for some years. Actually, I only saw her one more time.

Mama spent a holiday in Mexico City, and we thought of paying her a visit. The first thing that caught our attention was the wall around the Maestra's house, which was a few meters higher; as if this weren't enough, on top of it there was an iron fence with sharp points which would pierce whoever tried to climb over it. The Maestra herself had changed too: she was pale and emaciated. But I think she was happy to see us. She led us through the hydroponics, which filled the house so thickly that it was difficult to breathe. She offered us galletas Marias, biscuits, and she got ready to listen to the vicissitudes of the last few years.

After we had told her what had been going on in our lives, there was an embarrassing silence. It was obvious that the Maestra did not have the slightest desire to talk about herself, but nevertheless, the question was put to her. "And you, Maestra, how have you been?"

She had been doing well, thanks. She only had a few little frights. Therefore she had protected the house with a few additional security devices. And to tell the truth, if it were up to her, she wouldn't leave the house for anything. But this was impossible. She had to go out, at least to the market, which, thank God, had survived modernization, and to pick up her pension, which certainly wasn't enough to cover her basic expenses. Fortunately, she was making some money with her hydroponics. She was selling them to florists and was doing well. She didn't suffer from giving them away, because, as we could see, there was no more room for them in the house. Besides, the sales had made it possible to build up the wall and to protect the windows with aluminum bars, which we could also see. They definitely made the house look like a prison, but there was no alternative.

For it was the assault which taught her about the true dimensions of danger in the city. It was not that she didn't know about violence. Of course she did: she had lived through the repression of the teacher's movement in 1958. And also the snatching of her purse one afternoon as she was leaving the movies. And the shoot-out in the door of the corner restaurant, did we remember? But this new style, this. . . how do you say? this *spite*, this she hadn't known. The robbers were professionals. They had waited for her outside the bank where she had gone to pick up her pension. They followed her to the pedestrian crossing on Eje 16, a main city highway. As they were young, they had time to run and cut her off. There were three of them: their caps covered their faces and they pulled out their knives. Three armed youths against a miserable old lady! Can we imagine that? They asked for her money. This almost caused her to have a laughing fit. She gave them her purse with her entire pension in it. One of the bandits took it out up to the last centavo and got very angry. On this she agreed with him: the pension is ridiculous, but how can she be blamed? The same guy yanked the medallion from her chest and demanded her wedding ring. But it had been on her finger for ages and the Maestra could not pull it off. There was a moment of confusion. She did not remember whether they had pushed her or whether she had lost her equilibrium; the fact is that she fell to the ground. Another bandit made an obscene remark about her legs. How curious! Only that one moment really affected her; she would have liked to die. But she saw death, and she didn't like its face. It was very different from the sweet expression she had seen on her husband. This time it was all fright and solitude. She didn't notice anything else, not even the moment the bandits left. She was left there on the ground like an animal. . . or maybe worse. But why talk about such dreadful things? Fortunately, the event belonged to the past and now, to tell the truth, she didn't have anything to complain about. She was living—she owned this wonderful house, a privilege in this city, and she enjoyed the work with her plants. What else could she want at the age of seventy?

We said farewell in the middle of the patio. The Maestra excused herself for not accompanying us to the front door under the pretext of a sudden migraine. The last image of her walled-in house caused a feeling of dread which I didn't comprehend until today when I read the news of her death. The ending can only be understood in the light of these previous events. I can imagine how it all happened based on the testimonies of those people who had had contact with her during the last months. I'm not sure, however, if I'm grasping the truth.

In April, Maestra Arellano received an official notification informing her that a new thoroughfare would be constructed right through her block. Under those circumstances she should apply for compensation and leave her house as quickly as possible. First furiously, then desperately, she tried all legal recourses. But in the offices, the functionaries treated her paternalistically despite the fact that she could very well be the mother or grandmother of some of them. They explained to her that she only could gain with the exchange, that these days an old house is a bother, that with the compensation she could get a lovely tiny studio apartment with all comforts in a public housing project, and above all, she would have the opportunity to live among many, many neighbors. But when faced with her reaction, which they considered a senile foolishness, an absurdity, the despotism which is always behind the over-protective attitudes of the authorities surfaced: "This is how it's going to be whether you like it or not. These are orders from higher up."

Confronted with official deafness, the Maestra tried to organize the neighbors. She undertook a great effort to overcome her self-imposed isolation and visited house after house like in the old days. In each of them she gave a complete report about her case in order to propose that the neighbors organize non-violent resistance against the demolition.

The removal made most of the neighbors anxious, but for economic reasons, not because of its effects on the quarter. In the language of the hydroponics, they hadn't grown roots. But they hadn't had enough time for this elaborate process: some of them had arrived in Tacubaya only recently; others—the old neighbors—had their minds on something else. So her proposal seemed out of proportion to them. There was no comparison between the problems caused by a move and those which would be the result of opposing the authorities. However, nobody said so outright, because in accordance with the rules of Mexican courtesy, all assured her that they would think about it, and that they would come to the meeting which the Maestra was going to organize.

On Friday afternoon, the Maestra put chairs, benches and rocking chairs around the dining room table. Even though this room was too small for the number of people who had promised to come, it was also the one she liked best, especially when it was hot and the liquidambar tree gave its best shade. She prepared a basket with galletas Marias and there were two pots with hot water: one for tea and one for coffee.

She remained hopeful for a long time. She drank several cups of tea, and out of anxiety she devoured half the galletas. But when the night fell, she had to accept that nobody cared that all the houses in the block would be leveled.

The following day, for the first time in her life, she did not get up at six. She woke up at that hour because she couldn't go against her internal clock, but she stayed in bed listening to the boleros on the Voz del Recuerdo, Voice of Memories, radio program until midday. "Like the foam, which is carried by the mighty river, oh azalea, the avalanche of life carried you away. . ." What would be the solution?

Since she didn't find an answer to this unknown, she continued her daily life, doubling her workload and pretending that she didn't notice the moving vans, now a common sight in the neighborhood, until the day on which a machine noise announced the beginning of the demolition.

The Maestra jumped into her slippers, and, still putting on her morning robe, she went out into the open air, in defiance of the atmospheric inversion of the early morning. Carrying the weight of age on her shoulders, she took the spiral stairs leading to the roof terrace two by two, arriving just in time to witness the cutting of a big branch of the liquidambar tree.

"You over there. Stop it. What are you doing?"

A worker looked at her with scornful and reddened eyes.

"Can't you see? I'm cutting the tree."

"You say that so calmly? You can't do this."

"Well, now," said the man to himself. "Why not? The tree isn't even on your property."

"That doesn't matter, it's the only one left."

"Calm down, don't exaggerate. Besides, what about me? It's my job. I only do what I'm told by my bosses."

"Which bosses? Show me your orders, your permit. . ."

"Look, Ma'am, I'm getting tired of this. I don't owe you any explanations. Don't bother me."

The Maestra let her eyes drift off into the distance to gain some time to think about a diversionary tactic. Almost the entire landscape was filled with high buildings corroded from acid rain, leaving space only for a greenish brown spot: the leftovers of the once lush Chapultepec Woods.

"Look, there is nothing left."

The worker also looked over the city but couldn't see the losses to which the Maestra was referring. He couldn't compare this panorama to a panorama of former times. Instead of seeing it empty, he saw a universe full of possibilities: the city held everything that he could possibly wish and things that he even couldn't imagine. So he shrugged his shoulders and set off to continue his work.

"Wait, please," said the Maestra in an urgent tone. She felt that if she allowed them to cut the tree, she would be unable to stop the total destruction. At the same time she knew that this was absurd, but there was nothing else to be done. She wouldn't go back to her bed as if nothing had happened, and wait for the roof of her house to fall on her head.

"What can I do so that you'll leave the tree in peace?"

"I think you are a bit crazy. Don't you realize that if I won't do it someone else will? Besides, soon the demolition truck will come with a bunch of workers. They'll tear down everything: your house, this other house, three complete blocks."

The Maestra held on to the pole of the clothesline until it shook, making some of the clothes fall off. A handkerchief sailed down to the sidewalk, landing at the worker's feet; the other pieces were whirling around getting dusty. The Maestra didn't pay any attention to them: she was making a decision and this was of greater importance than all those things she had deeply cared about only five minutes ago.

"Let's see if they'll do it," she said, more to herself than to the worker, "but when it comes to me, they'll only take out my dead body."

And without waiting for the reply of the young man who was staring at her, bewildered, she went down directly to her patio where she kept the materials that had been left over from the construction of the wall. She checked them like an engineer, evaluating them and her own strength. If it was possible, she would do it, even though it might be her last act. There was no other way out. Not for anything in the world would she let them bury her alive in a two-by-four hole where not even her cupboard would fit and where the only daily landscape would be these horrendous concrete masses. This was already a coffin; nobody would fool her, it was a coffin.

Then she checked all the hydroponics, choosing those which were kept in bottles with narrow necks. She put those plants in other containers and set the bottles to dry in the sun. She didn't eat breakfast or take a bath; under the circumstances these luxuries had no place. She took time only to put on the most comfortable clothes she had. Actually it had been some time since the high heels and the tight skirts were stuffed into the bottom of the cupboard, and by now they probably had been eaten by moths, but today, especially today, she wouldn't have chosen them anyway; she would need all possible comfort and flexibility.

When she was ready she put some bottles in a jute bag she used to transport the plants, and she walked towards the door. Before she was out, she could hear the sharp noise of another branch of the liquidambar tree crashing onto the asphalt.

She spent all day going and coming in a rhythm that reminded her of the times in the classroom. She left with the bag filled with empty bottles and an hour later she came back with a liquid and smelly load. In between, she worked in the patio piling up wood and stones around the kitchen door. Occasionally it seemed to her that she was actually building a mock barricade to illustrate a history lesson. But a wheezy feeling in her stomach put her face to face with real enemies. They were men, or maybe women, because nowadays women were everywhere, even among those who carried out eviction orders. This idea made her uncomfortable: if she thought of people, of their eyes and voices, she would not be able to defend herself.

By dusk the liquidambar tree had disappeared. Now she only saw the huge mechanical arm of a demolition vehicle outside her dining room window. Exhausted, the Maestra sat on the stairs leading from the kitchen to the patio. In front of her were a little wall and the bottles arranged in a semicircle; the matches were in the small pocket of her skirt.

Somebody was ringing the doorbell. She got up, and she put her hand on her heart, which seemed ready to jump out of her body. Absolutely still, she waited for the next ring. Up until that moment she had not considered the possible failure of her plan: she might not dare to go ahead, or worse, the explosives might have been set wrong. After all, her knowledge regarding explosives was limited to some stories from the Spanish resistance and some other events which she couldn't remember at that moment. Finally she let herself be guided by common sense, which, in the past, had saved her in many situations, but it might not be enough for this emergency. She would know it soon, as soon as those outside would take the next step. The pause, however, lasted unbearably long. The Maestra realized that she wasn't wearing her glasses. The image of her desk, with the glasses and the book she was currently reading, provoked the first doubts: did she really want to take the risk?

Through a crack, the worker was observing the scene. Later he told the press that he had gone to the Maestra's house under the pretext of returning the handkerchief, but in reality he wanted to offer her his services. He knew that she had to move out within a few hours, and it was obvious that at her age she couldn't do it on her own, therefore it wouldn't be difficult to be hired by her. But it didn't happen that way: the Maestra was a little bit out of her mind, gone from this world, very strange. He had noticed it during the conversation they had had in the morning and his suspicions were confirmed when, instead of answering the door, she stood still behind the shades. Now that everything was over, he could understand the Maestra's behavior, but at that moment he believed that she was performing a spiritist ritual or something along those lines. And he was afraid. However, his need for money was so urgent, that he dared to insist, "Look. . . I got your handkerchief."

The Maestra felt her blood circulation return to normal. She approached the door and said in a low voice, "Very kind of you. Could you put it in the mailbox?"

The worker didn't find this demand unusual, because it matched her character, and because nowadays nobody opens the door for a stranger. But he didn't give up hope; he obeyed her instructions and proceeded to talk about his proposal.

"They already started. The last people in the block are moving out. Do you want me to get a moving van for you? At any moment they'll arrive at your house."

"Are there police?"

"Some. . . shall I get the van for you?"

"Thanks. I think I can do it on my own."

"It's better that I give you a hand, Ma'am. If they arrive before you are ready to go, they will throw your things out the house without giving a damn. There is a woman who is really pissed because they broke her color TV. Come on, let me help you. I won't charge much. . ."

"Really I can do it on my own, young man. Besides, I don't have a single centavo."

"Don't tell me! Then how are you going to manage?"

"I'll see. . . thanks anyway. Good night."

The man waited for a while at the door, hoping that the Maestra would reconsider, but she ignored him completely. She didn't even go to pick up the handkerchief. She was walking back and forth on the patio, like a suffering ghost; then she disappeared behind a pile of stones.

A few hours later, the cold started creeping into her bones. The Maestra improvised a bed on her watch post, and there she stayed looking at the sky, the same way any soldier would do on the night before a battle. Far away she could hear the first explosions.

After a brief doze she woke at dawn, and for a few moments she didn't know her whereabouts or the time. It occurred to her that she might already be dead and that the eviction was only a metaphor of her definite expulsion from this world. But she had too many pains all over her body to believe this hypothesis, and in the end a coughing fit made her straighten up and regain her sense of reality. She wondered whether she could have a bath and drink a cup of tea. The loud noise, however, made her aware that the demolition work was advancing fast. Therefore it was preferable to stay alert. The warmth of the house could also have a dangerous effect; she was so tired from the previous day's and night's activities that she wasn't sure whether she would resist sleep.

She settled on the ground again. There was nothing left but to wait. But what to do in the meantime? If one is waiting with someone else, there is always the possibility of confessions or, even better, a round of brisca or conquian, card games. But if there is nobody else, one is only left with the humming of one's mind. She tried to remember what she did during the long hours waiting for her husband's train. She saw herself walking on the platform, anticipating the embrace, the chat in the streetcar, the stroll later in the afternoon on the sidewalk under the cypresses, feeding each other dulces de yema, sweets. Now, however, which image of the future could she entertain? She only saw a long tunnel, incredibly long.

She didn't have time to become engrossed in this thought: the future was already here, having come with incredible speed. Several times there were knocks on the door, and at the same time a voice shouted something she couldn't understand. What followed was very confusing: maybe a kick against the lock, followed by strong hammering. The Maestra brought the match close to one of the big, green bottles: the burlap started burning slowly. With a brutal push the door's bolt was smashed.

"We have eviction orders."

Maestra Arellano threw the first and last bomb of her life. It provoked nothing but a panicky reaction: a very young cop fired a round with his machine gun. Fortunately it was a very short war. I believe that the Maestra didn't even have time to see death's real face, but went straight into the arms of her husband. At least I prefer to think so. There must be some consolation for people who lose their place on earth that way.

For myself, I'm getting ready to go to the cemetery.

*Translated from Spanish by Ines Rieder and Marlene Rodrigues*

# BARCELONA
## MARIA-ANTÒNIA OLIVER

*Barcelona is not only Catalonia's capital, but also
one of the oldest and now most important industrial cities
on the Iberian peninsula. The city's industrialization and
subsequent growth dates back to the beginning of the
eighteenth century. Since then, Barcelona has been known
as a center of radical politics, ranging from leftist to
anarchist movements. During the years of the Spanish Civil
War, 1936 to 1939, Barcelona was the headquarters of the
Republicans' resistance to Franco's right-wing troops, and
people from all over the world flocked to the city to fight
European fascism. The Republicans lost, and Franco came
to power. He punished the city for its role in the civil
war, and it took years for Barcelona to recuperate.*

*Maria-Antònia Oliver was born in Manacor, Majorca
in 1946. She has lived in Barcelona since 1969, and currently
divides her time between Majorca and Barcelona. She has
worked for print and electronic media, and has written
scripts for film and radio. She has published seven novels,
a number of short stories, as well as translating works by
Virginia Woolf, Mark Twain and others into Catalan. Two
of her novels,* Study in Lilac *and* Antipodes, *were
published in the United States by Seal Press.*

# Barcelona Love

Domènec: "You can find all the clothes you need just by going uptown, at night, and looking through the garbage. Clothes and shoes and furniture for the apartment. And not a single rat! The owners are all asleep and only a few cars go by, and the servants, well, the servants couldn't care less about garbage pickers. . ."

Dolors nodded her head without saying anything. She was wearing a gorgeous yellow mohair sweater.

Domènec: "Look at that sweater Dolors is wearing. It's from the garbage in Sant Gervasi. Those beautiful new houses up there are great for this stuff, I'm telling you. It's brand new, eh? The lady of the house must not have liked it, or it's last year's style, or whatever. And look, look at those shoes. We found them yesterday, you know where? What's the name of that street, no, it's an avenue, that curvy one, Pearson, Avinguda Pearson. We found them just down the way from the Pedralbes monastery. . . The filthy rich don't even use garbage bags. Oh, no, they just leave the stuff on the sidewalk in case anyone wants it."

Domènec and Dolors knew upper Barcelona, the Barcelona of the rich, like the palms of their hands. But you, Jaume, you weren't crazy about the idea of garbage picking or learning the secrets of the rich. I would have liked to, but I never did. Perhaps, deep down, we didn't believe that it would be so wonderful. We stuck to the center of town, to the Eixample. The left and right sides of the Eixample, which were very different from one another. And we did find a number of things. A table and a statue of a saint on the right side. Two fairly new kitchen chairs and some curtains on the left side. Remember how we loved the Eixample, Jaume? You because you'd grown up in a humbler neighborhood, and I because I was from Majorca. Besides, we didn't have to take a bus to get there.

There were no garbage dumpsters on the street corners then. Franco was alive.

And people didn't garbage pick. At least not many people, and they did it on the sly. Only us, a couple of twenty-year-olds with nothing better to do than parade our love through the sleeping city and make it ours. Or attend clandestine meetings: communist, or for Catalonia's independence, it didn't matter, as long as they were against Franco. We'd walk home alone, discussing something somebody had said, keeping an eye on the heaps of garbage in case there was anything of value piled on top. Once in a while we'd go to an evening movie and cover half the Eixample on foot on the way home, from the Passeig de Gràcia to the Hospital de Sant Pau, rummaging through the garbage and choosing (because we were choosy) something someone had thrown out that we thought we could use.

We were poor then. Seriously poor. But we pretended not to notice because we were only poor in terms of money, and that's of no importance when you're only twenty years old and have all the love in the world. Eh, Jaume?

Besides, we liked garbage picking: trash isn't so disgusting when you're twenty years old. Twenty years ago, with Franco alive and the cops keeping watch, the big city seemed smaller, more familiar. The city was whatever neighborhood we were in at a certain moment: charming Gràcia, with its narrow streets, so peaceful and homey you could almost hold it in your hand. The neighbors sitting in the cool air right out on the street—there weren't all those little restaurants that are there now, nor all those cars of all sizes that make it impossible to walk around.

Or Les Rambles, in the summer. Les Rambles, the belly button of the world, where you could buy a book at midnight and where you always ran into someone you knew in the crowd. And the sea at the end, the part of Barcelona that's always overlooked, how is it possible? Or La Ribera, with the church of Santa Maria del Mar, which I always found soothing. A Santa Maria del Mar that hadn't been fixed up yet, dirty and dark, and now it's so white, so clean. . .

Why did we always choose those neighborhoods, Jaume? How many times did we kiss in front of Santa Maria del Mar? And in the Portal de l'Angel? How many embraces on narrow, ugly Carrer Santa Carolina, near the Hospital de Sant Pau? A street devoid of all charm, except for the fact that our first home was there. A street with no personality, that belonged to no neighborhood, but that witnessed my first quarrels with your friends and my longing for Majorca. Later, there were neither quarrels nor longing. Everything calmed down.

What love in this city of Barcelona, great, luminous, dirty, alive, with police crackdowns, and us running at the front. Do you remember, Jaume, those two Sundays of "Freedom, Amnesty and Statute of Autonomy" at the bottom of the Passeig de Gràcia? I was with Xavier, in the car. And Xavier's dead now. Remember that day at the top of Les Rambles, we were running down a back street and I fell, and a thousand strange hands, friendly hands, grabbed me and put me on my feet so that I could keep running? And that time outside the Salón Victor Pradera, in front of the Parc de la Ciutadella, that horse running along the sidewalk, that horse, good God, and the rubber bullets, what a crush of people.

That was all twenty years ago. Twenty, or fifteen, or ten, it doesn't matter. But one day something happened and everything changed. The hospital. The stroke at age forty. I didn't realize the danger I was in, even as the ambulance took me to the hospital with half my body paralyzed. "Look at this girl's heart," the doctors said, "it looks like an artichoke." People called and wrote and came to see me. How wonderful to have so many friends who love me. It was a transitory cerebrovascular accident. An absurdity. I was on my feet in twenty days. With medication, and instructions to take long, long walks. . .

Do you know, Jaume, that this is the first time I'm writing this? I didn't think I'd ever be able to do it.

We've gone back to exploring the city, to kissing on street corners. Well, we'd never stopped doing that, but now we stroll arm-in-arm; we're a little older now, and there's a different taste to our kisses. I see Barcelona with new eyes. My first day out, I grew dizzy: the cars, the noise. It's a shame, this city. So beautiful, so alive, and the noise of the cars ruins it all. But I grew reaccustomed to it. The truth is that in Barcelona I like even the dirt, the noise, and the pollution.

We walked to the doctor's, in the nicer part of Les Corts (all neighborhoods have a nice part and a part that's less so, except maybe upper-class neighborhoods where everything is nice), but first we took a walk through Turó Parc. What did Avinguda Pau

Casals used to be called, do you remember? General Goded, that's right. See? I couldn't even remember, and it wasn't all that long ago that they changed the name. The way they changed Plaça Calvo Sotelo to Francesc Macia, and Victory Pradera to Lluis Companys. Yes, even if it were only because of the street names, the city would be a very different place. What did they call the Granvia? And the Diagonal? They were and are broad, beautiful avenues that cross the city, are part of the city, that adapt to every neighborhood, taking on a different look to fit each area as they cross through it.

We're strolling through Barcelona now. We can see the apartment buildings of the Eixample. They're cleaning them up, restoring them. They started a few years ago and they're keeping at it, and it's a treat for the eyes. The modernist buildings on so many streets were covered with dust, and filth, and shit, and now, look at that one, and that one! Every time you go out, you see another one, new to the eyes and the senses. Building modern-looking buildings is prohibited in the Eixample now; they've learned to restore the old ones. . . or make new ones like the old ones (which I find ridiculous, really, this making them like the old ones; it's fine to repair old buildings, but making them the way they used to. . .) We live in the Eixample now, but in a new building, because when we moved in it wasn't in style to buy an old apartment.

Now we're in Pedralbes, exploring its silent streets lined with high walls that hide the houses of the super-rich. We walk as if walking on the Ronda del Guinardó, with its mix of old and new apartment buildings, none of them very large, and with no gardens and few plants on the terraces. Two different neighborhoods, but they're both part of Barcelona. Now we're strolling through the old section, the Casc Antic, which hasn't changed, except that now there are pedestrian zones and the Plaça de Sant Jaume looks more beautiful than ever (remember, Jaume, the demonstration in favor of the statute of autonomy? We came down Carrer Ferran—what beautiful lights—to the Plaça de Sant Jaume, and I grew dizzy from the crowd) with the buildings sparkling clean, and plants all around. . .

Franco is dead now.

It's been fourteen years. Do you remember Franco? I do. I want to remember him always, so that he'll never come back to life.

There are garbage dumpsters on the streets.

That friend of ours who worked at city hall got them put in.

They're unaesthetic, and they smell, and you can't open them on an empty stomach.

We're a little better off than we used to be, and we no longer rummage through the garbage to find a dress or some curtains or a table or a sweater.

And Barcelona is the same city, unchanged, yet very distinct from the city that received me, at twenty, with open arms and a teasing smile. A city so great that no matter how much you say you've still left most of it unsaid, as I have here. Montjuic, for example, with its gardens, or the neighborhood of La Mina, with its delinquents. I'd never finish. That's what makes it a great city.

Our best friends are no longer Domènec and Dolors, although Dolors got in touch when I was in the hospital. Now our friends are Montse and Josep Maria, who live in the Putxet, where it's impossible to find a parking space at night; and Joan and Luisa, who live in an apartment his parents own in Poble Nou, that horrible transient neighborhood that will be completely changed after they build something or other for the Olympics there (I'm not sure which is better—perhaps neither); and so many others, too many to count.

All of them, though, were with me during my illness.

And love; what do you say about love, Jaume?

Jaume: "We have it trapped in our hands; it won't escape."

Barcelona love.

*Translated from Catalan by Sheila McIntosh*

# DETROIT
ROSALIND WARREN

*In 1914, Detroit, Michigan became the world's first automobile capital thanks to Henry Ford, who installed assembly lines in car factories and paid a five-dollar-per-day minimum wage to his workers, many of them immigrants. Detroit's big days are long gone—manufacturers in other countries now produce more cars than Ford, General Motors and Chrysler—and all attempts to revive the city—deeply divided along race and class lines—have so far failed. But the myth that everything in the city revolves around the automobile lives on.*

*Rosalind Warren grew up in Detroit. Though she no longer lives there, and probably will never return, she writes that Detroit is the only place that feels like home. She is a bankruptcy attorney, and is working on her collection of stories with the help of a Pennsylvania Council on the Arts fellowship.*

# Auto Repair

There is no place to go in Detroit that's half as fun as getting there. Especially in my daddy's Olds. The closest thing to heaven on earth is being on the freeway when Aretha comes on. Her soaring voice is telling me to floor it. I turn the volume up until the music is coming from inside me and go as fast as I can.

I don't want you to think that I don't drive responsibly. I am a responsible driver. Responsible, but accelerated. I go to the community college, though I'm just seventeen, because I'm accelerated. I still live at home, though. So I can drive my daddy's Olds.

My father taught me to drive when I was fourteen. He took me to the parking lot at the Tel-Twelve Mall, told me to get behind the wheel, sat back in the passenger seat, and lit a cigar. "Do your worst, babe," he said.

He put on the country-western station and Earl Scruggs and Ricky Skaggs sang love songs as we lurched around the lot. Dad slouched back in the reclining seat and gave me advice. "Don't squash that poodle, honey." "Watch out for the Winnebago." One morning he gave me a key ring with the keys to seventeen cars. "They're all yours, Mercy," he said. I gave him a bear hug and he smiled. "Sure wish your mom could see you now," he said.

Mom died when I was only two. She died in her car, a red Trans Am. Coming home from the supermarket one night, she was broadsided by a drunk car-door salesman in a Lincoln Continental. The car was totaled. She was killed instantly. The groceries in the trunk survived.

Dad didn't junk the car. He had it towed home. He rebuilt it. He wanted to salvage something, he says. Repairing the car made him feel better. He started collecting them. He buys wrecks and puts them back together again. It's like a hobby. He tells me it's therapy. "Auto repair—the poor man's analysis," he says. He must have over twenty cars now, plus junkers he keeps for parts.

Some of Dad's cars are stashed in friends' garages; some are out in our driveway or sitting in the backyard. We've got a peach-colored Studebaker down in the basement, because he took it apart in the driveway one summer and reassembled it down there, just to see if he could.

Everything in Detroit comes down to cars. If you don't work on the line like my dad, you work for a company that makes car-door handles or cruise controls. Or plastic saints for the dashboard. Or you're that company's lawyer, or the shrink the auto execs go to, or the funeral director that puts them all in the ground. Remember that guy who was buried sitting behind the wheel of his Caddy? He wasn't a Detroit man, but he had the right idea. Detroit is all auto showrooms, muffler shops, and intersections with a gas station on each corner. Motown babies are born groping for the steering wheel, and by the time a local kid is five she can call out the model and year of every car that drives by.

My dad never remarried. He's got girlfriends. He's got me. He's got reconstituted Chevys, Fords, Pontiacs, a Studebaker in the basement, and job security. He's got pals on the line to go drinking with.

When he gets too drunk to drive, he phones me from a bar and I drive out to get him. His friends help him into the backseat. He sits with his feet up and lights a cigar.

"Where to?" I ask.

"East of the sun, west of the moon," he'll say if he's really sloshed.

"Dad?"

"Anywhere you want, babe," he says. "It's all the same to me."

The streets around Detroit—long, wide roads under a big mid-western sky—are made for cruising. I'll drive down Woodward Avenue. We'll put the radio on or just sit quiet and watch the world go by. Woodward is the main drag—miles of glittering neon signs and fast-food stands. Everybody in this city learned to drive on this street. Sometimes we'll cruise all the way out to Dearborn to see Ford Motor Company World Headquarters, a complex of gleaming skyscrapers sitting all by itself in the middle of nowhere. Or downtown to the Detroit River to see the Renaissance Center, which was supposed to revitalize the inner city but didn't. Or to Canada, crossing through the tunnel under the river, driving through sleepy downtown Windsor, and returning across the Ambassador Bridge. I drive by my mom's cemetery. Over the entrance is a sign in lovely pink neon script—Roseview Cemetery—that I remember from way before I had any idea what it meant.

Eventually Dad falls asleep and I drive home.

I fell in love with Todd in his daddy's Eldorado.

My daddy didn't take to Todd at first. "He's too short for you," he said. "He looks like a hoodlum." Dad was wrong about that. Todd was a rich kid from Bloomfield Hills. He wore faded jeans and a beat-up leather jacket because it looked cool, not because he couldn't afford better. He had long dark hair, beautiful gray eyes, and loads of nervous energy, and he played lead guitar for the Clone Brothers, a local band. He was at our place watching television, with a crowd of my friends. A girl I didn't like had brought him, so I started flirting with him.

I could sense Dad lurking by the front door later on as I walked Todd to his car. The girl he'd been with was long gone. Todd got into the Eldorado, and I leaned in the window of that gorgeous black car and kissed him. That's when I fell in love. Todd didn't seem too surprised—as if strange girls leaned in his car window and kissed him all the time.

"Call me," I said, dizzy.

We gazed into each other's eyes. Then he turned the key in the ignition and the engine blew up.

The next thing I know I'm sitting on our front lawn, with Todd and my father running around the car yelling instructions to each other, trying to get our old fire extinguisher to work and swatting at the burning Eldorado with blankets. A crowd of neighbors came out to cheer them on, but the Eldorado burned to a crisp.

Dad decided to like Todd then, either because he felt sorry for him or because he wanted his car for parts.

But Todd didn't phone. Maybe because our kiss had set his car on fire. I didn't see him again until months later. His band was playing at a bar out in Ypsilanti, and Dad went to see them without telling me. I guess he was getting sick of my moping around the house telling him how the love of my life had passed me by. Dad ended up having a pretty good time. After the last set, Todd drove my father home.

Todd rang the doorbell. It was late, and I came to the door in my pajamas. He was the last person I'd expected to see.

"Guess what?" Todd said.

I didn't have to guess—I could hear my daddy snoring away in the backseat of Todd's new Chevy.

"Let him rest," said Todd. He got out his guitar and I put on a bathrobe, and we sat on the warm hood of Todd's car, where he recycled all the love songs he'd written for his last girlfriend. Between the songs we kissed.

Hours later the car door opened and Dad stepped out. "What a night!" he said.

He squinted at us sitting there on the hood. I could tell he didn't really remember Todd's driving him home.

"Nice car," he said. "Is it ours?"

He circled the Chevy, patting the hood, stooping to admire the whitewalls, tracing the chrome with a fingertip. Finishing, he bowed to us and shuffled toward the house, still wrapped in the blanket I'd thrown over him. He looked like the drawing in my grade school civics textbook of Pontiac, the Indian chief for whom the city of Pontiac and later the car were named.

He paused on the front steps. "Call me if you need help putting any fires out," he said.

Todd phoned the next night.

"Want to come over?" he asked. He gave me directions to his house. It wasn't till I got there that I recognized the neighborhood, a posh subdivision that had gone up a few years back. When it was new, my friends and I used to cruise through and laugh at how grand and silly the houses were. They were all monsters, each flashier than the last. And Todd lived in the grandest one. It was a little castle, complete with three turrets, a waterless moat, and a fake drawbridge.

Todd met me at the door with a skinny girl with wild red curls and thick glasses. She looked about twelve.

"I'm baby-sitting," he said. "My parents are out of town. This is my sister, Gladys. She's a computer nerd."

"Computer hacker," Gladys corrected. "Want me to access your school records and change all your grades to A's?"

"They already are."

"Cool." She grinned. "If you're so smart, what are you doing with my brother?"

Todd gave her a friendly shove. "Come on," he said to me.

He led me through the place, which looked like something out of a magazine, to his room, which was ten times the size of my room at home. Guitars and stereo equipment lined one wall, and his record collection took up half of another. I'd never seen anything like it. We sat down on his bed.

"Where are your parents?" I asked.

"Geneva." He sounded almost apologetic.

Silence.

"I missed you," he said finally. Then we started kissing, and I felt at home again, even in that outlandish place.

We got to the point where if we'd been in a car, we'd have dusted ourselves off and gone to get coffee someplace on Woodward and talk. I'd never known anyone whose parents vanished to Geneva and left them a castle to hang out in. I wasn't entirely comfortable about it. I began wondering how I was going to get out of this. Did I really want to?

Then Todd stopped kissing me and looked into my eyes. I waited.

"Want to climb a tree?" he asked.

Climb? A tree?

"We have to take Gladys, though. I'm responsible for her."

"A tree?" I asked.

"You'll see," he said. "It'll be fun."

It was. The three of us drove to Ferndale, a small residential neighborhood. "We used to live here," said Todd as we cruised through the quiet streets. "Then Grandpa died and Mom inherited." We got out of the car at a sleepy little park. There was an old beech with thick, sprawling branches—perfect for climbing.

"This is my favorite place," Todd said when the three of us had climbed up to the top. We sat in the branches, looking out over the park and talking. When we ran out of things to say, Todd and Gladys sang me Elvis songs. I'd never been happier.

"And what have you been up to?" asked Dad when I got home.

Todd and I started going out. We usually took his car. I'd sit beside him, my head against his shoulder and the radio playing. He'd chain-smoke and we'd cruise and talk for hours. Or I'd just sit, quiet, feeling so happy I wanted to freeze the whole thing and stash it in a time capsule somewhere.

All this bliss made Dad a little nervous. "Don't get in over your head," he warned one night while he and I watched the Tigers pulverize the Red Sox on television.

"Too late," I said.

"He's a real nice kid," said Dad. "But he's got a few problems."
I got a kick out of that. Dad spoke as if Todd were a faulty engine
that needed a few days in the shop.

"What kind of problems?"

"You think that boy spends a tenth the time thinking about you
that you spend thinking about him?"

"This is a relationship, Dad, not a seesaw."

"Do you two ever talk about anything besides his music and
his band and his plans? Ever talk about your plans?"

"I don't need to talk about my plans."

"That's not the point," he said, "and you know it."

Of course I knew it, though I wasn't going to tell him so. I
wasn't stupid. I knew deep down that I was in love with Todd
and Todd was in love with me being in love with Todd. As neat
and talented as he was, he was too insecure and unsure of himself
to be able to focus on me. But that would change. I'd make it
change.

It was as if Dad could read my mind.

"That boy's a do-it-yourself model," he said, "You deserve a
finished product."

I blew up at him. "I'm not one of your cars!" I said. "Don't
try to make me apart and put me back the way you want."

He smiled. "OK, honey," he said. "I'll back off. But maybe
you'll listen to an expert." He took a folded-up piece of yellowed
newspaper from his wallet and pushed it across the table to me.
It was an old Ann Landers column about how to tell love from
infatuation. I asked how long he'd been carrying it around.

"Five, six years," he said. "You never know when something
like this could come in handy."

"I was only eleven when you clipped it?"

"Just thinking ahead," he said, rummaging around in his wallet.
"The concerned single parent."

"The overprotective single parent," I said. "The nosy, interfer-
ing single parent." I told him I didn't give a hoot about what
some old lady had to say five years ago about love. I was happier
than I'd been ever with Todd. Dad would just have to trust me.

He kept poking around in his wallet. Finally he took out my
mom's high school graduation photo and sighed. "You're the spitting image," he said. "On the outside. But on the inside you're
just as pigheaded as your old man."

"I could do a lot worse," I said.

84

A few weeks later Todd and I were sitting in his car parked in our driveway, and Todd told me that he wanted to break it off. "It's getting too serious," he said.

I had the feeling that wasn't it at all. He'd found someone new to listen to his love songs. He just didn't have the nerve to tell me. I tried to joke.

"You want it to be more shallow?" I asked.

He stared at me, looking as if he were about to cry. I could tell he wasn't enjoying this, and my heart went out to him. Then I realized that if I didn't stop myself, I'd end up comforting him for leaving me.

"Ann Landers tried to warn me about you," I said. I got out of the car, slammed the door, and went to my daddy's Olds, parked right behind Todd's Chevy. I started her up and began searching for a good radio station.

Todd came over and leaned in my window.

"Where are you going?" he asked. "You live here."

"East of the sun, west of the moon," I said.

"Can't we be friends?" he asked.

I was so angry I wanted to back up my daddy's Olds, floor her, and smash right into Todd's beautiful new car. You break my heart, I'll wreck your Chevy. But I'm my father's daughter—I couldn't do that to an innocent auto. Instead I found Stevie Wonder on the dial and took off with a squeal of tires. Todd ran after me, but I floored it until he was just a tiny dot in the rearview mirror.

The music was good. It carried me through our subdivision and the quiet side streets over to Telegraph Avenue. I decided to drive down Telegraph, past all the Mile Roads. Ten Mile Road, by the all-night kosher Dunkin' Donuts. Eleven Mile Road, by my old high school. Twelve Mile Road. All the lights were with me and I was cruising. I love this car, I was thinking. Nothing can get me in here. It's when you get out of your car that the trouble starts.

There was a groan from the backseat, and my daddy's face appeared in the rearview. "Apparently a man can't take a little nap in his own Oldsmobile without getting hijacked?" he said.

"What on earth are you doing back there?" I asked.

"I was sleeping," he said. "It's usually real peaceful back here."

I glared at him. I didn't need this. Not now.

We rode a few minutes, silent. I could see it was funny. And I knew he loved me. Still, I had planned to drive for hours—a heartbroken blond racing down the freeway at night with tears in her eyes. A real American cliché.

Having Dad pop up in the backseat like that kind of ruined the picture.

"Are we headed anywhere in particular?" he asked a few miles later.

"Nope."

"Care to talk about it?"

I didn't really. I wanted to drive. Alone. I wanted to drive for miles and miles and dwell on my sorrow. But it was too late for that.

"There's a twenty-four-hour car wash out on Lone Pine Road," Dad said. "Your mom and I used to go there to talk. If we couldn't get things straightened out, we figured at least the car would get clean." He smiled. "We don't have to talk if you don't want to. But the car could use washing."

The most miserable night of my life and we're talking about whether the car needs washing.

Of course, on the other hand, the car did need washing. It couldn't hurt to wash the car. At the next intersection I turned toward Lone Pine Road, switched over to the country station, and gave the full weight of my foot to the accelerator. Dad leaned forward to squeeze my shoulder, then settled back in his seat, smiling, "No rush," he said. "We've got all night."

It wasn't that I stopped feeling sad. There was a heaviness in my chest that I knew would stay with me awhile. But as we cruised along, the idea of driving in the middle of the night to take a beat-up Oldsmobile through a car wash for a heart-to-heart talk with my old man didn't seem so bad.

## SÃO PAULO
### SILVIA FANARO

*"To many people the city of São Paulo is just an
accumulation of brick and concrete structures surrounded
by slums,"* writes Silvia Fanaro. *"To me, it
is that and much more."*

*"São Paulo cannot stop,"* was the slogan of the city's
four million inhabitants in the early fifties when it
celebrated its four hundredth anniversary. Now city
planners are saying *"São Paulo has to stop,"* and they
are trying to keep its population at the
currently estimated eighteen million.

*"I don't know if São Paulo will survive economic crisis,
growing violence, traffic chaos. I only know that my
destiny is deeply linked to this city. While waiting for our
apocalypse, I keep going, selling old furniture in an
antique shop and health insurance in my spare time. I
hope to become a very nice old lady who will still enjoy
the pleasures of the big city: speeding around in my old
car, in the eternal search for time, money, and love."*

Silvia Fanaro was born in São Paulo in 1942. She is the
daughter and niece of the architects of São Paulo's most
famous apartment buildings, constructed in the fifties.
She has been involved in the women's movement ever
since it gained a foothold in Brazil. More than writing,
she loves to tell stories, and if the city of São Paulo ever
hires an official storyteller, it will have to be her.

# The Day I Met Miss America

It's six in the evening on a rather cold day. My daughter, two
friends and I walk towards the entrance of the Bretagne, a big
L-shaped apartment building in Avenida Higienópolis. The Bretagne is completely fenced in and the entrance has a big iron gate
controlled by a guard sitting in a little room with thick glass
windows. The window looking out to the street has a little opening
allowing communication.

"Excuse me, could you possibly let us in for a few minutes?
We would like to take a look at the building. . ." Anticipating
any suspicion, I add, "This building was planned and built by
my father and my uncle. I would like to show it to my friends.
They are foreigners; they are interested in architecture, you
know. . ."

After a moment of hesitation and checking to see whether my
friends really look like foreigners, the guard opens the door and
we wander into the big entrance hall. My daughter, who is seeing
the interior of this place for the first time, is delighted. After all,
it's part of our family's history, a legacy of the days when her
grandfather and his brother were successful entrepreneurs. They
had introduced a new housing concept to São Paulo's emerging
middle class: the condominium, with its own possibilities of entertainment—swimming pool, playground, ballroom, music
room, bar—and promises of safety for the kids who could no
longer play in the streets due to the increasing heavy traffic.

While she entertains my friends with architectural details, I
stroll slowly towards the music room. I softly close the door
behind me and let my eyes wander around, following the last rays

88

of light falling on the big piano. Suddenly I hear the faded murmur of people and sounds of soft music begin to fill the air. Around me forms are taking shape; voices become more distinct and I recognize the heavy body of my uncle, smell his big cigar, and hear him talking loudly to somebody with a cowboy hat. A blond, very beautiful young woman is leaning against the piano, having a conversation with an old lady. Somebody calls me, and as I turn around, I see my father. He wants to introduce me to the smiling cowboy who is still listening to my uncle.

"Come here, why don't you shake hands with Roy Rogers? And you might want to exchange some words with Miss America. Do you see her? She is over there, by the piano. . ."

I can't quite figure out what is going on, but the noise of people around me increases; they are all chatting loudly, sipping dry martinis and champagne and eating snacks. There is a profusion of handshakes and flashes from the photographers' cameras. A neatly dressed woman wearing a nice hat looks at me. She seems ageless and lacking any kind of expression. I move towards her and when I come closer I see that her eyes are cold, penetrating and at same time searching for something. I'm about to ask her who she is, but she has already started talking:

"Your father is celebrating the inauguration of the Bretagne. I know that it doesn't matter to you because you are very busy following orders from these stupid nuns who run that school across the street. You're just interested in learning how to sit with your legs kept tight, how to address the Mother Superior and how to behave properly in front of men. You are always accusing us of nouveau rich materialism. You have chosen to go there because you know that we don't care about religion, and this is your way to show us how much you despise us. But as soon as you are out of the classroom, you and your colleagues are after some mischief. Why don't you take after your two older sisters? They are so well behaved; they are going to pick up the right men and be secure for the rest of their lives. You don't want to play our game, but you won't get anywhere in life."

I try to remember who she is, but my memory just draws a blank. However, her monologue helps me to recognize some of the people gathered in the room—they are well known, both from the city's government and the church; there are also celebrated Brazilian artists and even prominent international figures, like Roy Rogers and Miss America.

I close my eyes because I want to get out of this place, but someone else takes me by the arm and sits me down on a sofa.

He is an old man, and I recognize his voice at once. He had been my father's lawyer for years and years.

"Eh, eh, girl, you still look very pretty!"

I am very puzzled, since I don't know if he refers to me as I am now, a woman in her forties, or to the fifteen-year-old I was back then.

"Well," he goes on, "I'm a little sad today, because this building is the last enterprise your father will finish. The sixties are coming—the economic boom and the high inflation. Everybody's attention is already turned towards Brasilia. All available construction materials will be used to build this new city. Prices will soar, and your family's business will go bankrupt."

I sit staring at him, without moving a muscle, waiting for what is still to come.

"Right now you don't need to worry; you are going to the movies with your friends," he continues. "You sing and dance to the sounds of Elvis Presley; you are under the spell of the growing city.

"The building frenzy is attracting hordes of poor people from all over the country, especially from the northeast, because there people are dying of hunger. They live in a land forgotten by God and they are sucked dry to the bones by the local landowners. These Nordestinos will help to change São Paulo, but also because of them the city will grow faster and faster, devouring all the green that's in its way, and in the end all our lives will become intolerable."

I get bored with this speech since I know its contents only too well. I would rather think about my father the entrepreneur—a side of his personality I don't know much about. At home there was never any talk about his business deals. And the financial failings and the bankruptcy were a well guarded secret of my parents. The impression I have of him is of a good-natured, quiet man. A man who never dared to challenge my mother and who had a total fascination for his brother, the one with talent and endless imagination.

But I don't have time to go on dreaming. The old man looks at me, smiles and says, "The uncontrollable growing of this city matches your uncontrollable desire for something that cannot be reached. . ."

His image starts fading away and I touch my fingers, looking for something. A wedding ring, but it's no longer there. Miss America is coming towards me, her hands stretched out. She

Silvia Fanaro

greets me with "Hi," and I could swear that she's chewing gum. She looks me all over and starts talking before I can get away from her.

"Hey, good lookin'. . . too bad that you are going to choose that spoiled son of a landowner for a husband. And just because you want to make your family feel miserable. You know that they don't care for him. I know that you'll sleep with him before the wedding night, and I can promise you that you'll have great sex throughout your married life. But he will treat you like a whore and you'll have to hide that from your family. They will pretend they don't know that he is beating you. You'll have a big wedding and then you'll go with him to his cattle farm. Within a few years you'll have two children. The farm, his friends, your married life will become unbearable. You'll run back to the city, back to where you belong. Well, honey, growing up in São Paulo, the city always seemed at your feet and you under its spell. But coming back after a failed marriage, with two children to feed, and your family bankrupt, there will be no room for dreams."

"But the sixties," I say, "they will come. . ." My sentence is cut short by her sharp laugh.

"Oh, of course, you will come back to the city under the magic of the sixties, but the pink, yellow and blue colors of your golden fifties will have faded away and the army's olive green uniforms and black boots are now setting the tone. . ."

I feel a cold wind coming from the windows and I want to go to a warmer place, but there is nowhere to go. I'm surrounded by people, the air is thick with smoke and I'm shivering. A little girl resembling my daughter when she was a child comes to me and says, "I'm very sorry, but I can't help them."

Whom, I think, whom is she unable to help? At that moment Roy Rogers announces in his best American voice that he would like to show a few scenes from his latest movie. A screen is put up and the projection starts, but instead of seeing Roy Rogers on his white horse going after bandits in the Old West, I see some streets which I know only too well. They are the streets of São Paulo. I see the Praça da República packed with students, shouting and carrying signs, "Vai acabar, vai acabar a ditadura militar: Down, down with the military dictatorship." I see the building of the Faculdade de Filosofia, the Philosophy Department, going up in flames; I hear gunfire and the screams from dark prison cells. Suddenly the room is lit again; Roy Rogers has disappeared and the piano is making funny sounds. Someone is improvising, and I'm relieved.

The uptight woman with the cold eyes joins me again and resumes her talk as if there hadn't been a break.

"You will step into the seventies full speed. You are going to be involved in the political movement opposing the military dictatorship. You'll run from your work to political meetings and from political meetings to the new bars which will be opened throughout the city to shelter the intellectuals who survived to see the seventies, and who are now thirsty for political freedom and good beer. Political organizations will be founded and you'll get acquainted with many people returning from exile, among them all these women who will bring back feminist ideas from Europe and the United States. You'll neglect your kids, you'll spend all the money you have, but you'll have a great time.

"By then, I'll be gone, your father will be gone, the fine old houses and mansions still left in Avenida Higienópolis will be gone. Avenida Paulista will see its last mansions go down to be replaced by shining gigantic structures of glass and iron, and whole neighborhoods will be destroyed to make room for new avenues and the underground. You'll start talking about the impossibility of surviving in São Paulo without a car. You'll think that the city is livable only on the weekends. Like everyone else, you'll drive at night without respecting the red lights, and you'll spend hours on the telephone talking about your latest relationship. The city will be engulfed in poverty, uncontrolled real estate speculation and the increase of violence. You'll refuse to acknowledge your own impoverishment, you'll go on in the swing of the fifties, but oh dear, by then, they'll be long gone."

Suddenly I recognize the face, I see my mother in front of me, and before she can say another word, I manage to run out of the room. In the hall I'm stopped by Miss America. She grabs me and forces me into the waiting elevator. She pushes the button and up we go, to the terrace. Still holding me tightly, she says, "Let's take that spaceship stationed up there and go for a ride over the city!"

The aircraft is ready and we take off, flying over the countless skyscrapers. Looking down I see all kinds of concrete towers, ugly viaducts, and a huge rectangular gray structure in place of the old buildings which once used to be on Praça da Sé, the heart of the city. I see millions of cars, buses, trucks and people coming and going in a desperate frenzy. The spaceship goes lower and lower, passing over the streets right in front of windows, and I see the interiors of flats. Most of them have the same kind of furniture, TV sets are turned on to the same programs, and the faces staring at the screens all look frighteningly alike. I get desperate, and I want to get off.

Miss America is saying something about "all these McDonald's and shopping malls make me feel at home. . ." and we continue our flight. We are now in the southern part of the city, in the best neighborhoods. They have been extended and are rapidly taking over all the available land on the other side of the Tietê river. The river is a grey, foamy and slowly moving mass, filled with old tires and garbage; rats and human bodies are floating on its surface.

Then we fly back towards the center of town, crossing my neighborhood. We reach my building, a small structure surrounded by high-rises. As we drift by the window of my living room, I look in and I cry out—there I am, walking about the place, getting ready to go to work. I am in a hurry, trying to get dressed, brush my hair, eat some food, answer the telephone, all at once, and my face is very tense. Bills are scattered all over my table.

I want to go back; I want to be in that music room, the only place where I seem to be able to escape from all this. I want to be back in the fifties. But Miss America is having lots of fun; she is not interested in returning.

There is a sudden change of scene in my living room. I'm still there, but now I appear relaxed. I'm lying on the couch reading a book; occasionally I glance at my watch. The bell rings; I get up, open the door and my lover comes in and embraces me. She has brought a bottle of good wine, some food from the take-out place around the corner and a wonderful record by Marisa Monte. We are talking about today's events and we often interrupt each other with our laughing and kissing.

I turn away from that scene and look at Miss America. She seems pretty annoyed. Now she is the one who wants to go back to the Bretagne, but I want to stay a little bit longer to enjoy those moments of happiness. We start arguing and she gets really angry. She grabs me by the shoulders and starts shaking me. Suddenly I am back in the music room. It seems very quiet again, very empty and dark. My daughter is standing in front of me.

"Mama, we've been waiting for you for a long time; we thought you had gone to the bathroom. Now here you are, not even caring to go around to see the building with us. What a shame!"

We go out in the streets again. It's night and the traffic is heavy. I look at the Bretagne one more time. The music room is unlit, but the windows of all the apartments are bright; people are already at home, eating dinner, watching the evening soap operas, or taking a shower. I look at my friends who came from Europe where everything is so neat, so orderly, so controlled, and at my daughter who wants to have a university career and maybe spend a year in Moscow studying Russian.

I think of the evening ahead of me; my lover will come over and I hope that we'll have a good time. Before we get into the car, a young blond woman approaches us and asks for directions. She wants to know where she can find the Hilton Hotel; she has been sightseeing and has lost her way. She speaks broken Portuguese with a heavy foreign accent. I take a closer look at her face and I seem to recognize Miss America's features. I rush my daughter and my friends into the car and I drive off very fast, laughing and not looking back. After all, I'm planning to have a good evening. Let Miss America find her own way.

## BOMBAY
### SHANTA COKHALE

*Bombay, the gateway of India, was once a group of seven islands on the western coast, now joined to each other and the mainland by land reclamation that continues today. It is both the commercial and cultural center of India. Like all industrial cities, it is heavily polluted and boasts an increasing number of high-rise buildings towering over an increasing number of shanty towns. People pour into Bombay, the dream city, at the rate of three hundred a day and somehow manage to survive. Civic amenities are under severe stress yet manage to function. Always cosmopolitan in nature, its eleven million residents include Hindus, Christians, Muslims, Parsis and Jews from every part of India.*

*Shanta Gokhale was born in 1939 and has lived in Bombay most of her life. She has worked as a teacher and journalist, has written stories, a play and a novella in Marathi, her mother tongue, and translates Marathi literature into English.*

# Shifting Sands

It is a perfectly square room, two hundred feet off the ground. In the early morning, just as the sun has broken the sky above the low bungalows in the east, it strikes a dozen suns off the windowpanes on this floor of the building. Later, it throws an ever-widening band of light, pale yellow in this season, across the speckled tile floor, in which motes rise and fall and swirl tirelessly.

Ganga sits in this streak of sun, pulling her chair into it and into it, as it shifts slowly across the floor and finally disappears in the late afternoon into the northern wall. Neelam helps her move her chair and moves with it herself, sitting at Ganga's feet, or standing behind her or leaning out of the window watching the yellow-topped taxis and long limousines pulling silently up to the porch of the neighbouring five-star hotel and divulging Pierre Cardin-covered rolls of fat, hair dyed black or rinsed blue and clouds of chiffon hung with diamonds.

"Don't lean out so much," Ganga can't stop herself from saying.

Neelam, still leaning out, answers with a laugh, "Granny, you always worry."

"I do, I do," Ganga admits ruefully. "It is an old memory that makes me worry so." Her "so" is inflected upwards. Will Neelam turn round from the window, come and sit beside her and say, "What memory, granny?" Will she?

Ganga watches Neelam's back. It has stiffened. Neelam knows what granny wants. She pulls her head in, turns round and says, "What memory, granny?" Her feet drag her over to the old woman's chair. She drops down at her feet. Pulls her knees up. Puts her cheek on them. Looks up sideways at Ganga. And says in a flat voice. "Do tell."

Ganga hears the flatness in Neelam's voice; yet her own voice begins its narration, unwilled. "It is the memory of my brother Raja, who died when he was ten, leaning off the roof of our house, trying to reach the topmost branches of our bakul tree." She looks down at Neelam, whose eyes are now unfocused. "Have you ever seen a bakul tree, my girl? How large it is?"

Neelam has never seen a bakul tree. But Ganga has often told her about this one in their garden, its trunk that twenty little arms could not encompass, and its gift every morning of a carpet of delicate beige brown flowers—flimsy to touch, heady of scent. "No, I haven't," she murmurs softly.

So Ganga tells her again, and as she speaks, her voice becomes first a mumble, then a whisper until at last it retreats from the outer world into an inner dialogue with voices which emerge one by one, noiselessly, from the vast spaces of her memory, eternally young. Her mother, her favourite aunt, her little sisters, her best friend Yamu whose early death made Ganga's world go black for a time.

Neelam's eyes are drooping with the stupor of emptiness. Behind them, she is straining to shape a dream that will bring on that delicious ache in the heart and that spurt of warm flow. She wills before herself the image of a young girl—she, in a flimsy sari, for whom the man with the cruel eyes and flashing smile will sing a deep-throated song full of suggestion, and who, once the vows are shyly taken, will change into a becomingly chaste bride, modestly prepared to be adored all her life.

But the dream will not form. Even with her eyes tightly closed and granny suddenly silent, she can only see the boring emptiness of a square room into which comes the occasional caw of a crow and the damp saltiness of the sea.

She watches the sliding band of sunlight sulkily. When it disappears into the wall, she must take granny down for her daily walk. Slowly the tension in her dissolves. Her flesh readies itself for its chores, grows soft and pliant. No use straining after a dream that won't form. The sunband is slowly pulling out. She watches it with a fixed, alert eye. One moment it is there, a bank, then a streak, a sliver and then it's gone.

"Come, granny, it is time for our walk," Neelam says, lazily unfolding off the floor and stretching, feeling the muscles tauten over her belly and chest.

Ganga glances up at the movement. Her eyes are milky with displacement. Where did that voice come from? It was an outsider's voice. What did it say? "Granny. It's time for our walk," Neelam repeats patiently. Reluctantly Ganga focuses her eyes on Neelam.

"Has Aditi come home?" she asks, trying to connect the time and the place.

"No, it's her tuition day," Neelam answers. "I said we must go for our walk."

"Tuition day," Ganga nods as she shuffles towards her room to get ready for the walk. "Tuition day today, dance class tomorrow, tuition again the day after. . ." Ganga stumbles at the threshold to her room. "Spin, spin, spin. . ."

"Bai wants her to come first in the whole of Bombay." Neelam helps her to the mirror on the wall.

"Yes. First in this, first in that. . ." Ganga picks up the tall tin of talcum powder from the top of the little medicine chest that Kumar has had made for her. She shakes a little powder into the cup of her right palm. Then, rubbing both palms together, she smoothes them over the skin of her face, once luminous, now loose. Lifting her palms to her nose, she sniffs at them delicately. "Nice. But not like the flowers I know. The bakul. The Krishna kamal. The thick white champac. The double-petalled mogra."

As the traffic grates and clangs and rumbles by, the road under their feet reverberates, making Ganga's walk even more uncertain than it is in the house. "Why does Kumar insist on this walk?" The question comes querulously in a miraculous moment of silence, that still throbs with the noise that has gone and the noise that is coming.

"The doctor says you must go out into the fresh air every day. And you must have some exercise," Neelam answers in the flat voice of daily repetition.

"My throat scratches. My eyes water. My blood runs scared in your fresh air. You won't understand, you young people. . ."

Ganga's voice is lost in the rumble of a truck. But she continues to talk as she shuffles along, holding onto Neelam's arm for support, the two enveloped in sun-flecked clouds of road dust.

Ganga mutters because she must. But she is also happy that nobody can hear her to call her crotchety and unreasonable as do Kumar and Kalindi and even Aditi, with their painfully patient faces. Ganga mutters about the uneven pavement, the trench they have now dug in it, the overflowing gutters, the slum colony that

lies between the house and the park. She mutters fearfully about
the sea. She will not believe that the sea, which once rolled here
and was forced back, further and further, to make way for people,
will not suddenly surge in where it belongs and swallow up men,
women, children, television sets, wedding glitter, and fluffy dogs,
all in one sky-scraping tidal wave, then subside, satiated.

Kumar says people are not fools to build their highest structures
on shifting ground. But she doesn't know, she just doesn't know.
The fear of not knowing brings her unsteady steps to a halt. She
cannot go on. She does not want to go on.

"Let's go back home," she says in great weariness.

"Home?" Neelam shouts above the traffic noise. "Why?"

She watches Ganga's mouth as it says "tired."

"But the park's just out there," Neelam points out. For her, *he*
is just out there—the gatekeeper. Not the hero of her dreams,
but one who smiles at her in a special way.

Ganga says nothing, but doesn't move. Then she slowly turns
and takes a step homewards. Neelam follows, her face dark and
full with anger. "I'm going away for Holi, the spring festival.
Then there'll be nobody to take you for a walk anyway," she
shouts spitefully. "There will be no Neelam to bother you all day
long. You'll be alone then, all alone in the house."

Ganga shakes her head from side to side as she continues
homeward, saying to herself, the girl is angry. Kalindi will not
like that. I must get her to smile before Kalindi comes home.
Poor child, with hardly fifteen years behind her. And me with
seventy and hardly five before me. Years? Months? Days?

In the house Ganga says to Neelam, "It'll be nice for you to
go home for a while, won't it?"

Neelam shrugs.

"How far is your home from here?"

"I've told you, granny. It takes me an hour on the local."

"And yet it's in Bombay?"

"Of course."

"Dear, dear. I can't think of such bigness. Something that goes
on and on with no river, no hill, at which to stop and let something
else begin."

Neelam sits picking at a scab on her leg.

"And the strike in your father's mill? Is it still on?"

"Yes."

Neelam's face darkens at the thought of her father sitting at
home drunk, beating up her mother for the money she earns doing
people's washing. She shouts and abuses, but she gets beaten and

has her money taken away. "How awful for your mother to bring up the children single-handed. Do the others go to school?"

"Only the boys. My sister's at home to look after the youngest."

Ganga does not know how to go on from here. Neelam's face is still clouded. "Kalindi will be home soon, won't she?"

Neelam glances at the clock on the wall. "Hm," she answers.

"You should go to school, Neelam. I should tell Kalindi to send you to night school. I'm sure there's one around here. Once everyone is home, you don't have to be here with me." As Ganga talks, her voice takes on an almost crisp chirpiness. She has never thought of this before. How good it will be for Neelam, to have a future opened up before her. She leans forward in her chair to peer at Neelam's face. But where she expects to see a rising sun, she sees a brooding thundercloud. "Wouldn't you like to go? To school?" Ganga asks, suddenly unsure.

"No." The word shoots out of Neelam's tightly clenched teeth like a bullet. Her last employer had asked her the same question in the same tone of voice. She had said yes then, not knowing what it meant. The woman had enrolled her in a local night school, then given her extra work during the day to compensate for her absence in the evening. More—she had cut her salary as partial payment for the books she had bought secondhand for Neelam. That had made her mother scream. "What do you want to go to school for? Just get the money to shove some scraps down your brothers' throats. Books aren't going to stop your husband getting drunk and beating you up when the time comes anyway. I can tell you that."

Her mother had found her this job then, and Neelam had told the woman she was quitting.

The woman had gone red in the face and spat out one word again and again. "Ungrateful. You people are all the same. Ungrateful."

As she walked out of the woman's house, her belongings stuffed in a small cloth bag, she had learned about one thing she didn't want. She didn't want to be grateful to anybody. She would manage without kindness. Ganga is watching the scowl deepen on Neelam's face. Helpless, unsure about what to do but not willing to give up trying to bring a smile to the girl's face, she asks, "How many days will you be away for Holi?"

"Eight," Neelam says curtly.

"That'll be a nice time for you. Away from this old bag who keeps rattling last century's bones in your ears." Ganga turns moist eyes on Neelam. Her mouth is half open, her forehead puckered up. For a moment Neelam looks at her blankly. Then her eyes fill with a sudden flood of clear water and she throws her young arm around the old woman's shoulders.

"You with your nice smelling talcum powder? Who'll call you an old bag?" She grins. Ganga looks at her with an uncertain smile, then begins to laugh. Neelam too. They both laugh, neither knowing why, until the tears stream down their cheeks.

"So?" Kalindi demands as soon as she has closed the door to their bedroom that night. "What do we do with Ai when Neelam is away?"

In the next room Ganga pricks up her ears. The walls between rooms in these tall city buildings are matchstick-thin. Where she grew up they were massive. You wouldn't know if the man next door beat his wife black and blue. But here, closed doors put you out of sight but not out of earshot.

"I'm waiting for your answer, Kumar," Kalindi says in her firm no-nonsense way.

Kumar's voice is a reluctant grumble which Ganga, for all her straining, sitting up in bed and leaning over, cannot hear.

"That's not an answer. Holi will be upon us in ten days," Kalindi points out.

"She'll stay alone. . . she won't mind." Kumar's voice comes vaguely through.

"She won't mind, but I will." Kalindi is obviously standing facing him. "I would never forgive myself if something. . . happened while we were away at work. Her cataracts are really bad now."

"I know. She's my mother, isn't she? The only one I have." Ganga knows, when her son grows sarcastic, he has a worry without a solution.

"Oh, fine." Kalindi's voice comes through the wall like an arrow. "Then you will decide what's to be done. I don't have to worry."

Ganga can hear a body throwing itself heavily on to the bed. Then the bed creaks as the other rolls over.

A heavy silence follows.

"I was thinking, Kumar," Ganga says, standing in the doorway of the bathroom where her son is shaving. She makes her voice sound as if she has only just experienced the interesting thought she is about to speak of. "I was thinking, why don't I go spend a few days at Kamla's?"

"What for?" Kumar grunts, screwing up the right side of his face to tauten the left for the razor.

"Because she's always asking me to come, and I haven't been for years."

"With her youngest son married, they must have added a couple more to the family and the place is the same—two rooms and a common verandah. Where do you think you'll sit or sleep?"

"Kamla always says we'll manage."

"She says that to be polite."

"Not Kamla. She's not one of those."

"We'll see."

"I'll have to let her know."

"When do you want to go?"

"Any time."

"Let's see."

"Around Holi might be a good time."

"I wouldn't know where to park the car when I take you there. The place is crawling with people. But perhaps we could manage it. Speak to Kalindi, though."

"Of course," Ganga says and softly moves away.

Sitting with Kamla, her childhood friend, out on the verandah that runs down the length of the block of tenement flats where she has lived for forty-five years, Ganga is picking fenugreek leaves off their stalks for the evening's meal. She inhales the bitter aroma that rises with every snapping, swaying back and forth in quiet harmony with her work.

"It's been years since I've eaten fenugreek," she says, glancing at the heap of leaves gathered in the colander ready for rinsing in half a dozen waters before cooking.

"Years?" Kamla's voice is full of surprise. They eat fenugreek every fourth day. It's good for the health and cheap.

"Aditi doesn't care for it," Ganga answers. "We don't make things she doesn't like."

A double-decker bus draws to a halt at the bus stop in front of the house. A man at the window on the upper deck is at eye level with them. He looks inquisitively into the colander of fenugreek leaves. As the bus moves on, his eyes take in the clothes hanging out, the baby crawling, the woman tipping garbage onto the pavement. The bus leaves behind a veil of dust that settles noiselessly on the flagstone floor of the verandah, on fenugreek, clothes and baby.

"The noise is worse than it used to be," Ganga observes, not wishing to sound critical but unable to stop herself from saying so.

"Worse? Ten times. A hundred times. The traffic never stops now. Even the crows sometimes caw in the night thinking it's day," Kamla answers, sniffing.

Ganga peers down between the slats of the verandah banister at the viscous flow of people strolling, walking, rushing, squatting, sleeping, jamming into each other.

"They frighten me," she mumbles. "I want to die before it gets much worse."

"Why should you want to die? Up your way you probably don't hear a squeak even at peak hour."

Ganga hears again the hollow, echoing soundlessness of the square room. "I prefer the noise," she says quickly, picking up the colander and tossing it expertly up and down to loosen the heap of leaves in it.

"The noise doesn't worry me any more," Kamla says, a bubble breaking in her voice. "I've found a way out. I've gone deaf."

Kamla shakes with laughter. Shalini, who has just come into the verandah further down to see if her daughter-in-law is coming back from work, catches the remark and joins in Kamla's laughter, quickly adding to Ganga, "But don't think she's as deaf as she likes to make out. Things she wants to hear she can hear very well, can't you, Kamla?"

On Holi night the boys in the tenement and the neighbourhood light a bonfire in an open plot across the road. They have dragged a young tree all the way from somewhere and set it up in the center of the pit they have dug for the fire, surrounding it with piled-up logs, branches and twigs. The fire takes a long time to catch. The tree is too young and green. But when it does, the boys break into a whoop, clapping their hands over their yelling mouths, letting forth the broken yodels of Holi. The flames of the bonfire, leaping and dancing, turn the surrounding faces into heinous masks of orange light and black shadow.

Ganga's eyes screw up, not only against the smoke but against a block in her memory. "Where does that open ground come from, Kamla, where the fire is?" she asks. "It wasn't there the last time I was here."

Kamla sighs. "No, it wasn't. It wasn't there last year either. Don't you remember the old cottage that used to stand there?"

"Oh, yes," Ganga whispers, still straining to remember.

"It was the finest house in the neighbourhood when we first came to stay here," Kamla says. "Then the old man lost his all on the stock exchange and hung himself from the beams of his own roof. The son took to drink. Only the old woman continued as if nothing had happened. They said it was a kind of madness, the way she hung onto the house while its paint peeled, walls crumbled and a peepul tree took root in its cracked floor. The woman died last year. Quick as anything, the sodden son sold off the place for a song. They say the man who bought it will build a shopping complex here."

They watch as the flames of the fire claw the air. Coconuts are thrown in and taken out when the roar of the yellow fire quietens to a red sizzle and finally to a grey hiss. The coconuts are cracked open then and the flesh broken up into warm smoke-flavoured pieces which are distributed to the families in the neighbourhood as holy offerings from the fire.

The acridness of the smoke still hangs in the air the following day when the colour games begin. Gangs of boys and girls roam the streets with scarlet hair and rainbow-coloured faces. Water balloons sail out at unsuspecting passers-by. Coloured powders cloud the air. Sticky paints are smeared on any face that dares to look clean.

Ganga sits in the verandah with Kamla, watching and laughing, but cringing too, away from those young faces which show only as white teeth and eyeballs through lurid coloured skin; away from their dances of triumph at having found their targets.

"Why do the girls play colour?" she asks Kamla querulously, hating to see their wet and clinging dresses. "Holi is only for boys."

"Used to be," Kamla sniffs. "Now it's for girls too. The only thing girls don't do yet is curse and drink. And why not?" she adds. "I suppose it is right. They study like boys, work like boys, play like boys—nothing wrong."

"No, nothing at all," Ganga says and turns her eyes away.

Kumar looks sideways at his mother's face, turned to gaze out of the window at the clash of coloured wares in pavement stalls.

"How noisy this part of the city has become," he says, trying to draw her into conversation.

"Yes," Ganga answers. "Kamla says she's gone deaf to keep the noise out. Perhaps I have gone blind to keep the sights out."

Kumar laughs and pats her knee with his left hand. "Blind? Having cataracts is not going blind. You'll be back to normal when they are out next year. Come on, cheer up, Ai."

Ganga sits still and silent, weary at the thought of living to next year. The car is bumping over hard metal roads with holes in them. Nothing seems to give to her here. Everything is so rigid. The road is hard. The holes are jagged. The trees are sapless and dusty, the windows in tall buildings blank and unending. Suddenly Ganga wants to stand barefoot on earth. On soft black clods through which the cotton plants will shoot and fluff into a thousand white balls. Her feet twitch with the thought.

Kumar stops the car before their block. She feels heavy to herself as he gives her a hand out of the car. Her feet drag as she follows him to the lift. "Neelam's back," he says cheerfully, opening the door of the lift. "She's waiting eagerly to see you."

Ganga steps into the lift without a word. The door slides shut. The lift is now an airless box moving up, eerily up. Ganga cowers as always against a corner, tense and fearful lest it explode or go hurtling down. The numbers on the panel above the door flick on and off, on and off until at last the lift comes to a stop. The door opens and Ganga totters out into the open.

Kalindi opens the door when Kumar rings.

"You look terrible," she says, greeting Ganga warmly.

"Doesn't she?" Kumar agrees. "We should have never sent her to that terrible place," he says.

"I'm okay," Ganga smiles wanly. Neelam comes forward out of the shadows to give her a hand. Ganga doesn't take it, but walks on slowly, very slowly towards the back of the flat. From the narrow ribbon of a verandah here, she can imagine the shape and the colours of the sun setting even now out there, behind the tall, light-pricked, cement anthills that surround her. She sits here, imagining the yellow ball of the sun burning into an orange ellipse, pressed between sky and ocean, dipping lower and lower until it has gone, leaving behind a greying pink flush.

# CITIES ON THE EDGE

## BEIJING
### PATRICIA SIEBER

*Patricia Sieber visited Beijing in 1981 and 1982, and returned to study Chinese for two years, 1983 to 1985. "First I learned to read the huge white letters on red-painted stone squares placed at eye level at all major intersections. . . Then I learned to read the placards placed next to the gates in the walls surrounding most buildings. I had no business visiting any of these places, so I learned to read Chinese newspapers. One of my teachers, a party member, taught us how to decipher the news in the* People's Daily *according to font size and front page lay-out. The most popular paper, the* Beijing Evening News, *was four pages long and cost five cents. It featured stories about the latest archaeological finds, famous poet-officials in history, and letters to the editor on whether women should sacrifice their careers to family obligations."*

*She then began writing in Chinese. "I realized that Beijing is not only a city of walls, it is above all a city of letters. That is what the city revolves around: walls, words and the words on the walls."*

*Patricia Sieber was born in Tokyo and grew up in Zurich. She is a member of the editorial collective of* Connexions, *and is currently working on a collection of stories about death.*

# The Spirits of Beijing

I was atop Mount Tai, some four hundred miles south of Beijing. The day before, I had climbed the six thousand steps together with countless other travelers. Carved into the cliffs along the stairways, calligraphic characters, some legible, others artfully distorted, had punctuated our ascent. The rocks had guided us towards the lone summit—it was from there that everybody would watch the sun rise over the plains. It was still dark, but the darkness stirred with muted anticipation. It was hard to hear what anybody said, for coats, blankets and the icy air muffled the sounds. With the first batch of light, it became clear that the peak was completely engulfed by dense fog. Of course, it might recede, but suddenly everybody remembered the saying that only on one day of the year can the sunrise be observed from Mount Tai. A voice added, somewhat sadly, that he had known we would not see the sunrise, but he had come up anyway. He continued, "You know, it is just like I said over two thousand years ago; you know you cannot succeed, but you do it anyway."

The voice sent a chill through my body. I suddenly remembered that the dead enter and leave the nether world through Mount Tai. The spectral silhouettes all seemed to converge, looking for a human body to whom they could attach themselves. I listened to the sound of their steps. I heard them quite clearly—the chanting of the washerwomen at the well where a young maidservant had sought refuge, the silent tears of a young mother deprived of her girl-child, the defiant shouts of an orgiastic visionary as she was being paraded on the way to her execution, the angry cussing of a successful civil service candidate upon people's discovery of her true sex. Their voices were not simply in my ears, they were in my hair, even in my hands. I did not hear stories anymore. My skin was being torn open with raw sounds, with bits and pieces sent whirling in a void. I gave in—to what, I don't know, but I did.

I felt as if I had been sucked into Mount Tai and spit out into the labyrinthine back streets of Beijing. In the distance, at the end of a narrow alleyway, I noticed two red lanterns. I slowly walked towards them. As I came closer, I saw that they were hanging on either side of a vermilion gate. On the outer screen of the lanterns, tiny shadows of young women brandishing their weapons turned round and round. I could hear them singing:

> All in red
> Wearing red headbands and wearing red boots
> We do not do our hair
> We do not bind our feet,
> With small red lanterns, we light fires,
> With the wave of our red fans, we soar up into the sky.
> They steal our grain, they steal our children,
> but we fight,
> even if we have nothing left but our bare red hands.

The vermilion gate opened and I stepped inside. I felt exuberant. Something dramatic seemed imminent. I expected to see hundreds of women prepared to fight. The courtyard, however, was deserted. Only in the main hall a dim light flickered. I realized I was dreaming and I wanted to wake up, but I couldn't. As if tied to an invisible rope, I was pulled, ineluctably, towards the hall. I knew that was where the ancestral spirit tablets were lined up. I did not know whose ancestors were gathered there; perhaps they were mine, except I did not know what family I belonged to. Then the gate to the main hall opened—instead of tablets inscribed with black ink, thousands of tablets inscribed with red ink burst into sight. Black ink was for those who had already passed on, but red ink was reserved for those who were still alive. I stared vacantly at the tablets; I did not want anybody to die. I did not want to make out the names on the tablets. I wanted to say that enough of us had died already when a melodious voice said, "So you are here." And before I could think about an answer, I said, "Yes, I am here," as if I could not possibly have been anywhere else.

I did not know whom I was talking to. I did not know whether *I* was there, or someone impersonating me. But it did not seem to matter. I felt so immensely alive that nothing seemed to matter. It occurred to me that I should find out who had expected me. She wore a Western man's suit—and not because she wanted to be either a Westerner or a man. A dagger was dangling from her belt, nonchalantly, but it was clear that her hands were as adept at handling that weapon as they were at brewing explosives. Her hair wasn't just cropped, but completely shaved—short hair was not radical enough. Playing on the homophonous sounds of "anarchy" and "hairlessness" in Chinese, a willfully bald head conveyed outrage over injustice. I smiled at her. She shook her head: "You know, I was beheaded some eighty years ago on a summer day. It's summer again. It's summer again . . ." Ah, she had a red silk scarf draped around her neck, carefully hiding her wound. Her voice trailed off, heavy with the prescience of a seasoned revolutionary.

With her arm around me she walked me over to a writing table. Several pieces of paper were spread out. She picked up a wicker basket lying next to an inkwell and stuck the handle of a brush underneath the basket. She motioned me to hold one side of the basket. And then, as if guided by a will of its own, the brush started tracing characters, illegibly at first, until the ink turned crimson. As I deciphered the mysterious writing, "a debt of blood must be repaid with blood," I realized that blood had welled up in the inkpot. I looked at her in bewilderment. Somberly she asked, "Can you hear them?"

At first I did not hear anything. I strained my ears; I still did not hear anything. Then I saw the pained expression on her face—she seemed suddenly very old, as if she had seen too many deaths. As her gaze was fixed on something outside, I followed her stare—on the lanterns where women warriors had fought their battles, the shadows of tanks were spinning round and round. The vehicles seemed to take a perverse delight in rolling over the same spot again and again—they wanted to deaden what was already dead under their wheels.

I heard shots somewhere in the distance; here, there, then silence, then a series of sharp sounds. Then from the night on the other side of the courtyard burst sprays of randomly fired bullets. I saw a young man fall from his bicycle—then his brain was splattered all over the ground—even the bicycle was pressed flat. Was it a truck or a tank? I didn't know, I just stared at the smudges of blood splashed across the asphalt—they did not mean anything, they just spelled death. I dipped my finger into the pool. I knew what I wanted to write on the blank scroll on the table; I knew exactly what I wanted this death to mean, but as my fingers touched the paper, they were seized—abrupt blotches appeared, soaking the paper so rapidly that it dripped. The blood spilled onto the table; still there was more of it; I closed my eyes, I felt drenched, it seemed that the whole room was flooded. I suddenly had visions of Hell. I did not see mothers drowning in the blood of the children they had borne; I saw fathers drowning in the blood of the children they had shot.

Then I heard a voice, emerging from amidst cordons of young men and women. It was not just one voice, even though only one woman was speaking; you could hear her choke on tears, yet hers was a syntax of a different order. She spoke simply, but the words held together, tightly linked like the arms of the women and men surrounding her; she spoke so simply that at first I did not understand what she was saying, yet I knew it was true. I knew this because I had had dreams of sentences structured just like hers, structured tightly around a utopian void. "I am going to tell you a very old story which everybody knows. There was an anthill inhabited by about one billion ants. One day the anthill caught on fire. The ants realized that they had to get down from the mountain if they were to be saved. Thus some ants formed a circle and descended to put out the fire. As a result, many of those on the edge died, but even more ants survived. Fellow students, we are on the square, we are standing on the outer edge of our people."

I realized that she must be speaking from Tiananmen Square, the grandiose open space in the heart of the city. It is not even so much the square itself, it is the sky that seems to be too large to be at the center of any city. On crisp days, light floods the space, overpowering the smog issuing from the southeastern industrial quarters. It almost washes away the neo-Stalinist columns demarcating the eastern and western edges. The mausoleum in the southern part too seems afloat, its columns no match for the inundation of light. Even the crimson walls of the Old Palace at the northern end of the square fade into immateriality. On a day like that the sky harbors a promise. Something pregnant with something larger than itself seems to hover over the sky, just like the many kites over the square trying to fly beyond their tethers.

I saw the headlights of tanks piercing the dark square. I heard more gunshots. I wanted my companion to put her arm around me and tell me that everything was going to be all right. I looked around the hall—she was nowhere to be seen. Instead I found myself face to face with the spirit tablets. I did not want to look at them, but I could not help noticing that whole rows had turned black. I felt a scream ripping through my body, and a deafening pain spreading even to the tips of my hair. I shivered, but my shivering scared me, so I just stood there, motionless, feeling deadened, but pretending to be alive.

I don't know how long I stood there—perhaps days, perhaps weeks. I know, though, what brought me back to my senses. I heard voices; the voices were very far away and I could not see anybody. It must have been shortly before dawn. The voices were repeating one line of a song; they sang "the east is red, the east is red." It sounded like a whisper, or perhaps only the faint echo of a whisper I had heard elsewhere.

## BEIRUT
### MICHA WARDE

*In 1961, when Micha Warde was born, Beirut was already the financial and cultural capital of the Arab world. It was also the capital of Lebanon, considered the Mediterranean Switzerland by the many foreigners who came to the city. The delicate system of dividing power among various Christian and Muslim groups had already set the stage for the conflicts that would later tear Beirut apart. Religious and class conflicts intensified, leading to civil war from 1975 to 1977. The end of the war did not bring an end to armed conflict. Depending on the current political situation, Christian and Muslim militias fight both together and against each other. Due to its precarious border with Israel, Lebanon not only houses thousands of Palestinian refugees, but is also a frequent target of Israeli air and land attacks.*

*While completing her studies in sociology at French University, Micha Warde spent her nights and days locked into the fairly secure house of her parents, listening to gunfire, shells and Israeli war planes. She is currently studying the effect of war on the cultural life of Beirut. Since 1985, Micha has lived in Berkeley. She regularly visits Beirut and hopes to return to live there one day.*

114

# An Ave Maria for Beirut

"Ave Maria—don't let them destroy our house.
"Ave Maria—spare the children.
"Ave Maria—have they all gone mad?"

A tight white T-shirt exposes her breasts as they move rhythmically up and down while she prays. She has been kneeling in front of the Virgin for several minutes. Two candles are slowly burning. She lit those candles during the first round of gunfire. One was for Khawaja Raymond: the other one was for Nayla. Whenever fighting breaks out, she lights candles for those who are not in the house. They are put out only once everyone has returned safely.

She should have known that there would be fighting—after all, the moon is almost full. The militias always go wild at this time of the month. Just like some women who go crazy when they are having their periods. Right at that moment she hears two familiar voices at the front door. "They are back," she thinks, and she wets her fingers to extinguish the candles. "It's time to go to the kitchen and get dinner started."

The kitchen is now all hers; she no longer has to bicker with other women over this domain. Sitt Leila still comes in to help or just to chat, but there are no orders, and more important, no rivals. Fatima, the maid, left the house after she had fallen in love with a Sudanese and gotten pregnant by him. She knows that the family preferred Fatima's cooking to hers, but that can

115

be attributed to the fact that Fatima is Syrian, just like them.

To be truthful, only Khawaja Raymond was born in Syria; but he had raised his family right here in Beirut. Sitt Leila and the kids really were Lebanese, but with a slight Syrian touch—there was no way around that. Whatever Maria doesn't understand about them, she blames it on their Syrian ancestors. She doesn't care much for the Syrians, and she thinks that they have been trying for too long to boss around the Lebanese. But then, of course, there were times when they had been helpful . . .

She herself owes nothing to the Syrians; she has obligations only towards Frangieh's family. But then everyone in her village in northern Lebanon has responsibilities towards their feudal lords. Right next to the statue of the Virgin, she keeps a framed picture of Suleyman Frangieh, the current head of the family, and at one time Lebanon's president.

Khawaja Raymond and Sitt Leila are Christians—no, she wouldn't work for anyone who wasn't—but they are Greek Catholics, not Maronites like her. For Maria, Christians are Christians, since they all believe in the same God. The rituals change, but the Virgin doesn't care about the words of the prayers as long as they are addressed to her. What a pity that the Virgin doesn't have more influence on politics. Maria is sure that if politics were up to her, Christians wouldn't fight each other with the same passion as they were fighting Muslims and Jews. If political decisions were to be left to her, she would make sure that the Phalangists would no longer control the neighborhood, and after that everything would fall into place.

She sighs. There is no point thinking about what could be. She has to prepare dinner. If only she had the same ingredients as she had at home. She could make hummus that would make their mouths water. But the garbanzo beans sold in Beirut aren't the same; they lack a certain taste. For all she knows, they might even have been produced in Israel. Or some other foreign country where people don't know a thing about food.

Maria is very devoted to traditional Lebanese cooking, and it's a mystery to her how all those Lebanese can survive abroad. She is sure that many of them are starving. That's why they all come back—with or without fighting. Not too long ago she met this woman at the souk who had lived in Berlin for a year. She had fled Beirut because her sons were getting to the age where they might start thinking of joining a militia. For months they had eaten nothing but lousy food in Berlin, and she decided to return to Beirut. The risks on her life in Beirut seemed outweighed by the food she could serve her family.

Almost every morning she is awakened shortly after seven by the sound of people either trying to wade through broken glass or sweeping it up, producing an eerie sound audible throughout Beirut. After a cup of coffee she goes out to buy the daily news-papers. Sometimes she is back home within an hour, but after nights of heavy combat, it often takes her several hours to check on everybody and everything in the area.

The papers are sold right around the corner in front of the grocery store, but in a city like Beirut, papers can't tell all the stories, and Maria's main interest is to find out how the neighbor-hood fared, and, even more, to be involved in predictions of what might still come. In order to collect all the information, rumors and gossip, she has to go from house to house helping to clean up broken glass and giving often unsolicited advice on daily matters. Frequently she becomes involved in arguments, and upon her return home she repeats every single word that was exchanged. Maria spends the rest of the morning preparing lunch in the kitchen. Out of habit she turns on the radio without ever listening to it.

By eight-thirty, dinner is over and Maria is back in the kitchen doing the dishes. Soon all the neighbors will arrive, since Khawaja Raymond's house is the safest place to be during these nights of gunfire and shellings. With one ear she is trying to listen to the noise outside the house, and with the other she is trying to pay attention to what's going on inside. The fights seem to have slowed down a bit, but the night is still young. She remembers the rumors she heard that morning while walking around the neighborhood, and she is sure that there will be fighting until dawn.

"This must be the only war in the world where most of the fighting goes on at night," she thinks. "During the day we are made to believe that we live in peace—we go about our business, but at night, we are turned into prisoners. We cannot leave our homes, and the militias are playing Russian roulette with our lives. We never know where they'll hit and whom. No wonder everyone is popping Valium and drinking whiskey as if it were water. I don't take that stuff, because I don't want to fog up my mind."

The shattering sounds of glass interrupt her thoughts. She drops everything and runs into the living room, where the sound came from. Khawaja Raymond has broken a whiskey glass. Her nerves must be on edge, because she feared that it was a window. She goes back to the kitchen to get a broom and a dustpan. As she is sweeping up the glass, the doorbell rings and Sitt Leila goes to open the door.

Maria hears Sitt Rose's high-pitched voice and hurries back to the kitchen. She has never gotten along with Sitt Rose, who believes that she is a bit better than everyone else because she is in possession of a U.S. passport. "Why doesn't she go back to America, if she believes that everything is better there?" Maria thinks. Sitt Rose has been putting all the blame for having to stay in Beirut on her husband, who always claims that business is better elsewhere. Currently he is in Brazil making more money, adding to his comfortable wealth. "And what does he do with all his money?" Maria wonders. "He wastes it on his children. All good-for-nothing Phalangists." There is only one thing Maria has to say in favor of Sitt Rose—she has always been outspoken in her dislike for the Phalangists. And just like Sitt Leila, she is using her money to help those who need it most.

Another ring. This time Maria distinguishes several voices—all of them belonging to Nayla's friends. "I wonder if this Shi'a is going to be with them? He seems to be part of the crowd now. . . I just don't know where she picks up her friends." Maria doesn't think that religions should be mixed up, not when it comes to friends, or, even worse, within families. After all, the children will be confused and they will suffer. One parent turns towards Mecca, the other teaches them how to make the cross—and in the end they'll be carrying crosses to Mecca and getting into trouble. Maria is sure that Muslims are people just like Christians—they are all praying to the same God. But—and this is Maria's biggest concern—they don't have a Virgin. Whom can they rely on? It is obvious to anyone who has lived in, and survived, a city like Beirut, that they manage to get through because the city and its people are under *her* special protection.

There are nine people in the living room—not everyone has arrived yet. "I hope I got enough biscuits. And if Khawaja Raymond didn't get more whiskey, we might run out." She always has to think of everything. Without her there wouldn't be anything to eat or to drink in this house.

Nayla is quietly playing backgammon with Omar, one of her friends. The other three, Amin, Pierre and Jean-Louis, are continuing a heated political discussion which must have started much earlier in the day. Amin and Omar have crossed over from West Beirut, and they will have to spend the night with their friends on the East side, since going back is impossible. Crossing at the only open checkpoint took careful planning. A day before coming to East Beirut, Amin and Omar had to give their names as well as the number of their car's license plate to the Syrian Army.

Maria, who loves the shops in the West, rarely crosses over now. There is too much apprehension, too many searches, humiliations and insults. It is as if there were a competition between the Syrians, the Lebanese Army and the Lebanese Forces: who can be the nastiest?

"You have lived in Paris for too long," she hears Pierre say to Amin. "Ever since you've come back, you only want to listen to Arabic music, eat Arabic food, speak Arabic. Why don't you ask Maria if she understands half of what you are trying to say . . ."

"His Arabic is not a problem," Maria laughs, "but I don't understand his politics."

"But he learned both his Arabic and his politics in Paris. He might have an easier time in Morocco," says Pierre.

"Just be quiet, Pierre," Nayla says in her calm voice. "Not everyone is as lucky as you to have sucked classical Arabic with their mother's milk."

Maria is bored with these conversations. On a night like this she prefers gossip. But she can no longer entertain that thought because the shellings have intensified. As if by a silent command, everyone in the living room gets up and goes to the lobby, the safest place in the house. The noise has gotten louder and the gunfire seems much closer.

As soon as everyone is settled into the lobby, Pierre turns to Amin, and asks mockingly, "Any phone calls from Paris recently?"

"Of course, of course. We all receive phone calls from Paris, or any other place in the world. We live for these phone calls." Amin sounds a bit annoyed. "Whatever happens in Beirut is important to us, but let's face it, the real news comes from abroad."

"And then we sit around on nights like this and repeat every word that was transmitted via satellite," Nayla adds. "We take it apart, analyze it and make it come alive again. Does it matter if it has been changed in the process? We already have a thousand and one nights of storytelling behind us, and many more ahead."

There's a loud knock on the front door, followed by the entrance of Aunt Madeleine. Maria goes over to greet her and is surprised to see some tears in her eyes.

"What's the matter with you?" she asks with compassion.

"I just got a phone call from Marcel. He's planning to get married."

"But that's wonderful," Maria exclaims.

"It sounds better than it is. You haven't heard yet who will be the bride, and why they are getting married. She is some Muslim girl. . ." sighs Aunt Madeleine. "She is from a respectable family. I know that much, but they would never have given her permission to marry a Christian if she wasn't pregnant. It's all my husband's fault; he was never around to educate Marcel. A boy needs a father to tell him what's acceptable. A son never listens to his mother when it comes to choosing a wife, but he will listen to the father. But you know how my husband is, always thinking about some business. When he was in Europe he came back more often, but now with all his dealings in Africa. . . sometimes I'm even surprised that he still sends us money. You would think that he has forgotten his family in Beirut."

Maria has always heard rumors about Madeleine's husband's interest in other women, but she has never been sure whether they are true. She has seen with her own eyes, though, Madeleine's education of Marcel. If ever there was a spoiled child it was him; he ate too much chocolate, and as a teenager he spent most of his waking hours right next to his record player.

"Just take a few of those," Maria says, handing Madeleine some Valium. From past experience she knows that there is nothing worse than spending a whole night with an upset mother. She could drive everyone up the wall. Too many people locked into a tiny space with gunfire in the background and a silver moon in the sky—it takes lots of skill to keep such a situation under control.

Sometimes Maria wonders how these nights would be spent in one of the many refugee camps and makeshift houses around Beirut. She knows that people there have little protection—neither sounds nor bullets can be kept out—and a bigger shell might bring down the whole structure. How many people might be crowded into one single room? Mothers with five, six, often even more children. And nowhere to go. Just hoping and praying that the night will pass and that their homes will be spared one more time. How can these people go on living? How can the Palestinians continue to have hope?

She doesn't have any lost love for the Palestinians. Together with the communists they had put Lebanon on the spot; they had turned Beirut into this living hell. They are foreigners, but she knows that they are foreigners without a country to return to. They had come to Beirut in waves—1948, 1967, 1970. Each war had brought more of them, and the camps and some neighborhoods were taken over by them.

She could never forget that day in the late summer of 1976. They were all driving back to Beirut from the mountains, when they saw the smoking ruins of the Tall-al-Zaatar refugee camp and the Karantina neighborhood. Nobody said a word. Everyone was in shock. She was the one who had broken the silence, asking, "What happened to all these people? Where have they all gone?"

Later they found out that those who had survived the massacres at the hands of the Phalangists had moved on and taken over Beirut's fashionable waterfront. They are still there today; the beach cabins of the rich have become the homes of the poor.

Maria looks at the clock—it is past one. Another three hours before dawn. Another three hours of shelling. Even if the fighters take drugs to stay awake, they always seem to get tired with the nearing of sunrise. They can't afford to let go for just one second, or they might be killed.

She should ask whether anyone wants to lie down—the mattresses are all ready in the other room. She isn't tired yet because she took a long nap in the afternoon. She is in the mood for a round of card games with Nayla and her friends. Their political discussions have fizzled out, and they are all involved in setting up a new board game. Maria joins them, even though she would prefer a card game. Sitt Leila will put the other guests to sleep; she doesn't need to worry. And given the noises coming in from the outside, they all might stay up anyway.

From the corner of her eye, Maria sees that Khawaja Raymond is opening another whiskey bottle, his hands slightly trembling. "Is he just nervous, or is he getting old?" she wonders. "Compared to the danger of his twice weekly trip to West Beirut, this is nothing—just a night of distant fighting. Maybe we have forgotten what danger is and confuse it with fear."

A couple more hours of card playing, and then the sun will rise. All the things she has to do. . . Most important, she should not forget to buy more candles. She used up the last two this evening. A couple more hours and all the fighters will have retreated from the battle, and then all the Beirutis—in the West and in the East—will have their first cup of coffee and go out into the streets. Some of them to clean up the previous night's mess, some to conduct business, some to do shopping, some to go to school. And with the first sounds of gunfire, they will all run back home, lock their front doors and leave the streets to those who are fighting over the city's destiny.

# WASHINGTON D.C.
## CAITLIN RICHARDS

*Washington D.C. indeed proves to be the perfect capital
for the "War Against Drugs" declared by the U.S.
government. In 1989, Washington set a new city record
for homicides: four hundred thirty-seven. According to
the media, most of these murders are drug-related. Even
the city's current mayor is suspected of taking
drugs—"but he was doing them to keep them off the
streets," according to Washington gossip. As with many
other urban problems in the United States, the blame for
the city's crisis is put on the inhabitants rather than
administrative and financial inadequacies. Eighty percent
of the population of Washington D.C. is black and
mostly poor, in contrast with the large numbers of mostly
white and well-to-do government employees, who
occupy the city during the day and go home to the
suburbs in the evening.*

*After graduating from Hofstra University in 1986, Caitlin
Richards moved to Washington D.C. for the summer
to finish out her sister's lease. Four years later,
she is still there, with no intention of leaving.
This is her first published story.*

# August Passes

I tell myself that August passes, so January will too. But that doesn't make the days go any faster. Neither does their being so short. They get longer every day, any way you look at it.

There are twenty murders so far this January. I guess I'm not the only one who finds the short winter days too long. Or maybe it is the long nights. Rules change in winter, like in the children's poem: "In winter I get up at night. . ." But I'd always thought it was heat, not cold, that heightened tempers. I don't know why January was made the first month of the year. There must be a reason, but none that would make sense to me. The year should begin with the spring, when new things start to grow. The king must die, as our ancestors said.

But it's only the dull, cold, dark days of January that herald the new year. No promise of anything new. Just twenty more people murdered. In this city alone. I listen to the news each night to get the update on the death toll. I don't know why it fascinates me. It doesn't worry me. They are all drug-related, or so I am reassured by the anchorman each night. Nancy Reagan still ineffectually fights her war on drugs. I watch her on TV and wonder whether she knows she is talking to the wrong audience.

So January marches on, slowly. The deaths add up. I mark them on my calendar. They add up more quickly than the days. The anchorman tells me I have nothing to fear. I aim my Uzi at his forehead and pull the trigger. The soft rubber dart sticks to the screen on his forehead, between the eyebrows, just over the nose.

I wake up suddenly in the night. I hear a noise. My heart constricts in fear and my breath catches. I lie very still, waiting for another sound. I hear the noise again—it sounds like someone at the door. I look at the closet, wondering if I have time to put something on. I don't want to be murdered naked. I get out of bed cautiously and head toward the closet. The noise comes again and I breathe a sigh of relief. It's only in the alley behind my bedroom. I get back in bed, reassured. It takes me a long time to fall asleep.

The next day there is a dead rat and an empty bottle of wine in the garbage can. I wonder briefly if the rat drank himself to death, then decide against it. The alley smells of urine and booze so I don't linger. I am careful to walk around a frozen pile of vomit as I make my way back out.

At work the shopkeeper next door comes over to complain that he has rats in his yard. "Do something about it," he says to me.

"I already have."

"What?" he demands.

"I've sent them over to your yard."

"Funny," he says as he turns to leave.

"Hey, Ira," I call after him. He turns. "Buy a bottle of wine."

He looks at me briefly, then turns and stomps out.

At the check-out counter in the grocery store a man yells from the end of the line. "How much is this?" he says, holding up a loaf of bread.

"Dollar," says the clerk, busy passing items over her scanner.

He drops a dollar bill on the belt and shuffles out. No one minds. He is dirty and smells; we are relieved that he is gone. Outside I see the bread man walking down the street with a shopping cart full of his possessions. Though it is only thirty-four degrees he has no coat on. I think he doesn't own one. He stops the cart and pulls out his loaf of bread. Then he starts breaking the bread into pieces and throwing it to the pigeons. I look away and see another man bending over and picking up receipts from an automatic teller machine. They are only scraps of paper, garbage people leave behind. He looks at them as though they are lottery tickets and he may suddenly win a fortune. I turn away and hurry on.

On the news the anchorman confides that another D.C. youth

has been slain. In an argument over a jacket. Drug-related, he reassures. I remember the jacketless man feeding the pigeons and feel sad. I shoot the anchorman dully. I come back from marking the total for the day on the calendar and stare vacantly at the TV. When I come to I see Johnny Carson. He's making jokes about a presidential candidate who keeps jumping in and out of the race. When he is through I watch David Letterman. He's making jokes about a presidential candidate who keeps jumping in and out of the race. I wonder if it is possible to snort cocaine through a crazy straw.

I dream about a presidential candidate feeding pigeons. Suddenly a rat comes and shoots him. The man falls to his knees, clutching a red jacket to his chest and saying, "No, no." The jacket turns into Nancy Reagan saying, "Just say no," and then into the anchorman. "It's all drug-related," he reassures.

I wake up to the sound of the garbage truck in the alley. It is too early to get up so I pull the blankets over my head and try to sleep again. I wonder why I always wake up craving sex.

At work the gallery owner next door comes over. "We should have a party one night and shoot the rats out back," he says.
"Ira doesn't like the rats," I tell him.

That night I don't turn on the TV.

Somewhere in January is my birthday. I look at my cards and open a bottle of beer. I switch on the TV. Surprise, surprise. Another murder. I begin to think that January will never end.

At the drugstore I stop to look at the magazine rack. Cher stares back at me from the cover of every paper. It takes me a minute to realize they are all different ones. I think that she is on as many covers as there are deaths in D.C. this month. I wonder how she would react to this news.

The anchorman hurries past the deaths to talk about football. The Redskins are going to the Super Bowl and the city is having a hard time trying to think of anything else. They are excited because this will be the first time there is a black quarterback in the Super Bowl. I digest this information with some surprise. I tend to think of football players as being black. I quickly censor this thought.

Ira comes into the store to complain about the rats again. He says I should call an exterminator. "Why?" I say. "We don't have a problem."

He insists that his rats come from my store, so I should get rid of them.

"OK," I say.

In the grocery store an old woman follows me down the aisles. Everything I put in my basket she duplicates in hers. She follows me to the check-out line and stands behind me. I pick up a magazine and glance at an article about Cher. When I look around again the woman's cart is still there, but she is gone. As I leave the store I see her following someone else.

I stay up late reading a mystery novel. I am frustrated because it is nearly the end of the book and I haven't figured out who the killer is yet. The detective in the book has, and we've seen all the same facts. I keep getting the characters mixed up. At the end the detective tells me everything, including how he figured it out. Was it the pretty girl with the libido or the quiet girl with the glasses? I decide I don't care and try to sleep.

One morning I buy a bottle of wine on my way to work. I walk into Ira's shop. "Ira, come on, we're going to kill your rats." I hold up the bottle. He doesn't understand, but follows me outside anyway.

"This always seems to work in my neighborhood," I tell him. I open the bottle and drink its contents. It's only eleven-thirty and the wine is cheap, but somehow it all goes down. Then I wait for a rat to come by.

"Watch," I say to Ira as a rat emerges from under the fence. I throw the bottle at the rat. Ira looks from me to the dead rat and says, "There must be a better way."

I go home and don't open the shop that day.

It's January 27, and there have been thirty-two murders so far this year. I look at the calendar and wonder how many of us will make it through the next four days.

On Saturday I sit in my window and watch people move. There are three people moving from my block. I would like to know where they are going. Maybe to a city that doesn't have so many murders. Maybe to a country where presidential candidates don't jump in and out of the race. I figure they'd have to go pretty far to get somewhere that doesn't have Cher on all the magazine covers.

The next morning is finally the last one of the month. It is unseasonably warm, says the weatherman. There is a carnival atmosphere about the city and I wonder why. Then I remember the Super Bowl.

That afternoon I open a bottle of beer and turn on the TV. I don't notice the game until after it is over. Then I don't notice the game, just the noise. The city has erupted. I don't remember ever having heard so much noise. I look at the TV and wonder what would have happened several hundred years ago if the original redskins had won.

In the early hours of the morning the anchorman comes on to confide to me that the total number of murders for January was thirty-seven. I aim at his head and fire.

I wait a minute until the dart has dropped off the TV. I reload the gun and put it to my head. Then, just to see what it's like, I pull the trigger.

# SOWETO
## MIRIAM TLALI

*Soweto, an abbreviation for southwestern townships, is home to many black people who work in Johannesburg, South Africa's largest city, founded in 1886 as a result of the discovery of gold in the Transvaal. Soweto has become internationally known as a center of resistance to apartheid. The townships are linked to the "white" city by rail, but the numbers of trains allocated to service the black community are not enough and subject black people to a daily humiliating train ride.*

*Miriam Tlali was born in Doornfontein in Johannesburg and grew up in Sophiatown. She enrolled in the University of the Witwatersrand just before blacks were barred from entering. Her novel,* Amandla!, *was banned in South Africa within six weeks of its publication in 1980. This ban was recently lifted. Her earlier novel,* Muriel at the Metropolitan, *has been reissued by Longmans' African Classics Series.*

# Fud-u-u-a!

Dikeledi, or Nkele, as she was called, hurried towards Park Station in Johannesburg. She mingled with the other pedestrians dodging, winding and scuttling along without slowing down. It was five-fifteen in the evening. She knew that she would arrive in time for the Six-Nine—the First-Stop-Naledi train. The thought that Ntombi, her friend, would be anxiously waiting for her at the station made her smile.

It was never easy to make one's way through the hundreds of people, all competing for passing space. The two parallel streams on either side of Von Brandis Street looked like human avalanches. Nkele had avoided Eloff Street, thinking that Von Brandis would be better.

"Ke semphete-ke-go-fete ka Morena!" Nkele remarked. "We are like bees," she complained softly to herself, pausing for a split second before she crossed Pritchard Street, holding tightly onto the straps of her shopping bag.

It was mainly black faces. She dismissed with a smile the thought which came flashing into her mind that most whites seemed lately to avoid moving along the main thoroughfares leading towards Park Station at that time of the day. She mused at the many arguments which often resulted in black-versus-white free-for-alls at such times. She remembered, chuckling, how she herself would become involved in the skirmishes, all through the shuffling and colliding of opposing waves of human traffic—whites maintaining that the blacks should remember to stick to their "place" by keeping "out of the way" and the blacks stubbornly refusing to accept this "order" and dismissing it as a sign of

130

nonsensical arrogance! The adjacent never-ending flood of cars in the street itself only aggravated matters. What would happen if the traffic lights were not there? Nkele asked herself, reflecting, and allowing her mind to wander freely. It was a typical Friday evening.

"Shall I make it?" she asked herself, wondering doubtfully. She was going to take a chance and leap into Jeppe Street just as the robot was about to turn red against her when someone reached for her elbow, holding her back gently. She had kept moving and moving without presence of mind. If it had not been for the timely gesture of the man, Nkele would have darted right into the flow of cars which came rushing impetuously down that street. She stopped abruptly and gasped thankfully, "Dankie Abuti!" She sighed, looking up at the face of the person whose arm had steadied her and had perhaps saved her from certain disaster. "Our brothers are usually so protective towards us in town here," Nkele thought, gratefully. When the green light came on, she hurried on, shuffling, brushing and bumping against one person after another.

Again the question kept creeping into her mind. "Shall I make it?" she asked herself once more. "That stupid Boer guard of the Six-Nine has the filthy habit of blowing the whistle a whole three, even four minutes early; a ka go seleka, he can make you fed up!" Nkele remarked, adding, "Kajeno ho na ha ke batle ho e supa ka monoana, ka Morena—today of all days I do not want to point my finger, honestly. Not on a Friday—and it's even month-end for that matter." Nkele whispered to herself, "Thank God I did all my shopping during lunch time. At least this week I will not have to come to town tomorrow for shopping."

It had been one of those rare good Fridays when the white woman, their wage clerk, had been in a happy mood and handed the black staff their pay envelopes before lunch time.

The pressure exerted by the straps on her fingers became increasingly unbearable and she transferred the heavy bag from one arm to the other, repeating the act of alternating almost automatically.

The familiar Friday evening stampede for trains, buses and taxis had now become, to her, as to the other commuters, just one of those phenomena one had to live with and fight one's way through. She had to be alert all the time. She quickly stepped into the station concourse in the direction of the line of the temporary stalls the black women had erected to display fruits and other wares. They were smiling and chatting with each other.

They, too, were alert, all the time keeping an eye on their merchandise—apples, pears, oranges, naartjies, peanuts, which were neatly arranged in attractive cone-shaped little hillocks. "Business is good," Nkele imagined they might be saying to each other, peering at each other through the throngs of passing commuters, some of whom stopped now and then to buy.

The fruit sellers were obviously in a good mood, and they had reason to be thankful, too. The white policemen in their usual packed pickup vans, who always seemed to appear from God-knows-where, had not come today. The women were smiling, watching and giving each other all the moral support women in need of help ought to give each other. "We're all alike; we're women," she thought. "We need each other when things are difficult because we have given birth to children. Wherever I go, I hear women say, 'We have to feed our children, haven't we?'"

On this particular day, a Friday which also fell on the last day of the month, the white dogs, as they called the white police, had not dashed in to kick the rows of boxes on which the women had exhibited their hard-earned wares. They had not come to load the hawkers mercilessly onto the pickup vans and to disappear swearing and threatening. At times they would just smash and destroy the products, throwing them into the nearest rubbish cans and trampling maliciously over them in disgust. The persistence and determination of the women was a pain in the necks of the police, especially because whenever they chased them, they never succeeded in getting hold of them. They would vanish without a trace into the black myriads in the corridors and station platforms. And one black face looks exactly like another when one is confronted with the task of identifying them from the milling thousands. What is worse, in the spirit of black solidarity, the passengers never helped to expose the "offenders."

Nkele smiled. Ntombi must be waiting, she thought. There is nothing like the knowledge that the help of another woman is available to you whenever you need it—when the going gets tough, as the saying goes. Ntombi was her bosom friend. It had been like that for years, ever since she left school and started travelling to work in town on board the Soweto trains. And now they were both married and they had children to work for.

All Nkele needed to be conscious of was that she had her shopping bag; everything was meticulously packed with every packet squeezed in so that nothing would be damaged along the journey. She remembered that she had checked the zip again and again to make sure that it worked. And her purse. . . of course her purse with all that had remained after she had bought what she thought were essentials for the weekend was inside. It was right inside—on her person, over her pubis—between her panty-hose and her tight step-in corset. No one could get his hand in there. The purse was quite safe there. Anyone who would have the guts to dig in there would be very brave indeed. She would scream and by the time he got hold of the purse, she would have made so much noise that people all around would come to her aid. No pick-pocket would want to be the center of attraction. She and Ntombi would help each other. They would stand face to face in the train, clasping their shopping bags tightly against their legs, each breathing over the other's shoulder and watching. "You need to have someone to see what is happening behind you too," Nkele mumbled to herself, her face brightening into a broad smile.

Just as she descended the second flight of stairs on Platforms 1 and 2, the whistle went, its shrill piercing sound stabbing pain-fully right through her heart. She nearly stood dead still. In fact, she might have done so if it had not been for the force of the moving stream behind her. The torrent of male passengers tore even more hastily past her, forcing her—amid loud squeals of female voices—to float towards the wall. She could imagine this as a race track, the whistle giving the final take-off "Go" signal.

"Die bleddie naalertjie van 'n vark; ons sal hom wys! Bloody swine, we'll teach him a lesson!" Some cursed loudly as they sprinted past; others hurled their sprightly figures over the sloping walls, landing over the edge of the platform, and expertly making it into the moving train. Others jumped over two, sometimes three, steps at a time to scale the distance. To them it was just one of those things. They swore, "Die hond; hy wil ons los! That dog; he wants to get rid of us!" But they knew all the time that they would get into the train, come what may. And as they gasped, adjusting their jackets, they pointed accusing fingers towards the rear of the moving train where the uncaring pink face of the guard was just disappearing.

Nkele's delicate body had been pressed against the hard wall for what seemed like hours when in fact it could only have been for half a minute. She had kept her eyes shut, holding on to her bag with all her might. Someone was clinging to her. From the faint subdued squeaking cries the person had made, she knew that it was a woman. The distressed stranger had dug her face into the nape of Nkele's neck. When the weight on her back started easing off slowly, poor Nkele was relieved, knowing the worst was over.

"I'm sorry, my sister. I hope I didn't break all your bones," the woman apologised, their eyes meeting and smiling at each other. She was a little older than Nkele, and she tugged at her sleeve, indicating the desire to help her carry the heavy bag. Together they scuttled quickly out of the way, moving as carefully as they could and as closely to the wall as possible. At the end of the stairs, the two hustled away from the joggling, propelling throngs and sought momentary shelter in the angle formed by the tall concrete pillar and the wall.

"Come, my sister, let us whisper," the kind, strange woman proposed, just as Ntombi was making her way towards them. Ntombi was twisting and pushing, struggling to disentangle herself from the nest of wrestling bodies. She shouted, "Nkele o e, Nkele!" to her friend.

"Oh, there's Ntombi. She's my friend. She'll help me. Thanks and don't worry; I'll—"

The other interrupted her. "It's all right, Nkele my sister. Let Ntombi come along. Both of you. Come, Ntombi; my name is Mashadi. Come, let us whisper. This corner here looks safer. They won't crush us here." The three laughed loudly. There were no formal introductions necessary. Women in distress just accept each other without much hesitation because they know that they need each other.

"Re basadi bo batlhe; tlaeang re itshebeng. We are all women; come, let us whisper to one another," Shadi repeated, retreating deeper into the safe nook. "What shall we do? The Six-Nine has left us; so we have to wait for the O-Five."

Nkele was disappointed. She very much regretted the unfortunate occurrence. She remarked, "We really have no luck today. . . That silly guard, fancy just letting the Six-Nine take off like that. And a whole three minutes early. Now we have no alternative but to take the O-Five—and I hate going into that train!" She turned to her friend. "Shame. You must have been looking around for me, Ntombi my dear."

Ntombi nodded in response, adding, "Yes, Nkele my sister. But don't worry. We shall make it somehow. You know we are used to fighting. And you, Shadi my sister, you were going to tell us something, weren't you? You had something on your mind; let's hear it. We're women. We're all alike."

Shadi looked around, stammering reluctantly, "You know. . .
I hate the O-Five, I never want to set my foot in it! Come, listen;
we have to whisper. I don't want the other people to hear us. I
once had a most nasty experience on the O-Five."

Ntombi could not stand the suspense any longer. She asked,
"What nasty experience? Tell us. You'll be surprised to find that
we know all about it. That we have also had even worse experiences, my sister. Tell us. There's too much noise. People are
straining their ears trying to hear what the announcer is saying.
Sometimes I wonder why they introduce that howler at all!"

The three women looked around them. The usual Friday evening
stampede was at its peak. The formal announcements seemed
quite useless on such days. They only served to confuse passengers
all the more. In any case, most of the people were either too
excited or too involved in their own varied conversations to listen.
Even what was said over the loudspeaker was not always reliable.
"Anything can happen!" you would hear a person say, annoyed.
"You come rushing into Platforms 1 and 2, and you see the train
you want unashamedly rattle right on over to the other side into
Platform voetsek, departing, and you have to jump over rails and
break your legs or lose your life, just like that. They don't care!
You just have to be on the alert and read the train numbers
yourself!"

No one was listening to the announcer. He bellowed the numbers
and the words away, melodiously adding twists of tone, crooning
in a heavy bass as if he was imitating Paul Robeson and failing
hopelessly. It could be that he, too, had the Friday fever. He was
sitting there with his pay packet in front of him, serenading it,
and enjoying listening to his own voice.

Nkele reminded Mashadi, urging impatiently, "You were still
telling us, by the way, Mashadi my sister. We shall just have to
go into the O-Five. There is nothing we can do. . . OK, what
happened? Go on."

Shadi tried hesitantly to proceed. The words just would not
come out. She gurgled, "It happened on the train. . . the O-Five.
I was not aware what had happened. I did not feel anything at
the time, you see. The train was packed and everyone was
sandwiched into everyone as usual. The train kept swaying from
side to side as if the wheels had moved out of place. . . 'gadlang-
gadlang, gadlang-gadlang, gadlang-gadlang,' it was noisy, you
know. . ."

The others nodded, smiling sympathetically. Shadi was amazed.
She asked, "He bathong, le a tshega, people, are you laughing?"

"Siza'thini, Shadi, my sister? It hurts so much. What's the use of crying?" Ntombi asked.

This very sad sensitive subject, sparked off by Mashadi's dilemma, was not merely an isolated case. It was a painful harrowing experience, always related in bated breath by helpless, misused, derogated, bitter women of all ages.

There was complete silence. Each one of the women was thinking what they would now have to do. They would have to keep together and give each other moral, and, as far as possible, physical support. One had to be strong to face the daily hazards of travelling in the trains of Soweto.

Ntombi was sad and bitter. She wondered why they, the black women who were trying to make a living, should be the victims of all the evil in the land. She spoke softly and said, "We all know about these terrible occurrences, Shadi my dear, and are only smiling because, baholo ba re loso leholo ke ditshego— people laugh even when they are under the threat of death. It happens all the time and we have no way of fighting against it."

Ntombi declared, "What is annoying about this congestion is that you never see it happening in their trains—those white only coaches. They make sure that the white passengers sit comfortably. You very rarely find them standing even at the very busy hours like early in the morning when most people board trains, and at this time of night when everybody wants to go home. Sometimes this very difference between black and white is so bad that it can easily lead to a black against white war. Look at what happens in the trains serving Randfontein, Krugersdorp, Roodepoort, Pretoria and so on. See what the white coaches are like compared to the black ones. The carriages for whites are always so many! Why can't they have more for blacks when there are so many of us? Why? They provide more for people who do not need them; like with the buses in town. This whole one-sided way of treating people can sometimes be dangerous. You know one morning when our sardine-packed train got to the Langlaagte junction, the comfortable all-white Randfontein train was just crossing to the other line and the two moved side by side. Some of the whites on their train were looking at us smiling as if they were sneering at monkeys in the zoo. As if we were deliberately put there for their entertainment."

Before Ntombi could continue with her story, Nkele and Shadi were already smiling in that we-know-it-all manner. Nkele, unable to restrain herself from interrupting, added, "Yes, of course they would. . . the same way they bring white tourists into Soweto, in luxury buses to come and study us like their mute animals."

"On that day, we nearly saw something terrible," Ntombi continued. "The young men in our train became irritated and abusive. They hurled insult after insult at them: 'Komaan, maak jou groen oe tow, jou lelike nyoertjie!. . . Jy lag jou bleddie fokken Boer!...Come on—face your front, you swine!. . .' It went on like that. People lose their self-respect when they are made to feel like they are dogs. There was nothing anyone could do to calm them down. They were furious! They even wanted to throw knives and other weapons at them. You know they carry such things on the trains, especially on weekends. The whites were wise enough to draw the blinds to prevent serious fighting from starting. You know what I mean. Anything could happen."

Just then Mashadi interjected, "Honestly, they treat us just like dogs."

"Even dogs are better, my sister," Nkele emphasised sadly. "They don't treat dogs like that; they nurse them like small babies. They even give us rotten dog's meat—what they would rather not give to their dogs."

"Yes, I know," Ntombi agreed, adding, "in their kitchens. It's awful, I know."

The three watched the Pimville-Midday-Line trains come and go, and the jostling and rubbing and the deafening noise continued. They were looking on and reflecting, anxiously awaiting their turn to be caught up in what was virtually the front line of a black woman's battle for mere existence in the bustling city of gold. Ntombi broke the uneasy silence again, her voice penetrating the variable sounds all around them. Her mind had suddenly gone back, focussing on experiences she and her bosom friend had had, and the very first battle they had fought, which had cemented them into practically a team of comrades in action. She recalled, "The limit was the early morning Four-Six First-Stop-Braamfontein. Do you remember, Nkele?" she asked, looking at her friend and smiling.

"What happened, people? Tell me," Mashadi pleaded, looking from the one to the other of her companions.

"How can I ever forget that?" Nkele enquired rhetorically. She began narrating, "It was just after I had left school and got my first job. I had to take the Naledi Four-Six. Moo ke ntoa e a lefu le bophelo, ke u joetsa, my sister, there is a battle for life and death, let me tell you. I remember seeing the thing for the first time. I saw the veterans, bo-Nkatha ba basadi—women who had become tough and brave—remove their wigs and stockings and stuff them into their handbags as we approached Naledi Station. You remember those days black women used to wear wigs?"

The others nodded, smiling expectantly. Nkele proceeded. "When the train came bouncing into that Naledi platform, I was surprised to see people turn their backs away from the doors ready to propel each other with their shoulder blades and backsides. 'Fudua!. . . Fudua!. . . Fudu-a-a!' Stir the pot! St-i-i-r the p-o-t! The push-push yelling started as everyone, man, woman and child alike, strained all the muscles in their bodies to get inside. I just allowed myself to be carried along. I thought I would be flattened dead by the time I got inside. On that Four-Six, no one dares sit down on the hard wooden benches or on the floor. You did what everybody else was doing if you did not want to break your back or lose your limbs. I jumped onto the bunk and was forced into an upright position by the many bodies around me. All along, when I was being carried, I could feel that my clothes were moving from around my calves upwards and there was nothing I could do to lower them. How could I? I had to keep my arms firmly crossed over my breasts all the time because I had to make sure my handbag would not drift away from me. It was then that I saw Ntombi. The poor girl's face was flushed as if someone had dipped it in boiling water. Her hair, which had been neatly brushed, was now standing in unkempt irregular heaps. Although it was winter, there was steam all over inside the train, caused by the vapours from the mouths and nostrils of the passengers and the closed windows. The windows were closed because otherwise the ice-cold air would rush in and those standing near them would suffer. So we remained in that upright position, and the train took off.

"Someone—a woman—started singing a hymn. Her voice was sharp and loud. I tried to turn my head to see her but so many people were packed and squeezed against each other that it was impossible to see her. Soon after, other voices, women's voices, joined in the singing. They were singing a hymn from the popular apostolic hymnals—'Lifela Tsa Sione.'

"'Hosanna ho Morena! Praise be to the Lord!' yet another woman yelled loudly, like someone already possessed by the Holy Spirit.

"'Amen, Alleluia!' the men and more women shouted loudly in reply.

"'Khotso ha e be ho batho! Peace be unto the people!' she cried in a piercing voice as if in thankful appreciation to the welcome response from the men. The people answered, joining eagerly in the singing.

"'Peace! Alleluia! Amen!' Everybody roared.

"There was a whole deafening chorus. But at that moment, I really wished they would stop singing and praying. . ."

Women, regardless of whether they have children of their own, are always mothers. At a critical moment, when they find themselves plunged into an awkward precarious situation, they become immediately inventive and they rally around one another. Then they cease to be childlike but they appeal to their latent inner strength of character. In this diabolical setting, there is a lot at stake. The moral strength of a whole proud nation is faced with cruel challenge. The young, the weak, have to be guided along the correct path of human and not animal behaviour. An urgent appeal to their conscience has to be made.

Why do you think our regular churchgoers are predominantly women? Why do you think in the whites-only kitchens there is what is known as Sheila's Day and we never hear of John's Day? I have never heard of white Sheila's Day, either. Why do you think on Thursday afternoons our black mothers leave every other activity, garb themselves in holy consecrated garments, seaparo, and converge on the altar with the sole united purpose of praying, Bo-'Me-ba-Merapelo? Do you think the sins of the members of our black mothers' households, compared to those of the white mothers, are much greater? Never! In fact, the very opposite prevails!

It is precisely because—M'a-Ngoana o tsoara thipa ka boahalen—the child's mother grabs the sharp end of the knife. It is because they, our black mothers, have to carry the cross on their seemingly frail shoulders. When the father plods his way to the place of worship, more often than not, reasons other than those of the one who must "grab the sharp end of the knife" impel him. It is the black mothers who must pay the ultimate penalty. No black mother, or even a snow-white one for that matter, will stand by and bear to watch passively while her young go to ruin without facing the foe herself.

We forgive our black mothers in their sad predicament for resorting to the ecumenical spear. It is perhaps the only weapon they are familiar with. It is certainly the only one they are ever so readily offered to arm themselves with whenever they have to carry out an onslaught. . .

"Those who could lift up their hands started clapping them—hard. I wanted the music to stop because, instead of helping, the very noise was being used as a shield. I was trying to scream that someone was busy massaging my thighs and backside, trying to probe into my private parts, and nobody was paying attention. It was embarrassing and awful! That day, I thanked God for having given me powerful thighs, because all I did was cross them over one another and squeeze as hard as I could. I clenched my teeth and wished that I were grinding those fingers between my thighs. You see, with so much congestion, it was impossible to see who the culprits were. We suffocated and suffered in that terrible torture of it all, and there was nothing we could do. By the time the train got to Park Station, we were too hurt, too shamefully abused, to speak. Whom could we speak to? Whom could we accuse? Who would listen to us even if we tried to complain? Everyone would tell us, 'It is all too shameful to say anything about this.' I used to hear women whisper about this and never believed it. I used to hear them swearing and spitting. . . On that day I remember hearing a number of powerless women cursing and shouting on the platform, adjusting the wigs on their heads and, like myself, trying their best to look ladylike and presentable. I resolved never to get on that Four-Six again. That day it was our turn, Ntombi, wasn't it?" Nkele asked, smiling and turning to her friend.

"Yes it was; I'll never forget it as long as I live," Ntombi replied, smiling back thoughtfully. She remarked, frowning, "What is even more annoying is that no one wants to even talk about this whole nonsense, as they regard it. It is not nonsense because who suffers? We suffer. They just don't care. They treat us exactly like animals."

"Here's the O-Five!" someone shouted loudly. Others whistled. Nkele, Ntombi and Shadi scrambled into position. It was now time for business. Serious muscle business: the tooth-and-nail fight for survival. "Fudua! Fudua! Fud-u-u-a!" several gave the word of command.

Some youthful men wasted no time. Even before the train stopped, they held tightly on to the sides of the open windows, and then swung their bodies, legs first, into the coaches. As soon as they had secured sitting space, they reserved places for their female companions who, of course, had no alternative but to join

# Miriam Tlali

the fudua routine at the doorways. In another two or three minutes, the train had come to a complete standstill and the three women had succeeded somehow in battling their way in. They had at last found space to stand next to each other. It was an achievement and a victory which deserved to be celebrated. Alert and as watchful as ever, they stood smiling into each other's faces. They sighed. They had won. . . The whistle went. The O-Five rambled on and on, noisily and indifferently, towards Naledi.

## DELHI
### Mridula Garg

*Delhi—whose borders blur with those of New Delhi—has the distinction of being both the oldest and the newest city of India. Chosen as India's capital seven times, Delhi is a historian's delight, bearing pieces of each of these periods. It is also a motorist's despair, with its myriad lanes and congested neighborhoods. Delhi is a confusing city, full of parks and spacious buildings, narrow lanes and a suffocating density of people. It is a city which has as many historical moments as it has bureaucrats.*

*Most of the time, Delhi goes its leisurely way, gossiping and telling tales with or without malice. But once in a while, the old city erupts in anger and frustration. Ethnic violence, called communal violence here, is the lava Delhi spews. But once that volcanic anger settles down, it's difficult to believe such violence could occur in a city with such an interplay of arts and culture among so many different languages and diverse ethnic groups. Delhi is violent, indolent, as changeable as the seasons.*

*Mridula Garg was born in 1938 in Calcutta; her family moved to Delhi a year later. Except for some years in the mid-sixties spent traveling throughout India, she has lived there since. She has published twelve books in Hindi, and three in English,* A Touch of Sun, Daffodils on Fire *and* Skyscraper.

# The Morning After

Downstairs they were shouting again. The Bansals. Her landlord's family. They were forever shouting. If someone were to ask her to describe Delhi in one word, she would say, "Noise." Noise that assaulted your senses from all directions at all times. A constant uproar made up of meaningless sounds that you had to suffer shut up in a small room closed on all sides by other rooms full of noise. Thirty-seven years it had been since she first took refuge in this city and she still had not gotten used to the noise. No, she was being unfair. Khairpur in Punjab had been no less noisy. But she had the advantage of space there. A medium-sized cottage with a small garden outside. They had grown fruits and vegetables there, even flowers occasionally. They had been the prosperous ones there.

Why remember it now? That was before the partition of the country, before they had turned into faceless refugees. Delhi had given them refuge; she should be grateful, and she was. Only she wished the Bansals were less voluble or less loud. At least sometimes, they could be silent; could they not, now, at least for a little while, when they had received such shattering news? The prime minister, Indira Gandhi, had been shot, killed by her own bodyguards! It was not two hours since the transistor had announced it. She had been struck dumb. Her sons Ashok and Ajay and their friend Sarabjit were there with her in her little room but no one had a word to say. They had been sitting quietly all of the last two hours. But not the Bansals.

"Sattoji! Satto Aunty!" There they go again. Good God, it was

143

her name they were calling, father and son together. Now what? Shanti-shanti, Peace be on earth, she intoned, Om shanti-shanti, as she came out on the little balcony outside her room.

"Keep your sons home," Bansalji said as soon as he saw her. "There's a riot on in the city."

"Saw four Sikhs being cut to pieces myself," his son Manku added.

"Sikhs? Why Sikhs?"

"She was killed by the Sikhs."

"By her guards, the radio said."

"Yes, yes, they were Sikhs."

"So what?" Ashok was at her side questioning them. Out of the corner of her eye, she saw Sarabjit come out of the room with Ajay. In a flash she had turned round, sending Sarabjit to the inside wall of the room with a violent push. At the same time, she shouted loudly for Ashok, startling him into coming in. Quickly she bolted the door from inside and stood panting before them.

"What's wrong?" the boys asked at the same time.

She came close to them and whispered. "No one is to go out and no one is to know he is here."

The three of them burst out laughing. She had Sarabjit gagged with her hand in an instant. "Silence. Not a sound," she hissed.

"You've gone mad!" Ashok sounded angry.

"You heard. There's a riot in the city. People are killing the Sikhs."

"Crazy. Ma, you know the Delhiwalas, born rumour mongers."

"With solid lung power."

"Bansals the proven champions." Sarabjit had removed her hand from his mouth and was chuckling with the rest.

"Let's go see." Ajay turned to the door but she was there guarding it, a wall before the door.

"Sarabjit is in danger. We must hide him," she whispered.

"What danger?" Sarabjit interjected. "Everyone knows me here."

"That's the danger. Everyone knew Papa in 1947. He was the station master in Khairpur. That's how. . . but I am wasting my time. Come with me." She took him by the hand and pushed him into the store. "Sit here and don't put on the light. Open only when I knock thrice thus." She demonstrated.

"Some detective story you have been reading. OK, I'll sit here. But what if I suffocate, Auntyji?"

"You won't. The skylight is there." She showed him the small hole in the outer wall that opened into the back lane. She was about to close the door when he held her hand. "Will you starve me then, my dear Aunty?" he said and laughed.

She did not. With utmost seriousness, she put a few chapatis and some vegetables on a plate and handed it to him, along with a bottle of water. She closed the door, locked it and turned to face her scowling sons.

"What is all this in aid of?" came from a bitter Ashok.

"You were not there in 1947. I was; I know," she said.

"That was different. The country had been partitioned. Why will people kill each other now? They are not mad."

"They go mad."

"All of them?"

"No, some."

"Silly."

"It is not. One lighted match is all that's needed to ignite a damp of coal. Once a crowd gathers, it soon becomes a mob. A mob out to celebrate or annihilate. A man in a mob is a mob, not a man."

"Which book is that from?" Ashok teased but before she could answer, Ajay suddenly said, "But where do they come from?"

Yes, where do they come from, the rioters and the killers? Until yesterday everyone was busy earning his bread; no one had time for anyone else. How could they suddenly come to know each other so intimately today to form cohesive groups, with separate identities, organised to kill each other? Who were those people, where did they come from, and where did they hide again once it was over?

"Where do they come from, Ma?" Ajay repeated his question.

"No one is coming from anywhere," Ashok cut in. "Ma's got 1947 on her mind."

"Sattoji!" Her name rang through, bringing her to the balcony before it could be repeated. Bansal again.

"Is Ashok at home?"

"Yes."

"And his friend. . . that Sikh fellow?"

"He left right after you did, at three, after the news."

"Don't let him in if he comes back."

"Never. Who can trust them now?" she said bitterly.

"And why not?" Ashok butted in. "Have you no shame, Ma?"

"Shut up."

"They were there, all around the Medical Institute, distributing sweets, dancing the Bhangra, while the poor lady lay dead. Won't the Hindus want to kill? Have they no blood coursing in their veins?"

"You saw them dancing and eating sweets?"

"Am I lying then?"

"You saw. . . did you really?" Ashok grew shaky.

"There was no other way to teach them a lesson. They have been killing Hindus for so long in Punjab, we did nothing. . ."

"Why didn't you! If you had gone there to take revenge, that would have been something; what's the fun in killing innocent Sikhs here?"

"Why are you so eager to defend the enemy? This is self-defence, son. If we don't kill them now, they'll run over the whole country tomorrow. Am I wrong, Sattoji?"

"No, absolutely right," she said in a strong voice.

"You think so. . . truly you do. . .? I don't, you hear me, I won't." Ashok cried out as if in pain.

"No point hiding under your Ma's sari, son; come out and see for yourself, if you dare." Bansal laughed at his face.

"I will!" He shoved her roughly aside and ran down the stairs into the street.

She went back into the room and began a chant of prayer to Bajrangbali, the great monkey god Hanuman, the protector of the weak and the young. Bajrangbali, look after him, protect my son, she intoned again and again. Bajrangbali-Bajrangbali-Bajrangbali. . .

Inside the store, Sarabjit heard them and froze with terror. He was about to put a piece of chapati into his mouth when he heard Satto Aunty say, "Who can trust them now?" What about him! He had put himself completely in their hands and there they were plotting his. . . he let the chapati fall and went to the door. There was a gap between the door and the floor, where a thin stream of light filtered in from the room. By now he had gotten used to seeing by that dim light. He examined the door thoroughly. There was no bolt inside! The door was bolted or locked from outside. He could not protect himself by bolting it from his side. When they decided to open it, they would have him at their mercy, alone, unarmed, with his back to the wall. He went over the cage-like room with his hands, inch by inch, searching for something that could be used as a weapon. All he found was a board of wood. He clung to it with both his hands, ready to strike at the first sound.

Mridula Garg

It was the first quarter of the evening when even Delhi fell into an uneasy silence. The daytime cacophony died down, albeit slowly and with spasmodic grunts and growls. This happened every night. Only this time she did not welcome the silence; she left the radio on to keep her company in her lonely vigil. She found it soothing with its mournful rendition of religious songs and tunes appropriate to the passing away of a leader. It brought her own sorrow back to her; it was but seven years that her husband had died. With him had died her dream of living in the other Delhi, the Delhi of green parks and wide roads. The Delhi of the tourist brochures, the beautiful capital of a lovely country. Delhi of the movies and the television, that's what she had always called it. It was only in the movies and later on the TV in Bansal's house that she had ever seen that Delhi, the one that boasted of being a garden city, where the rich had huge one-story bungalows filled with colourful flowers in the winter season and coolers and air conditioners in the summer. Not only were there gardens inside the houses, but the traffic islands also erupted in a blaze of colour with the advent of winter. Then there were the huge, well tended public parks, which reminded her of her native town in Punjab, each of them as big as the whole town. But it had not the wide smooth roads of Delhi, on which the cars of the rich ran merrily, unmindful of rules or the less fortunate ones who walked along. Why, in that Delhi of movie sets, there were even fountains spouting water at the height of summer, when the tap in her house did not yield the thinnest trickle of water. She and the likes of her had to depend on the municipal tanker for their minimum needs.

That was her Delhi, this motley jumble of closely built small tenements amid narrow lanes and alleys in Sadar Bazar, a part of Old Delhi, as they used to call it once. They had stopped doing that for some time now; why, she did not know. All she knew was that there was a newer Delhi that was even better than New Delhi and it lay in the south of the city. She knew it, bless the TV at the Bansal's house, not only by hearsay but from the pictures they showed of it. She had a glimpse of the spacious flower-carpeted city each time a foreign dignitary came to visit and did a round of the capital. They always saw the tour on the box. In colour too. The Bansals had plenty of money, what with their hardware shop and rooms to let. Not that she meant to be ungrateful. They were not bad people, never threatened her with eviction or demand of higher rent like so many other landlords she heard of.

They knew how to twist the arm of the law, tenant protection or no tenant protection, and she a widow with two young sons. Not the Bansals. How nicely they invited her to come and watch TV at their place, the Sunday feature film, the cricket matches, everything. The only thing she had never gone to see there was the republic day parade—not that they did not ask her, but she wanted to retain the memory of the parade she had seen live on India Gate as it was. Her husband had taken her there, had purchased the most expensive tickets—well, almost. That was the only time she had seen the Delhi of the movies and television in real life. Indira Gandhi had been the prime minister then and now she was dead. Killed! Om shanti-shanti-shanti.

May her soul rest in peace. Peace was the important thing, not money or comfort. It's true that she, Satto, had to sell the small plot of land her husband had managed to buy in the south of Delhi, then a patch of wilderness but well on its way to prosperous development now, or so she had heard. She had to sell because she had no money to build even one room and the municipal authorities were not willing to let the land lie waste. Destiny: who could fight it? She was better than millions of others. She had a confirmed job as a teacher of domestic science in a government school close by. She earned her living and lived in an independent room with a store and even a small, very small balcony to breathe in the fresh air. Ah, she was a lucky one.

The silence grew more palpable. The dogs had stopped barking, she realised. The bhajans, religious songs, from the radio filled the silence of the room with their sweet sound and her with peace. May her soul rest in peace, she murmured again. May all their souls rest in peace. Yes, peace was what was most important. That was what her mother always said when they had first come as refugees to Delhi. Satto, pray that never again may anyone lose his loved ones in a riot, pray that all souls rest in peace so that none roam around inciting people to hatred and violence. Pray not for money or comfort but peace. Peace to all, each and everyone. Om shanti-shanti-shanti.

Filled with peace, she got up, went to the kitchen and called Ajay to come and eat.

"Are you going to keep Sarabjit in the store all night?" he asked.

Suddenly she laughed and said, "I'm a crazy fool, am I not, to worry so, shutting the poor child in the store to lull my own wild fears. Let me go unlock him."

She got up and almost immediately heard a long drawn-out human scream rend the air. She stopped, petrified, then turned to Ajay and asked, "Did you hear it too?"

She did not give him time to answer. Cautioning him to silence, she put up the volume of the radio, then went to work with furious but hushed speed. Motioning Ajay for help, she moved the old, high-domed almirah that stood in a corner of the room to block the entrance to the store. Fortunately it covered the door fully. No one could know at first glance that there was a door to another room there. Carefully she changed the position of the bed, the wooden box and the chairs, to make the room look properly laid out. They had to use all their strength to ensure that nothing dragged along the floor to make the slightest sound that could make the Bansals suspicious. She did not forget to carefully wipe out the dust marks with a wet cloth. She could not possibly start using a broom at that hour after sunset; they would immediately know and wonder at her doing something so inauspicious with the poor lady not yet consigned to the flames.

And Ashok. . . where was Ashok? Why had he not returned home yet? Her heart cried out, sick with worry for her son as she made preparations to protect the other one. Bajrangbali, look after my son, bring him back soon. You know the murky narrow bylanes of Sadar Bazar are no place for a young boy to be out at night. You know what crimes are committed there in the dark. Make him come back, Bajrangbali, take care of him tonight of all the dark terrifying nights. Ashok, come back, come back safe, come back soon before the night goes into its second quarter.

Inside the store it suddenly grew pitch dark. The thin pencil of light disappeared. Fools! Why did they have to put out the light in the room? Didn't they know that this would put him in total darkness? He knelt down to peer under the door and was surprised to find a wall blocking his view. Now what! How could the wall shrink to come so close to the door? Wahe Guru, he prayed, was his brain getting addled in this airless room? He shook himself. No, he must not imagine things. He remembered Satto Aunty telling him not to put on the light. So there was a light inside. See, no need to panic. He was going to put it on once just to see.

Carefully he groped along all the walls looking for a switch. Nothing. No way to put on the light from inside. So she had lied to him! Oh God!

He did not expect this of Ashok's mother. For five years, he had come to their house and been treated like a son. Ashok and he had been through school and college together; they were even now planning to be partners in a scooter repair shop, with the mother pitching in with funds. And now this!

Was it his fault that Indira Gandhi had been killed by her Sikh guards? Why did they kill her, the bastards. Had they not vowed to protect her, eaten her salt, been chosen to guard her? Then they had gone and shot her, sixteen times, a woman and unarmed. That was not like a true Sikh warrior, a Khalsa. Why, we do not even hit an animal twice. If it is beheaded the first time, fine; otherwise the meat is taboo for us. Who knows—the Hindus might have killed her themselves, grown beards and hair to do it. To let the Sikhs suffer! The effeminate bastards! They were quite capable of it. Our people might be hot-headed, but not cheats. Traitors never. Then why am I hiding here like a coward? Are not my hands and feet enough to break the door open and confront Ashok's mother? I don't wish her ill; I'll tell her she has been taken for a ride by them, the eunuchs. It is not right to heed strangers and reject your own; am I not like your own son?

Suddenly the store was filled with a red glow: flashes of light that blinded him for a moment, then a red afterglow. Where had he seen it before? Yes, he remembered, it rose out of the funeral pyre of his father, which he had lighted himself only last year. There were red glints like this all over the crematorium, so many pyres there had been that day. I suppose that is how it is every day there, he thought. Today. . . but the crematorium was miles away; how was the glow shining in his room? "Wahe Guru, help me, this is a fire!"

He could see angry red flames streaking the sky from the skylight. "It's in this neighbourhood, behind this very house. Wahe Guru, it is this house which is on fire! Have they all gone, leaving me here to be burned alive? Motherfuckers! You don't know me, I'm a Khalsa, equal to a hundred thousand of you. I'll not die trapped like a rat. I'll kick the door and be out to take vengeance. I'll kill you all before I die. Jo bole so nihal, Sat Sri Akal! I'm ready to die for the faith. So help me God!"

He worked himself into a frenzy and gave the door a powerful kick.

What was the boy up to? Satto felt the kick on the door vibrate through her spine. Does he want the whole neighbourhood here?

150

Should she go into the store and see, remove the almirah and. . . She was still undecided when she heard the footsteps on the stairs. They were on their way up! She ran out of the room to bang against Manku on the top step.

"The Sikhs have attacked!" Both father and son shouted together. "They are firing from inside the Gurudwara."

"Ashok," she muttered.

"Has he come back?"

She shook her head.

"Why did you let him go? Didn't we warn you? The Sikhs cannot be trusted. Look at the fire outside."

Meanwhile Ajay had run out on the balcony. He came back and said, "What have the Sikhs to do with the fire? It's the Gurudwara which is on fire."

The Gurudwara! On fire! The house of God! Mercy! She had gone so often to the Gurudwara in the past to hear the Gurbani, the readings of sacred texts, which both Sikhs and Hindus attended. So what if she was a Hindu in the Gurudwara, the house of worship for the Sikhs. Had they not always lived like brothers of one faith in this city? The Guru was their teacher too, their ladder to God. Mercy. Forgive them O Lord. Protect my son. "Ashok. . ." she muttered faintly.

"So the Gurudwara is on fire, eh? What did you expect? If they fire on us won't we hit back?" Manku had his hand on Ajay's collar.

"Ashok. . . what about Ashok?" she started wailing.

It had its effect. Manku turned to her and said, "I'll go and look for him. Come with me." He took Ajay by the hand and clattered down the stairs.

"Bansalji, my son. . ." she was weeping in earnest now.

"Don't worry, Sattoji, we are already there. Manku will find him and bring him home. Has he gone?"

"Who?" her voice shook.

"That friend of Ashok's?"

Sarabjit had held back after that one powerful kick on the door. He could hear the shouts and accusations of the Bansals clearly. He stood close to the door with the wooden board clasped firmly in his hand and waited for the woman to answer the question Bansal had asked her.

Despite total concentration, he could not catch her answer. Why was that woman speaking in such low tones? The Bansals were shouting loudly enough. Wahe Guru, what plot were they hatching against him? This was not the time to run out; the house was on fire. It was the Gurudwara. . . curse the bastards, they had destroyed the house of God. But he must wait, catch the woman alone.

"Has he gone or not?" Bansal repeated in a menacing tone.

"Long ago," she said amid sobs, so softly that Bansal could hardly hear her. "It must be all over with him by now. But Ashok. . ."

"I'll go see." Bansal went down.

She flung herself on the cot in the room and started praying to Hanuman, the protector of the weak and the young.

Sarabjit stood alert, clinging to the door with his body and to the wooden board with his hands. There was just this door between him and death. He was ready. If he had to die, he had to. But he would die like a true Khalsa, after killing the enemy.

The night claims its own, however sharp the blades of fire. A time came when both Sarabjit, clinging to the door, and Satto, moaning her prayers on the cot, fell into an uneasy sleep.

Each night has a dawn. Only some are darker than the night before. Such was the first morning of November, which marked the end of the night of October 31, 1984.

He entered his own house like a thief, tapped on the door as if the slightest noise would bring the house down. A single tap was enough for Satto to be up and at the door. She opened it only after ascertaining who it was in a muted whisper and just wide enough to admit him.

She looked at him aghast. Her husband had returned from the dead! But how? Had she not seen him consigned to the flames and reduced to ashes with her own eyes? She was there when her young sons had collected the remains of the charred bones from the crematorium and taken them to their final resting place in the river Ganges at Haridwar. He had grown old in his youth with the sickness that had wasted him, but he had found rest in death. Not once had he come to haunt her in the past seven years. Why now?

He took firm hold of her hand with his and bolted the door with the other. "He can't be kept here, Ma," he said.

Ma! She looked at him mesmerised and realised with a shock that he was not the ghost of her dead husband but her younger son, Ajay. But what had happened to his face? How could he turn from fourteen to forty in one night?

"What. . . what. . ." she fumbled.

"It was a blunder. I went to the police station last night."

"Then?"

"I asked them for help for him. They said to me, 'You call yourself a Hindu! We would help you if you had come to us after killing him.'"

"What will we do?" Satto cried.

"We'll have to cut his hair."

"He'll never agree."

"He will. I'll tell him all that I saw last night," he said in a cold dry tone.

Was he the same boy who had asked her last night, "But where do they come from?"

"Hurry. We must have him out."

"Why, what's the danger here?" she asked and got the answer immediately. From both sides of the streets rose a crescendo of slogans. Kill. Kill. Kill the enemies of the nation!

Ajay pulled her behind the almirah. She opened the door of the store and went inside.

Sarabjit had woken with a start from the mad din in the street to find that the wooden board had slipped from his hands. The woman was upon him before he could find it. He clenched his fists and raised them to bring them down on her head. But she was quicker than he was. She had him in a tight embrace before he could move.

"Son! My child! Hurry! Let Ajay cut your hair and take you with him." She was sobbing.

Ajay was there too, with scissors and a razor ready in his hands. Sarabjit stood frozen with his hands raised above his head. Outside, the slogans were punctuated with tortured cries of pain.

They heard a truck and a few motorbikes rattle past, and then the house opposite theirs was on fire. And the cries. God, those fearsome cries of human agony. Yet they went on pruning his hair like high-powered machines. She had pulled Ashok's well-worn shirt and trousers on him even before Ajay had finished the shave. The neighbours had seen the clothes so often, they were sure to mistake him for Ashok, as they were the same height and build.

But Ashok—where was Ashok? Her heart cried out but there

was no time for thoughts of anyone but Sarabjit. He tried to thank her, to say goodbye, but there was no time for that either.

"Quick." Ajay was hustling him. "The mob's enjoying the fire. Let's get the bike. You ride, I'll drive."

That was right; that way the crowd would see more of Ajay's face than Sarabjit's.

The Bansals were all on the rooftop to enjoy better the tamasha, the show on the street. They got out of the house and managed to reach the road without being accosted. Satto locked the store and pulled the almirah back before it. She stood there with a silent prayer on her lips, afraid to go out and look, yet drawn to the balcony by the wild hunting cries of the crowd.

Could one call it a crowd, or was it a stampede of wild animals turned into men or men turned into rapacious beasts? Were the boys out on a jihad, a crusade, or a jashan, a celebration? Not one face bore a tinge of grief or pain. There was nothing but the fever of the chase. There had been an assassination then also, in 1948, of another Gandhi; people had come out of their homes in droves to gather on the streets. But that was a crowd of mourners, gathered together by common consent in self-condemnation and a will to expiate. No kitchen fires had burned that night and the morning after. This morning the houses themselves were afire in a murderous aftermath.

She stood transfixed on the balcony and wondered what she was a witness to: a mourning gone berserk or a celebration of a windfall violence? A jashan, maybe a jihad, but on no account a demonstration of grief, no, not that, ever.

With a prayer on her lips, she scanned the crowd below and saw that Ashok and Sarabjit had not yet reached the safe precincts beyond the frenzied mob. Bajrangbali-Guru Kirpal, help them, she called out to both the protectors together, and leaned a little further to keep them in sight. She was appalled to see four young men drag an old, white-bearded Sikh on the road right in front of her house.

"Let the old man go, you beasts," she screamed and screamed but to no avail. She was about to run down when she realised she still had Sarabjit's long hair in her hand. Before she could decide what to do with it, a white car came to a stop before her house and a man looked out with a smug smile. Why, he was the man she had voted for in the last elections. So had her Sikh neighbours. But she did not have the time to shudder or recoil, for the man was out of the car, shouting like a hunter with a buck in sight.

"Stop. Stop the shaved Sikhda on the bike."

"No!" she held the hair aloft. "I have him inside the house. See. See the hair. I cut them to lure him into the store. I have him locked in. Come and get him. Those are my sons on the bike. Come quickly, he must not escape."

She was like the bloodthirsty goddess Kali seeking destruction of evil. The tongues of fire touched the visage of the goddess with an awesome allure. The long black tresses swung back and forth in rhythm to the dance of the flames, inviting the faithful to keep in step. The crowd ran up, like a pack of wolves with their tongues hanging out, scenting blood.

"There," she said and pointed to the almirah in front of the store. It did not take bare hands more than a moment to wrest the locked doors apart. They growled at the stuff packed inside and turned to tear her apart. She was still in control. "Behind it, inside the store," she said firmly.

They pulled the almirah away with all its weight as if it contained nothing but feathers, they wrenched the lock off the door as if it was not there, they were in and out of the store and upon her almost in the same instant.

"Lies! Hand him over or. . ."

"You call yourself Hindus; you shameless brutes, is this what your religion has taught you?" she said evenly, framed by the fire and black tresses. "What if it was your son Manku being burned alive! Or trampled to death! You have sons and daughters too. Have mercy, my brothers, if you want mercy for your children." She folded her hands and the hair formed a shield. "Come with me, brothers, let us go and save the old Sardarji. Come." She pressed against the railing and started to point at the man being kicked and stamped on the road, but stopped, petrified.

She would have flung herself down as all composure deserted her, had not an iron rod landed on her head. Her skull broke open. Sarabjit's hair was splattered with Satto's blood. "Ashok. . ." she managed to mumble as darkness engulfed her. She had seen her elder son on the outer fringe of the murderous crowd on the road.

## BERLIN
Lydia Schend

*Berlin. Separated since 1945, but one city. Filled
with history, felt in every corner. In the East, capital of the
German Democratic Republic (GDR), and in the West,
headquarters of the Allied Control Council. Berlin is an
island in the middle of the GDR, surrounded by a wall,
now tumbling down, piece by piece.*

*Berlin is still more open, more free, than all other German
cities; all those looking for that freedom move to Berlin.
Lydia Schend has been living in Berlin since 1979. "I want
to stay and write, and fight for the possibility of
living in peace and with cultural tolerance."*

*Old and new fascists gather in Berlin. Lydia reports, "In
January 1989, they gained seats on the City Council for the
first time since World War II, calling themselves—rather
misleadingly—the Republican Party. They dream about a
big, united German Empire; since the dismantling of the
wall, they are trying to expand into the GDR, where they
agitate loudly and try to get votes from those who
think of themselves as the ones being left behind. . ."*

*Lydia Schend was born in a small village in West Germany.
She moved to Berlin 1979. She has studied anthropology
and sociology, and has worked in publishing in Berlin.
Currently, she is working on a multi-cultural writing project.*

# News

"Nazis out! Nazis out!" was the slogan people yelled over and over again right outside City Hall. They were angry and desperate, because the Nazis were already in City Hall, thanks to the Allies, who had permitted the participation of the "Republicans" in the January 29, 1989 elections, and the people, who had voted for them. Schönhuber, their national leader, appeared on television. He was radiant, charming, eloquent: his party had received eight percent of the vote this time, but in the next national elections they expected close to twenty-five percent. They would be the third largest force in this country, he had no doubt! And then there was Andres, their Berlin representative, who spoke about the rights of the Germans and their virtues: cleanliness, honesty, punctuality. A former policeman with the face of a pimp. Puffy, a cynical smile, cold eyes. He didn't say, "Ausländer raus, Foreigners out!" He said, "We are humane. We are in favor of keeping families together—in their home countries."

I called my friend Eva.

She had been in front of City Hall. She had shouted herself hoarse. Her voice was almost gone; she was only croaking. "I'll come over to your place tomorrow."

The following afternoon Eva stood at my door. She seemed taller than usual, somewhat stretched, with overtired, wired eyes. As she was hugging and kissing me, she pulled me out of my flat into the hall.

"Have you seen this?" she asked breathlessly, her finger pointing to a swastika right next to our door. Clear, thin lines, drawn with dark blue chalk.

157

"There is one scratched into the wood of the front door. They are in fact everywhere. And those slogans. . . Maria, we left them there! Why on earth did we leave them? Out of laziness? Or indifference?"

"Or as something which can't be simply erased," I replied. "I also thought about it last night—probably we didn't want to recognize it. . ."

Eva laughed. "I've had enough, really, once and for all. I've brought some paint along. Come on, let's go to the zoo. I have to get out, I need to move, I can hardly breathe."

It was time for us to go; it was already getting dark. The first crows drifted towards us, as always on winter evenings, in throngs from everywhere. Silently we followed them along the rails, carrying the paint, passing by warehouses, workshops, and the smelly butcher right across from the morgue.

GERMAN REMAIN GERMAN. Paint a white bar over it.

FOREIGNERS OUT. LET THE FOREIGNERS IN, YOU NAZI PIG. Away with it.

A few steps further:

BEAT THE NAZI BALD HEADS, UNTIL THEIR BRAINS ARE SMASHED.

BEAT THE RED JEWISH KIDS, UNTIL. . .

It was the return of sheer madness.

At the Bellevue Castle, we had the performance of the crows, fluttering and shrieking around the castle's gable and the highest treetops, all the way downstream the river Spree to the Kongresshalle, which lies like a big shell on a Spree curve, very close to the Reichstag and near the new Carillon. Right behind it towers the Hotel Berlin and the pointed globe of the Television Tower in the East, then further in the West the Axel-Springer-Haus, all appearing to belong together.

"It's the same with André and me," said Eva. "As if there was no wall between us. I often ask myself if I have to blame Germany, or if we would have had a chance in Senegal. André tells me that he is different there, but I only know him here. When we go there next year, I'll find out. But tell me, what difference does it make if we are going to live here in the coming years? I can't go on like this, I have to change my life; otherwise I'll go mad."

Eva and André.

They were separated from the very beginning.

He likes silence and she likes words; he wanted to remain the man, but she didn't want to remain the woman. Africa and Europe. A disastrous story.

Eva had a dream: to be free, equal and different.

But she couldn't stand the tensions kindled by their polarities. Harmony was impossible, even though she was looking for it.

"I can't expect any support," Eva continued. "I have to ask for it, demand it. I'm tired of it—I'm giving up the struggle. . ."

"And how will it continue?"

"I don't know. Maybe not at all. He will have to make up his mind, but what it comes down to is that he doesn't really live here. . ."

"And the children?"

"The children. They won't lose their father, I'm sure about that. They can spend as much time with him as with me—unless André goes back one day—or is forced to go—but I don't want to think about it. He has applied for German citizenship; that way they just can't kick him out one day. André will go, that's quite clear, but he'll go when he's ready to. He wants to; of course he wants to go back to where he is king. He can't stand the hostility, the cold—and I, I can't take him like that."

Eva became silent, and I didn't say anything either.

We passed a chopped-up tree trunk behind Kongresshalle. Silence—there was only silence around us, impossible during the summer when the place is overflowing with people, with grass and sun and a wide sky. Turkish families all over the place on blankets, chairs, hammocks, ready to spend the whole day here. Jugs filled with tea, bowls of salad, the smell of barbecue in the air, constant movement. A few Germans sit around too; the others are on the paths that lead like a spider web from the Castle to the Reichstag to the Philharmonie and to the Victory Column, interwoven with the noisy thoroughfares, all cut off at the wall. Colors and symbols from all over the world melt into each other. Half sentences, only a few legible:

TOI L'ABSURDE.

FREEDOM FOR TRANSYLVANIA.

ONE DAY EVERY WALL FALLS.

ATTENTION—YOU ARE NOW LEAVING WEST BERLIN, warns a sign. HOW? is scribbled above.

The path took us to the Amazon, the weathered one on the horse, armed, composed and noble, and from there all the way to Luiseninsel. The statues of the royal couple, Luise and Wilhelm, separated by the water. Through the bushes, to the place where the Euthanasiezentrale used to stand, and where now, in bright yellow, stands the most beautiful of all the Philharmonies.

We returned much faster. The wind was pulling us; night had fallen. Running along the Grossen Weg, the Great Path, toward the Victory Column, crossing the Street of June Seventeenth. High up in the haze the victory angel, golden like her cannons. In the Rüsternallee, stone soldiers with their mourning wives. Faded letters: NEVER AGAIN WAR.

We hurried on along the row of little trees planted to celebrate Berlin's seven hundred and fiftieth anniversary. A historic reconstruction, a re-naturalized nature. A few old chestnut trees on Zeltenplatz, one with five trunks like elephant legs.

We sat down on a bench in a half circle. The place of dancing and revolution, where people demanded freedom, where Clara Schumann used to live, and also Bettine von Arnim, with her dream about unity among peoples and the harmony of wisdom. Unrecognizable, forgotten a long time ago.

Seven avenues start here.

The sign on a post in Kastanienallee:

AUSLÄNDER RAUS, FOREIGNERS OUT, NF. A gunsight, the National Front's symbol.

They want to shoot. They are practicing. Madmen, who continue, sometimes behind bars, then again set free. The way they march, brazen, with Heil and Fatherland and We will win. Loving weapons, playing Hitler. They would not win, I knew that; but they were on the upswing, ready to cause mischief.

This I saw that day, with this sign, which I had seen before. But now I was wiping. I spat and wiped and spat and wiped it all off.

On the other side, beyond John-Foster-Dulles-Allee, there is the brightly lit Kongresshalle. I didn't know then that three days earlier the House of World Cultures had been opened there. I only knew it as a building financed by the U.S.A., a power I feared. Kongresshalle had collapsed a few years ago, and it was rebuilt in its old shape, but now it was to become the House of World Cultures. I was very happy when I heard this, and that James Koothongsie had sanctified the place. The wise man of the Hopi had not been invited; he came on his own and handed holy blue corn flour into the winds, praying silently on January 26, 1989.

*Translated from German by Ines Rieder*

# CITIES TIED TO THE PAST

# DAMASCUS
## ULFAT AL-ADLIBI

*Damascus, Syria's capital, is considered one of the oldest constantly inhabited cities in the world. Many traditional Damascene houses—with patios and water fountains, ideal for the desert climate—have been destroyed as the city's architecture has evolved over the centuries. In today's Damascus, as elsewhere in Syria, one has to use one's imagination to find what's left of the past. The world wars, fights against French colonialism, and the ongoing hostilities with neighboring Israel have left their marks on Damascus. But the traditional souk, the market, the old mosques and bath houses remain, providing the special flavor of a particular way of life that has been passed on from one generation to the next.*

*Ulfat al-Idlibi was born in Damascus in 1912. When she was seventeen, her family decided to marry her off and she was forced to give up her studies. She began writing in the fifties and has published three collections of short stories.*

# The Women's Baths

Our household was troubled by an unusual problem: my grandmother, who had passed the age of seventy, insisted on taking a bath at the beginning of every month at the public baths.

In my grandmother's opinion the market baths, as she called them, had a delicious ambience which we, who had never experienced it, could not appreciate.

For our part we were afraid that the old lady might slip on the wet floor of the baths—which often happens to people who go there—and break her leg, as her seventy years had made her bones dry and brittle; or she might catch a severe chill coming outside from the warm air of the baths and contract a fatal illness as a result. But how could we convince this stubborn old lady of the logic of these arguments?

It was quite out of the question that she should give up a custom to which she had adhered for seventy years without ever once having been stricken with the mishaps we feared. Grandmother had made up her mind that she would keep up this custom as long as she was able to walk on her own two feet, and her tenacity only increased the more my mother tried to reason with her.

Yet Mother never tired of criticizing her mother-in-law, arguing with her and attempting to demonstrate the silliness of her views, even if only by implication. Whenever the subject of the public baths came up my mother enumerated their shortcomings from the standpoints of health, of society, and even of economics.

What really annoyed Mother was that on the day she went to the baths, my grandmother monopolized our only maid from the early morning onward. She would summon the maid to her room to help her sweep it and change the sheets and prepare the bundles to take to the baths. Then she would set out with her and would not bring her back until nearly sunset, when our maid would be exhausted and hardly able to perform her routine chores.

In our house I was the observer of the relentless, though hidden, struggle between mother-in-law and daughter-in-law: between my grandmother, who clung to her position in the household and was resolved under no circumstances to relinquish it, and my mother, who strove to take her place.

Although girls usually side with their mother, I had strong sympathy for my grandmother: old age had caught up with her since her husband had died and left her a widow, and little by little her authority in the home shrank as my mother's authority gradually extended. It is the law of life: one takes, then hands over to another in one's turn. But that does not mean we obey the law readily and willingly.

I used to feel a certain prick of pain when I saw Grandmother retire alone to her room for long hours after being defeated in an argument with Mother. Sometimes I would hear her talking bitterly to herself, or I would see her monotonously shaking her head in silence, as though she were rehearsing the book of her long life, reviewing the days of her past, when she was the unchallenged mistress of the house, with the last word. I would often see her vent the force of her resentment on her thousand-bead rosary as her nervous fingers marked off its beads and she repeated the prayer to herself: "Oh merciful God, remove this affliction!"

And who could this affliction be but my mother?

Then little by little she would calm down and forget the cause of her anger. There is nothing like the invocation of God for purifying the soul and enabling it to bear the hardships of life.

One day I saw my grandmother getting her things ready to go to the market baths; I had a notion to accompany her, thinking that perhaps I might uncover the secret which attracted her to them. When I expressed my wish to accompany her, she was very pleased, but my mother did not like this sudden impulse at all, and said, in my grandmother's hearing, "Has the craze for going to the market baths affected you as well? Who knows—you may catch some infection, like scabies or something, and it will spread around the family."

Thereupon my father broke in with the final word: "What is the matter with you? Let her go with her grandmother. All of us went to the public baths when we were young and it never did any of us any harm."

My mother relapsed into a grudging silence, while my grand-mother gave an exultant smile at this victory—my father rarely took her side against my mother.

Then Grandmother led me by the hand to the room where her massive trunk was kept. She produced the key from her pocket and opened the trunk in my presence—this was a great honor for me, for the venerable trunk had never before been opened in the presence of another person—and immediately there wafted out of it a strange yet familiar scent, a scent of age, a smell of the distant past, of years which have been folded up and stored away. Out of the depths of the trunk Grandmother drew a bundle of red velvet, the corners of which were embroidered with pearls and sequins.

She opened it in front of me and handed me a wine-colored bath-wrap decorated with golden stars. I had never set eyes on a more beautiful robe. She also gave me a number of white towels decorated around the edges with silver thread, saying, "All these are brand new; no one has ever used them. I have saved them from the time I was married. Now I'm giving them to you as a present, since you are going to the baths with me. Alas. . . poor me. Nobody goes with me now except the servants."

She gave a deep, heartfelt sigh. Then she called the servant to carry the bundle containing our clothes and towels, and the large bag which held the bowl, the soap, the comb, the sponge-bag, the loofah, the soil of Aleppo—a special clay found around Aleppo, which is mixed with perfume and used in washing the hair—and the henna which would transform my grandmother's white hair to jet black. She put on her shawl, and we made our way toward the baths, which were only a few paces from our house. Countless times I had read the words on the little plaque which crowned the low, unpretentious door as I passed by: "Who-ever the Divine Blessing of health would achieve, should turn to the Lord and then to baths of Afif."

We entered the baths.

The first thing I noticed was the female intendant. She was a stout woman, sitting on the bench to the right of people coming in. In front of her was a small box for collecting the day's revenue. Next to it was a nargileh, a water pipe, decorated with flowers. It had a long mouthpiece which the intendant played with between her lips, while she looked at those around her with a proprietorial air. When she saw us she proceeded to welcome us without stirring from her place. Then she summoned Umm Abdu, the bath atten-dant. A woman hastened up and gave us a perfunctory welcome.

She had penciled eyebrows and eyes painted with kohl, and was dressed very neatly. She had adorned her hair with two roses and a sprig of jasmine. She was very voluble, and was like a spinning top, never motionless; her feet in her Shabrawi clogs made a rhythmic clatter on the floor of the baths. Her function was that of a hostess to the bathers. She came up to my grandmother and led her to a special bench resembling a bed. Our maid hastened to undo one of our bundles, drawing out a small prayer rug which she spread out on the bench. My grandmother sat down on it to get undressed.

I was fascinated by what I saw around me. In particular my attention was drawn to the spacious hall called al-barrani, the outer hall of a public bath. In the center of it was a gushing fountain. Around the hall were narrow benches on which were spread brightly colored rugs where the bathers laid their things. The walls were decorated with mirrors, yellowed and spotted with age, and panels on which were inscribed various maxims. On one of them I read, "Cleanliness is part of Faith."

My grandmother urged me to undress. I took off my clothes and wrapped myself in the wine-colored bath-wrap, but as I was not doing it properly Umm Abdu came and helped me. She secured it around my body and then drew the free end over my left shoulder, like an Indian sari.

Then she helped my grandmother down from her bench, and conducted us toward a small door which led into a dark corridor, calling out at the top of her voice, "Marwah! Come and look after the Bey's mother!"

With a sigh a shape suddenly materialized in the gloom in front of me: it was a grey-haired, emaciated woman of middle age with a face in which suffering had engraved deep furrows. She was naked except for a faded cloth which hung from her waist to her knees. She welcomed us in a nasal tone, prattling on although I could not catch a single syllable of what she was saying, thanks to the babble of discordant voices which filled my ears and the hot thick steam which obstructed my sight. There was a smell which nearly made me faint, the likes of which I had never encountered in my life before. I felt nauseous, and was almost sick, leaning against the maid for support.

Nevertheless, in a few moments I grew accustomed to the odor and it no longer troubled me; my eyes, also, became accustomed to seeing through the steam.

We reached a small hall containing a large stone basin. A

number of women circled around in it, chatting and washing at the same time. I asked my grandmother, "Why don't we join them?"

She replied, "This is the wastani, the middle hall of a public bath; I have rented a cubicle in the juwani, the inner hall of the public bath. I am not accustomed to bathing with the herd."

I followed her through a small door to the juwani, and found myself looking with confused curiosity at the scene that presented itself. There was a large rectangular hall, at each corner of which stood a large basin of white marble. Women sat around each one, busily engrossed in washing, scrubbing, and rubbing, as though they were in some kind of race. I raised my eyes to look at the ceiling, and saw a lofty dome with circular openings, glazed with crystal, through which enough light filtered to illuminate the hall. The uproar here was at its worst—there was a clashing of cans, the splashing of water, and the clamor of children.

My grandmother paused for a moment to greet a friend among the bathers, while I found myself following a violent quarrel which had arisen between two young women. I understood from the women around them that they were two wives of a polygamous marriage, who had met face to face for the first time at the baths. The furious quarrel led at length to an exchange of blows with metal bowls. Luckily a spirit of chivalry among some of the bathers induced them to separate the two warring wives before they could satisfy their thirst for revenge.

As we advanced a little way, the howling of a small child drowned the hubbub of the hall. Its mother had put it on her lap, twisting one of its legs around her and proceeding to scrub its face with soap and pour hot water over it until its skin was scarlet red. I averted my gaze, fearing the child would expire before my eyes.

We reached the cubicle, and I felt a sense of oppression as we entered it. It consisted of nothing but a small chamber with a basin in the front. Its one advantage was that it screened those taking a bath inside from the other women.

We were received in the cubicle by a dark, stout woman with a pockmarked face and a harsh voice. This was Mistress Umm Mahmud. She took my grandmother from the attendant Marwah, who was being assailed by shouts from every direction: "Cold water, Marwah, cold water, Marwah!"

The poor woman set about complying with the bathers' requests for cold water, dispensing it from two big buckets which she filled from the fountain in the outer hall. I pitied her, struggling along, so weighed down with the buckets.

I turned back to Grandmother and found her sitting on the tiled floor in front of the basin. She had rested her head between the hands of Umm Mahmud, who sat behind her on a low wooden chair, only slightly raised above the level of the floor. She proceeded to scour Grandmother's head with soap seven consecutive times—not more, not less.

I stood at the door of the cubicle, entertained by the scene presented by the bathers. I watched the younger women coming and going, from time to time going into the outer hall for the sake of diversion, their fresh youthfulness showing in their proud swaying gait. In their brightly colored wraps decorated with silver thread, they resembled Hindu women in a temple filled with the fragrance of incense. Little circles of light fell from the domes onto their tender-skinned bodies, causing them to glisten.

I found the sight of the older women depressing: they sat close to the walls chatting with one another, while the cream of henna on their hair trickled in black rivulets along the wrinkles of their foreheads and cheeks, as they waited impatiently for their turn to bathe.

Suddenly I heard shrill exclamations of pleasure. I turned toward their source, and saw a group of women gathered around a pretty young girl, loudly expressing their delight at some matter.

Mistress Umm Mahmud said to me, "Our baths are doing well today: we have a bride here, we have a woman who has recently had a child, and we have the mother of the Bey—may God spare her for us!"

It was no wonder that my grandmother swelled with pride at being mentioned in the same breath with a bride and a young mother.

I enjoyed standing at the door of the cubicle watching the bride and her companions. Then I caught sight of a fair well-built woman enveloped in a dark blue wrap, giving vent to overflowing joy with little shrieks of delight. I realized from the words she was singing that she must be the bride's mother:

*Seven bundles I packed for thee, and the eighth in the chest is stored;*
*To Thee, Whom all creatures need, praise be, oh Lord!*

A young woman, a relative or friend of the bride, replied:

*Oh maiden coming from the wastani, with thy towel all scented,*
*He who at thy wedding shows no joy, shall die an infidel, from Paradise prevented!*

The bride's mother continued the song:
*The little birds chirp and flutter among the trellis'd leaves;*
*How sweet the bride! The bath upon her brow now pearly*
*crowns of moisture weaves.*
*Thou canst touch the City Gate with thy little fingertip, though*
*it is so high;*
*I have waited for long, long years for this day's coming nigh!*
But the best verse was reserved for the bridegroom's mother:
*Oh my daughter-in-law! I take thee as my daughter!*
*The daughters of Syria are many, but my heart only desires and*
*wishes for thee!*
*Pistachios, hazels and dates: the heart of the envious has been*
*sore wounded;*
*Today we are merry, but the envious no merriment shall see!*
The singing ended as the bride and her companions formed a
circle around a tray which held cakes of Damascene mincemeat,
and a second one filled with various kinds of fruit. The bride's
mother busied herself distributing the cakes right and left, and
one of them even came to me.

In a far corner a woman was sitting with her four children
around a large dish piled with mujaddarah, a Syrian dish of rice,
lentils, onions, and oil, and pickled turnips, their preoccupation
with their meal rendering them completely oblivious to what was
going on around them in the baths. When the dish was empty,
the mother reached into a basket by her side and took out a large
cabbage. Gripping its long green leaves, she raised it up and then
brought it down hard on the tiled floor, until it split apart and
scattered into fragments. The children tumbled over each other
to snatch them up and greedily devoured them, savoring their
fresh taste.

Then my attention was diverted by a pretty girl, about fifteen
or sixteen years old, sitting on a bench along the wall of the
boiler-house. She seemed impatient and restless, as though she
found it hard to tolerate the pervasive heat. She was surrounded
by three women, one of whom, apparently her mother, was
feverishly fussing over her. She began to rub over her body a
yellow ointment which exuded a scent of ginger; it was considered
strengthening ointment. My grandmother explained to me that it
reinforced the blood vessels of a new mother, and restored her to
the state of health she had enjoyed before having her child.

The attendant Umm Abdu came up to us and inquired after our
comfort. She brought us both glasses of licorice sherbet as a

present from the intendant. Then she lit a cigarette for my grandmother, who was obviously regarded as a patron of distinction.

It was now my turn. My grandmother moved aside, and I sat
down in her place, entrusting my head to the attentions of Umm
Mahmud for a thorough rubbing. After I had had my seven soap-
ings I sat down before the door of the cubicle to relax a little. I
was amused to watch the bath attendant Marwah scrubbing one
of the bathers. Her right hand was covered with coarse sacking,
which she rubbed over the body of the woman sitting in front of
her. She began quite slowly, and then sped up, and as she did so
little grey wicks began to appear under the sacking, which quickly
became bigger and were shaken to the floor.

After we had finished being loofahed and rubbed, Umm
Mahmud asked me to come back to her to have my head soaped
an additional five times. I surrendered to her because I had promised myself that I would carry out the bathing rites through all
their stages and degrees as protocol dictated—no matter what
rigors I had to endure in the process.

I was not finished until Umm Mahmud had poured the last
basinful of water over my head, after anointing it with soil of
Aleppo, the scent of which clung to my hair for days afterwards.

Umm Mahmud rose and, standing at the door of the cubicle,
called out in her harsh voice, "Marwah! Towels for the Bey's
mother!"

With a light and agile bound Marwah was at the door of the
wastani, calling out in a high-pitched tone, like a rooster, "Umm
Abdu! Towels for the Bey's mother!" Her shout mingled with that
of another Mistress who was standing in front of a cubicle opposite
ours, likewise demanding towels for her client.

Umm Abdu appeared, clattering along in her Shabrawi clogs,
with a pile of towels on her arm which she distributed among us,
saying as she did, "Blessings upon you. . . Have an enjoyable
bath, if God wills!"

Then she took my grandmother by the arm and led her to the
barani, where she helped her to get up onto the high bench, and
then to dry herself and get into her clothes.

Grandmother stood waiting her turn to pay her bill. There was
a heated argument going on between the intendant and a middle-
aged woman who had three girls with her. I gathered from what
was being said that the usual custom was for the intendant to
charge married women in full, but that widows and single women
paid only half the normal fee. The lady was claiming that she

was a widow, and her daughters were all single. The intendant listened to her skeptically, obviously not believing that the eldest of the girls was single, since she was an adult and was very beautiful. But at last she was forced to accept what the woman said after the latter had sworn the most solemn oath that what she was saying was the truth.

My grandmother stepped forward and pressed something into the intendant's hand, telling her, "Here's what I owe you, with something extra for the cold water and the attendance."

The intendant peered down at her hand and then smiled; in fact, she seemed very pleased, for I heard her say to my grandmother", May God keep you, Madam, and we hope to see you every month."

Then my grandmother distributed tips to the attendant, the Mistress, and Marwah, as they emerged from the juwani to bid her goodbye.

I have never known my grandmother to be so generous and openhanded as on the day which we spent at the market baths. She was pleased and proud as she listened to the blessings called down on her by those who had received her largesse. Then she gave me an intentionally lofty look, as if to say, "Can you appreciate your grandmother's status now? How about telling your mother about this, now that she's begun to look down her nose at me?"

As she left the baths there was a certain air of haughtiness in her step, and she held herself proudly upright, although I had only known her to walk resignedly, with a bent back at home.

Now she was enjoying the esteem which was hers only when she visited the market baths. At last I understood her secret. . .

*Translated from Arabic by Michel G. Azrak*

# LONDON
ELIZABETH WILSON

*Elizabeth Wilson has always responded to the "untidy intimacy" of London's districts and the "melancholy charm" of its enclosed squares and Victorian streets. "As I have changed, London has changed around me, both for better and worse, but however worn or altered, I wear the city like a comfortable, familiar coat, whose darns and patches I have come to value for themselves. . . . I am passionately opposed to those who attack city life, and especially to the planners, philanthropists and politicians who have so often tried to regulate and control ordinary people by crushing the vitality out of city life."*

*Elizabeth Wilson is the author of several books, among them a book of essays,* Hallucinations: Life in the Post-Modern City. *She has just finished writing a book about women in cities, to be published by Virago Press, London.*

# Summer in the City

I meet my friend Lenore in the bus. She's looking marvellous. Red T-shirt and espadrilles match her lipstick, the color of tomatoes, and she's wearing wonderful Bermudas, black, red and parrot green. Her hair stands out in a bob that looks like it's been carved from black foam rubber.

So what's changed? She's still having trouble with the custody of her children, and has to go back to court again in another two weeks. This saga has gone on for months. So has the racial harassment in the flats. And the council's done nothing about it. These hot nights it's worse if anything. There's been another incident. Bottles were thrown.

Yes, today she's full of energy, she's left the kids with her mum; she's on her own, going off to see a friend. She leaps off the bus and strides away through the petrol fumes at the junction, the heat a source of energy, of defiance.

Another hot day. It's like a winning streak at Vingt et Un. Against all the odds, when you turn the cards up it's another ace, another king. With a sly smile you slip them into view, and you feel not lucky, but smug. I can't lose now: my lucky day.

A sense of excess and transgression invades all areas of life. You know it was never meant to be like this. How far can you push your luck? You spend afternoons in the cool darkness of almost empty cinemas. You experience sudden desires and unexpected encounters; yet making love becomes a slithery, passive experience—you might melt before anything happens. You swim at the Highgate ponds. The grass by the Ladies Pool is jammed with municipal strikers.

'Isn't this wonderful—I don't feel stressed, I'm not tired. I don't think I'll go back to work ever.' No winter of discontent. This is the summer of serenity; who wouldn't rather water the garden than sit in a crowded commuter train?

In northern winters you hardly feel you're outside at all; the street is like a corridor, an interior, some cheerless antechamber: the city as total institution. Now the sun splits it open—bomb damage, waste ground, cracks in the facades and grass that grows as pale as wheat; this is an open city, the rules are relaxed, routine is made strange. The heats rolls you in warm treacle. It presses up close to you, rubs itself against you like a great invisible cat. Sunlight flashes a steel blade off the wings of cars. Mirrors glitter, and a breath of wind through the hair, and a casual elbow protrudes from every rolled-down window. This is the freeway; driving to work was never like this. This is a science fiction city.

Another hot day. To the chorus of pale old women on the bus, as faded and whitish beige as their clothes, the heat is an added source of misery. So close, so humid, that's what they always say. This heat is cruel. God, I think, can't the Brits ever stop moaning? When it's wet they whine, and when it's cold. Now this brilliant weather becomes another scapegoat for their discontent. But in the flats, those little rooms are ovens and the caretakers are on strike, so the waste shute's blocked and the stench from the bursting plastic bags of rotting food gets so bad you have to have the windows shut. Someone found maggots crawling everywhere. It's a health hazard; they're frightened of rats.

Another hot day. Two months of it and this is a third world city. In southern suburbs they're queuing for water at standpipes a twenty-minute walk from home. Fighting broke out. The water has to be boiled. Civilisation begins to break down. And people demand compensation. Don't they realise it was always like this? It's hot and cold running water that's the aberration. In the desert the women toil for miles with their buckets and gourds. Before 1945 in the English countryside, and in the slums, they had one tap on a landing.

There's outrage on the radio because some petty entrepreneur is selling water for two quid a bucket—a thoroughly appropriate thing to do in Thatcher's Britain, I'd have thought, Victorian values to the nth degree. They got their water from standpipes then too, in the summer of 1859, the summer of the Great Stink when the Thames was like an open sewer. They thought you could catch cholera from the smell, so they hung great sheets that had been soaked in chloride of lime over the windows along Whitehall. Think of those Victorians in their thick, black suits, their waistcoats, their corsets and crinolines and bodices and gloves.

Remember the hysteria in 1976—the droughts, the subsidence, the riots at Nottinghill? They said it would never get cold again, that instead of the ozone layer there'd be a copper dome of exhaust fumes to lock us into some European Bronx forever.

The hysteria's starting again. Yet something has changed. Now the young, at least, are taking the heatwave in their stride. And, like on Come Dancing, they wear fewer and fewer clothes. No Victorian values in the way we dress. You need (whatever sex you identify with) a vest (black or white), shorts (black, white or jeans), a tattoo, an elastic band for your bunch and tiny round sunglasses the size of a sixpence, framed in steel. And you need muscle. The young are working out. Hard muscle; tough times. Young women wear vest bras and shorts like school locknit knickers; or items from the Marks and Spencers lingerie department— languorous camisoles and bikini panties with frills: the street as boudoir. Or men and women alike encase their thighs like shiny black sausages in cycling shorts that must be hotter than any garment on earth.

So? That's fashion these days. Gaultier himself said all you need is a white shirt, a jacket and jeans (and he meant women).

Minimal dress, though, while just the thing, can also be the end. Except in the City, where they're pretending nothing has happened, there's a T-shirt for every walk of life, the bottom line in industrial dress. The outsize lager drinker's T-shirt is the ultimate sartorial dustbin into which a suet-coloured body, oozing fat, can be flung while its owner goes on eating and drinking like there is no tomorrow. Women of fifty wear them fitted, pulled over a preformed, separated bra and carefully pastel to match the gathered cretonne skirt. They must think they're still in the fifties. Meanwhile it's message T-shirts for the young: "I'm an S/M dyke" announces one, its wearer scrupulously non-aggressive in the bus queue melee during a train strike rush hour.

Every sash window of the squat on the High Road is pushed up to the farthest extent. Three punks sit on the front steps of the eighteenth-century mansion. Inside a forty-watt bulb makes a pinpoint of light, denoting a continuing radical commitment to indoor life, but the house gapes open and what furniture there is lies strewn around the grass at the front. Their full punk regalia, which adheres strictly to a wholly urban style bearing no relation to comfort or nature, suggests a resolute refusal to modify one's dress to suit the climate.

Nature, however, does figure here in London, unlike, perhaps, Detroit, Manhattan, Palermo, Athens, Limassol—southern cities whose very names speak of heat and dust. In any case the dusty, arid countryside out of which they have grown is more like an excavated ancient site than anything we would call the country. But here, in the mauve dusk of Hampstead, the grasses sigh, and the foliage of trees thickens into a rural glade as theatrical as the Forest of Arden. White bodies tumble off the diving raft into a green lake. There are picnics, pastoral settings, suburban gardens with splashing pools.

That's another dream, though, far from the heart of the city. It's in this stony landscape that the truth of the summer city is found. Through its uninhabited ravines some far-off music echoes from the open window of an empty room, a woman's voice aching with melancholy, stale music washing through the hot, stale air: a weekend city in which you're the lone survivor, while its millions crowd the parks, the pools, the freeways.

Only in dark mansion flats, a few survivors float through watery green interiors like alligators at the bottom of a lagoon.

## DUBLIN
### EILIS NI DHUIBHNE

*Eilis Ni Dhuibhne was born in Dublin in 1954 and has lived there for most of her life. She says she was born at a lucky time, just as Dublin, and Ireland, were moving out of the depression, authoritarianism and rigid nationalism of the first half of the century, and into a new era of growth and liberalism. She was among the first group of Irish students who received free secondary school and university education, and feels she straddles the fence between an old, rural, superstitious society and a modern cosmopolitan world. It is an interesting vantage point.*

*Eilis Ni Dhuibhne's collection of stories,* Blood and Water, *and her novel,* The Bray House, *are published by Attic Press, Dublin.*

# Rootlessness

My family did not, at least until very recently, practice exogamy. For hundred of years its members have married their cousins and neighbors in a small parish in Donegal. It is true that my father and mother met in a dance hall in Dublin. . . which one I do not know: that is not the sort of detail they would divulge. She—my mother—had a job in Jacob's at that time, packing biscuits. She got, as a result, bags of broken marshmallows, club milks, mikadoes, at cut price every Friday for the rest of her life—an important heritage for me and my brothers. My father was an electrician with a huge building corporation which constructed most of the public buildings in the city during the fifties and sixties. Bus Arus, Belfield, Liberty Hall: he worked on all of these. Sometimes, when I grew up and walked in these places as someone who belonged, had every right to be there, I remembered this, that he had been in the same place when it was still a heap of muck and rubble. I tried to get a sense of him, from the locations. But I invariably failed: somehow I could not think of him as a worker; I could not imagine him in connection with these sturdy urban constructs. And possibly I cannot imagine myself in connection with them either, in serious deep connection, even though they are and always have been the setting of my life.

My parents, although they met for the first time in a Dublin dance hall, were both natives of the same parish, of Carrick. But he was fifteen years older than she was, and had left for Glasgow when she was still a toddler, not even started school. Their families lived in neighbouring townlands; however, they might as well have been childhood sweethearts, for all the difference it made. It was

178

their shared origin that drew them together, more than anything else. More than sexuality, perhaps, although that is something which I do not know. It never struck me that there was any sexual relationship between my parents. The only time they touched one another, as far as I saw, was when my mother pecked my father on the cheek as she said goodbye to him in the morning. And that was more a ritual than a display of affection. But probably the absence of display meant nothing. People still kept secrets in those days; they kept money in mattresses and old Christmas puddings in rusty tins and they went to bed in long nightdresses made of flowered wincyette. Perhaps they made love in flowered wincyette too. No child would have known, as children know now, what went on between adults. They were not meant to know. And, in my case, at least, didn't want to.

My parents were the only ones in their respective families who stayed in Ireland. All their brothers and sisters emigrated, to Liverpool, Glasgow, Philadelphia, and Sydney, Australia. Dublin was probably just as strange to them as America was to their siblings, but they did not have the stigma and the glory of immigrants. They did not live in ghettos, with other people from Carrick; they did not have a club to go to with other people from Carrick; they did not have a club to go to, to talk Irish in and do old-time dances and reminisce about the old days. They had to mix in, with other people from other places in Ireland. From Kerry and Tipperary and Mayo, they had to mix in with real Dubliners. Perhaps they lost more of their real identity in this way than the people who really went far away and established a home away from home. They did not need to hold onto that identity so badly, because the one that was replacing it was not so different from the original anyway. Or it did not seem to be, at the time. There was no ocean dividing the old and the new cultures, and so they let their natural ways slip away, gradually, without noticing what was happening. Language, manners, mores vanished. They did not seem to, but they did, until my parents, now, are totally different people from those who emerged from Carrick fifty years ago. Their minds are filled with other images, their ears with other sounds. Their tongues shape other words. They are not, in one sense, the same people. Or are they?

The many brothers and sisters never came home on a visit. They never went to Carrick, as we did, every summer. But they too, in the main, married other people from the parish, or the surrounding district. Men and women from places like Teelin, or Glencolumbkille. Roots were what the couples had in common, and I could imagine a long tough tap, the kind you get on shrubs such as broom or woodbine, shrubs which are difficult to transplant. . . wandering all over the world, sending up shoots in the oddest places, but having a constant base in south Donegal.

There was one person who broke this pattern, who married outside Carrick, and that was Uncle Park. He had been Patsy in Ireland, but in America he'd changed that, and my mother, whose brother he was not, accepted the new name. My father didn't refer to him much: he was older than my father, and perhaps they had not even known each other all that well. I did not know him at all, I'd never seen him, because he'd never come to Ireland. Once his wife, Ingrid. . . yes!. . . had sent us a photo of him, sitting at a table in their kitchen. The table was set for a casual meal, and Uncle Park loomed behind a milk bottle, fat and aging, with receding hair which was either very thin or very greasy.

"A football head, like your father," was my mother's only comment on his appearance, which did not impress me, either. But she remarked in detail and at length on the milk bottle, and the state of the table, and the overall untidiness of the kitchen, which could be imagined rather than seen in the small snapshot. She was quite offended by it; we all were. We had high standards of table-setting in our family, and a large selection of jugs, sugar bowls, butter knives, napkin rings, and numerous other utensils to ensure that meals were eaten with due formality. We would have died rather than put a milk bottle on the table. And in a photograph! We put on our best dresses, and lined up against the railing in front of the house, smiling, when anyone took a picture. It wasn't often, and they usually got lost afterwards, because our tidiness did not extend to documents: we had no filing system or album or any of the bureaucratic paraphernalia of the modern household, so the snaps seem even fewer than they were.

"If that's America, they can keep it!" my mother said.

When I was ten, Uncle Park died, of cancer of the liver. I did not learn this, or of the fact of his death, for some time after my parents knew. See what I mean about secrets? The first hint that something was amiss came when I returned from school one day, and found that my mother was not in the kitchen. I buttered some bread and dipped it in sugar, and put on the kettle for tea. While

I was eating my snack, she came in and said one sentence, "You needn't bother to change your clothes today." Then she went away again.

Because of the way our house was built, higgledy-piggledy, with bits and pieces tacked on by my father whenever he felt like it, or my mother felt like it, you could see into the dining room from the window of the kitchen. When I went to wash my cup, I saw my mother, sitting at the extending table, staring out at an apple tree in the back garden. It was not one of her usual attitudes and anyone could see she was worried. I went upstairs, took off the navy blue gymslip which was my school uniform, and put on what I usually wore after school: an old blue dress and pink cardigan, which had been my Sunday dress two years earlier and was so small and shabby that it was an act of mortification to wear it, even around the house. My mother was as a rule very adamant about this changing business, however, and now I planned to cheer her up, by doing it even though she had said I needn't bother.

But when I went back downstairs she was annoyed, not pleased.

"What did you put that old thing on for?" she demanded petulantly.

I could not tell her it was in order to please her. Although I was still very dependent on my mother, although I still loved her, I was not in the habit of telling her this. The word "love" was not used in our family, except, occasionally, as a form of address. "Will you run up to the shop and get the paper, love?" The word "like" was not used either. We did not talk about feelings at all, really. We cried, got angry, laughed, but we never verbalised our emotions. We did not, in fact, use words much for any purpose. My mother related gossip, information about food prices, things like that. My father cursed as he listened to the news or drove the car. We—my brothers and I—asked for things. But I do not think we talked to our parents, or to any adults, and I do not think they talked to us. Perhaps that was why my mother had not bothered explaining why I was to leave on my uniform. She was used to giving orders, not information, to children.

"Uncle Park died three days ago," she said at last. "They're flying back the remains. They'll be all here this evening. So go up and put your gymslip back on."

I did, mystified. It did dawn on me that my gymslip, short in the skirt and shining in the seat, was my mother's idea of mourning.

After tea, two uncles, from New Jersey and Philadelphia, and Ingrid, also from Philadelphia, arrived in a large taxi, laden with shining cases and plastic bags full of whiskey and cigarettes. The uncles wore dark, perfectly new suits and their shirts and teeth flashed brilliantly in the November gloom. Their faces, too, beamed, red, bursting with laughter, greetings, bonhomie: they were genuinely delighted to be home.

Ingrid, however, seemed as pale and subdued as any widow could be. Thin and tall, she was dressed in a coat of heavy black, and under her large grey eyes were dark rings. Of sorrow, I assumed, touched and awed. Her hair, however, was not black, like mine and my parents', but perfectly flaxen, and, for an adult woman, unusually long. She wore it heaped on her head in coils. These coils were held in place by a large shining black slide, shaped like a bow.

She did not speak at all, beyond making the most essential exchanges, and she spent the evening ensconced in the sofa in the corner of the sitting room, sipping tea. She complained of tiredness but that was all: it was such a busy evening, such a lot of things had to be said and done, that it was not really possible to pay attention to her, and nobody knew how to approach her, anyway. The focus of attention was the uncles: they had not visited Ireland in twenty years, and now, here they were, unencumbered as they had been before they took the boat from Cobh and sailed to jobs and families and responsibilities. Home and free! No wonder their bronze-red faces were wreathed in smiles! No wonder they smoked their king-size cigarettes with slow, deliberate pleasure, and poured another glass of whiskey, and settled into the smoky hot festive room, the room never used except at Christmas and for very special occasions. No wonder they ignored Ingrid, foreign and strange, bereaved: in every way, a creature of ill luck.

I was up early the following morning, preparing breakfast for all the visitors. Ingrid came into the kitchen.

"Here you are," she said, "so busy, cooking!"

Already I was used to her voice, not a mixture of Donegal and American, like the uncles', but a mixture of American and foreign.

"I'm not cooking!" I protested. I hated praise of this kind; housework was something I did because I was forced to, by my mother, and I took no pride in it. What I was doing was cutting grapefruit. "It's not real cooking!"

I ran the breadknife between the flesh and the peel, so that the fruit could be eaten easily with a spoon, and then I sprinkled the pale yellow moons with white sugar.

"No?" she asked, pleasantly. "It sure looks like cooking to me!" She smiled. Her smile had an unusual quality; it was a foreign smile, not innocent and sweet, or cute and sour, as Irish smiles were, but cool, elegant, inscrutable. She helped me carry the glass dishes to the table.

What an odd woman, I thought; any other woman would have taken offence at such cheek from a child like me!

"What do you like to eat for breakfast?" I asked, looking at her morning housecoat, which was not black, but pink, edged with snowy fur.

"Oh, not so much! Bread and jam."

"*Yam?*"

"*Yam.* Can I tell you a joke, from Wisconsin, where I lived before I lived in Philadelphia? It's a Swede talking, like me, who's been in America for a long time. 'It's taken me ten years to learn how to say "jam" and now they call it jelly.'"

She laughed, excessively, I considered, for what seemed a rather feeble joke. But I laughed with her, for politeness' sake, and from admiration, not of her humour, but of her skill: I had never heard a grown woman tell a formal joke before. At wit and repartee the women I knew were excellent, but they did not know how to tell jokes. I felt close to Ingrid; for a minute I felt the hope and excitement that a new good relationship can promise, before it has properly begun. She felt it too, it seemed. And for that reason I was chosen to accompany her and the uncles to Carrick, in a hired black limousine, while my parents and brothers went in our old Anglia.

We were following the hearse which contained Park's coffin, but when we stopped at Ardee for drinks, the hearse did not, and we did not see it again after that. In a small pub the uncles drank whiskey with the chauffeur, and Ingrid and I had bronze-coloured lemonade, made by a local firm I had never heard of: Setanta Mineral Water Company. Ingrid did not drink alcohol, she told me, and I realised from the set of her lips as she said it that she did not approve of my uncles' habits, that she did not, probably, approve of my uncles at all. Or of my father or mother, or perhaps of anyone in the family. This answered something in my own attitude to them, and for that reason made me uncomfortable. I wished I was with my mother, or even my brothers; suddenly I did not feel capable of sustaining these new relationships, if such they could be called, on my own.

But the journey was very long. The limousine hurtled along, over potholes the size of wells, up and down, up and down drumlin after drumlin, until I was thoroughly nauseated. We stopped at Monaghan for lunch, a long lingering affair, during which nobody ate very much but more whiskey was consumed by the uncles. We stopped at Omagh, and would have stopped again if the driver of the car had not refused, pleading the pressure of time. After that, they all slept, the uncles and Ingrid. Only the driver and I were awake, entombed into the dark stuffy car, gazing at blackness all around, hearing nothing except the loud hum of the engine and the loud snores of the sleepers: even Ingrid, who looked like an angel, sounded like an elephant in heat. Probably something to do with the uncomfortable position she was obliged to take.

Carrick always presented a striking contrast to Rathmines, which was the only pole of comparison I had, and at the same time seemed as familiar as my gymslip or own bed. I had no respect for it, for any of the people in it, but I was also aware that I loved it, and all its little effects, quaint, inconvenient, or beautiful: the dirt track that served instead of a road; the plastic bin in the barn that served as a toilet, the range, the well, the hens, the bony brindle cow. The hills, the sea, the fuschia, the corncrake. It was a far cry from the narrow cul-de-sac of prim, shabby houses where we lived, a far cry from the number twelve bus, and the queue outside the Stella on Saturdays. But as familiar to me, after my holidays, as much a part of me, as all of that. As much, and sometimes, I thought, more, although now I am not sure. Now I think it was stranger than it seemed, then, and more interesting, and more important.

The house we arrived at was, now as always, inhabited by my bachelor uncles. My father had two in Carrick; the three in America had married, and we did not know about the other, Seamas, in Australia, the youngest, who'd disappeared suddenly one day, and never forwarded his address. I don't know how they knew he was in Australia, unless it was simply that he didn't crop up in any of the other likely places. And I don't know why he disappeared. Why do people suddenly go away, not saying good-bye or telling anyone where they're going? Losing contact, I can understand. In the context of my family, it was the easiest thing in the world. They were out of touch more often than not, losing addresses, never writing letters even when they had them. Now that I am an adult it is the same, with my brothers, who live in Dun Laoghaire and Bray. From one end of the year to the other, I do not see them, except by accident. Or at a family occasion: a Christmas dinner at my mother's house, a christening. Among my siblings, we have had no funeral, not yet, but at them we will meet. Otherwise, blood relationship is something taken for granted in my family; it is not considered important to keep up friendships with those who are, after all, inextricably linked anyway. But I know where my brothers are. And I know they will not emigrate without ringing me up to tell me where they are going, and I imagine they will send me an address, when and if—it is far from impossible—they go. But Seamas upped and left, without a word to anyone. A row? Rows occur in this family as in others. But they are not spoken of, they are pushed away as if they had been doses of flu, best, indeed inevitably, forgotten.

They were at the door, in their suits, the uncles, and they took off their caps before walking shyly up to Mike and Ned—the Americans—and shaking hands stiffly with them. Ingrid, who had stepped out of the car after the uncles, they looked at, but did not approach. I nodded at her, and indicated the door of the house, rather stupidly, since it was perfectly obvious where it was, but some sign had to be made, and no one was making it. Silently, we all trooped through the low portal to the kitchen.

Transformed. Usually the kitchen was hot, empty, and messy. Now it was packed with people. Everyone from the parish was there, talking, eating and drinking tea or whiskey. It uncomfortably resembled a pub. I could see my own parents in a corner, chatting with Mags Gallagher from down the road. I could not see my own brothers. Fighting through the crush, embarrassed by the greetings, the "sorry for your troubles," a phrase I could not stomach, for some reason—snobbishness, probably—then or even now, although there is no formula in my vocabulary to replace it. . . I reached my mother.

"Where're Colin and Donal?"

"I don't know," she said. "Come on now, you, and say a prayer at the remains."

She took my hand and pulled me out of the kitchen, across the hall and into the parlour. Seeing Ingrid standing in a corner, surrounded by a narrow barrier of empty space, I took her hand and dragged her along with us, a gesture so brave and so uncharacteristic that I can only suppose I was in some sort of hallucinatory state, induced by tiredness or smoke or alcoholic air.

The coffin had been placed on the table, in the center of the small room. Candles were lighted at its head, and a group of old women and men knelt on the floor around it, clinking beads and praying in murmuring voices. The lid had been opened. It hung to one side, black and lined with white quilted satin, like a jewelry box. The coffin itself had the same kind of lining, and resting against it, in a charcoal suit and white shirt, dressed identically to the other uncles, was Park.

He looked different from the Park I had seen in the photograph, who had been like my father, or Ned or Mike. He looked different from anyone I had ever seen, and resembled, really, a plaster mannequin from a shop window: a menswear shop. He could have modelled a sports coat or a burberry very well, the Park in the coffin, with his white, chiselled features, his contemptuously curved mouth, his downcast eyes.

"Kiss him!" my mother hissed.

I felt this was unfair. I had never even seen Park during his lifetime. Why should I have to kiss him now? He looked white and immaculate, but the room was filled with a sweet smell. The smell, I thought, of the ointment used in embalming him. It did not strike me as being healthy.

Ingrid looked at him stonily, and after a minute said, in an ordinary speaking voice (insofar as her speaking voice was ordinary), "The casket was not to be opened."

One of the old men, kneeling on the floor, lifted his bleary eyes and stared at her. Everyone else in the room acted as if they were deaf, and my mother averted her gaze, as from a person who is behaving in an unseemly manner.

"It should not be opened. That was known to everyone," Ingrid said again, in tones which were calm and measured. My mother pushed me towards the coffin.

"Kiss him!" she repeated.

I looked at Ingrid. She shrugged, and left the room.

I hissed at my mother, "They weren't supposed to open the coffin! I don't want to kiss him!"

I felt ashamed. Not of him, lying in state, perfumed, glamorous as he had never been during his lifetime. But of my mother and father. The openers of the coffin. They had been here first. They had known that the coffin was not to be opened: it was a point that much had been made of the night before, in our house in Dublin.

Again and again, the uncles had said that they had been allowed to bring over the remains on condition that the coffin was not opened, and everyone had taken some sort of pride in this injunction, pleased that the authorities, the customs officials, the powers that move dead bodies from continent to continent, had trusted them, put them on their honour. They could have their corpse, if. . . And now the trust had been broken, the coffin had been opened, by those untrustworthy rule-breakers, my parents. Who but they opened the coffin? Who but they had that power, in that house, at that time? I knew them to be more than capable of it: they kept no rules, at least, none of the modern ones that I was familiar with, that I was a stickler for. Rules, moral codes, ethics which my parents did not abide by or understand. In them I saw—or thought I saw, although I was wrong—my salvation, escape from the class and traditions which encoffined my family. What was I escaping to? The prim world of the nuns in my convent school, the boring dull world of the lower-middle-class girls who were my companions, daughters of minor civil servants, national teachers, who would not let them undress on a public beach, later would not let them date boys, stay out after half past ten? Not that, not that, which was after all so much worse than my own life, governed by traditional country people, old-fashioned, maybe, in some ways, but with the power of adaptation. Intelligent and sensitive to change as my schoolfriends' parents could not be. Nevertheless, knowing all this, I envied their ways, narrow, petty, ladylike. Their snow-white socks. Their little rules. Thou shalt not wear a skirt above the knee. Thou shalt not shop at a street stall. Thou shalt have a credit account in Arnott's.

Thou shalt not open coffins, play games at wakes, bury your own dead.

"They opened the coffin," my mother passed the buck, in a tired voice, knowing me and my ways, "as soon as it got here. Sure they had to look at him."

The smell was not perfume; it was heavier and more cloying than that. It was must, a sort of sweet musty odour.

"Go on," she whispered, "kiss him."

I went to the coffin and looked at the alabaster face, with its brush of hair combed back from the forehead, its even black brows. I bent over it and pretended to kiss it, but did not. The smell of old flesh. He'd been dead five days, this glamorous Park.

He was going off. I knew it, bending over his head, which had the exact shape, I could see, of my brother's, also of my own. I joined my hands and muttered a Hail Mary very fast, and withdrew.

He was buried in the graveyard across the road from the village church. Ingrid did not come to the burial: she claimed headaches, tiredness, and after the first day I did not see much of her: she went home, back to America, earlier than the uncles did, and without calling us in Dublin. I was disappointed. Ingrid had promised something, she had interested me, with her coiled fair hair and her accent, and her foreign name. It would have suited me to remain in touch with her. But after the funeral we never saw her or heard from her, ever ever again.

I cannot remember where exactly the grave is: my family does not visit or tend graves. Even those of my grandparents, in Glasnevin, we ignore, although we knew and loved them, and were genuinely sorry when they died. We do not go to the anniversary mass, either; in fact, I do not remember its date, although my mother, I think, does. Our contact with dead members of the family, as with those who are alive, is minimal.

What causes this casualness is something I wonder about. This lack of care for rules and courtesies, the inability to keep in touch. At the Carrick funeral the chaos stopped suddenly and brutally: death, and such a death, had a miraculous power to shock and catalyse and transform attitudes. Death is always potent in Ireland. But codes were broken at Carrick, too, and the links which fail to join me to my family all have to do with rule-breaking: the garage erected without planning permission, the doses of penicillin not completed, the coffin opened, to release something for a brief period. And then closed again.

Where such broken links are forged I do not know. Below the clay, taproots mingle; is that it? Or is it something overground, something that is always, after all, there and available, but not always visible? A brick in a skyscraper, a stone in a road? Or something deeper than any of those things? Deeper, farther down, and completely lost.

# VIENNA
### INES RIEDER

*Vienna's dream of becoming the greatest city in Europe died with the downfall of the Austro-Hungarian Empire at the end of World War I. Since then, the city's population has shrunk, with more than half its inhabitants over fifty—a quite unusual phenomenon at the end of this century. No surprise then that Ines Rieder grew up with stories of a (selectively) praiseworthy past and false fantasies about lost glory.*

*Even though Vienna likes to think of itself as the gateway from West to East, it seems to belong more to the East, with the majority of the population coming from Czechoslovakia, Hungary, Poland, Yugoslavia and Turkey. Cut off from its lifeline by the now-defunct Iron Curtain, Vienna's destiny as a dying city seemed sealed.*

*The winds of change which have swept through most of Eastern Europe have been felt in Vienna: almost forgotten relatives and friends are showing up again; many come for a short shopping or sightseeing trip, others for a longer stay to earn some hard currency. Western visitors wear business suits and carry briefcases filled with cash. The new glory may be another fantasy, but the fact still remains: the open borders in the East, only a few kilometers away, will once again influence Vienna and maybe even save it from turning into a big cemetery.*

# After Life in Vienna

OFFERING SECURE POSITION. LOOKING FOR WOMEN INSENSITIVE TO ODORS. REQUIREMENTS: FLUENCY IN AT LEAST FIVE LANGUAGES. NO AGE LIMITS. THOSE INTERESTED, SEND PICTURE AND RESUME.

My friend, who reads every paper from cover to cover, told me about this ad, and since I know more than five languages, I decided to try my luck. I knew that I would have to lie a bit: I only knew Czech and Hungarian real well—I picked them up without studying, because my mother was from Pilsen and my father from Sopron. After many years in Vienna, they ended up speaking more German with us, but with their old friends and relatives, they stuck to their native languages.

Later with the Allies, I learned a bit of Russian, and French and English. Enough to make deals whenever necessary. And then in the sixties, we could afford to go on vacations to Italy. The Italians talk to you until you understand them. And nowadays with all the Yugoslavs and Turks living in my neighborhood, I can't help but learn a bit here and there. No, I'm not particularly gifted with languages, but I do want to talk with people. If I am asked to read or write in any of those languages, I'll tell them that I left my glasses at home, and I'll walk out. I tried to figure out what the job was about, but I couldn't guess. I thought I might have to smell odd fluids and give them their proper names in different languages.

It was a job offer from the city. They needed someone to take care of the public toilet in front of the Hundertwasserhaus. The house isn't that old—it was only built in the early eighties—but

190

very quickly and to everybody's surprise it had turned into one of Vienna's main tourist attractions. Soon the people in the neighborhood were complaining about desperate tourists trying to piss in unlikely locations. At first I thought that I wouldn't go that low, but at my age it isn't that easy to find employment, so I decided to give it a try. I could, of course, live on my retirement, but then I wouldn't be able to save anything, and that might mean trouble ten years from now. My kids say that I might be in my grave by then if I don't stop working, but the problem is that I don't have a grave I like. I want to have my very own, and I'm planning on having some nice music at my funeral. All those things have their price.

The price I pay right now is high: I have to look at the Hundertwasserhaus every day. It seems as if the whole world knows about it, and they all want to see it. They think it's some architectonic marvel, but if you ask me, I think it's nothing special. Anybody who is given lots of money can do it. I think the toilets I clean are worth more shit than Mister Hundertwasser's architecture. And the people living in the house aren't satisfied because nothing works properly.

Occasionally I have to think about all the money that was poured into this, just to tickle the fancy of some artist. He doesn't even need to live in this building; he has several villas and he owns a palazzo in Venice. But in this city there is always money for those with the right connections. They get the best apartments and the fanciest funerals. Only people like me have to work hard for them.

I was lucky to have grown up in a Gemeindebau, a city-owned apartment building. All these tourists who waste their time with Hundertwasser would be better off taking a look at those buildings. Well, there are a few tourists, the ones who are interested in politics, and they go and take a look at the Karl-Marx-Hof. They go there because of the name. Nobody comes to the George-Washington-Hof, where I grew up. Wouldn't that be something to show to the Americans? Have a nice coffeehouse, where we serve them Apfelstrudel, play some working-class music, tunes like "Wir sind die Arbeiter von Wien" ("We Are the Workers of Vienna"), take some pictures in front of George's bust, and send them off with a few postcards. They'll mail those cards to their relatives and friends back home. . . then they'll get all excited about Washington, and next year they'll book a trip to Vienna. Once we have them in our hands, we can tell them a bit about how socialism works.

I should say how socialism *worked*, because I'm not so sure how it works these days. We had our golden period in the twenties; those were the heydays of Red Vienna. The socialist government taxed everything and everybody and used that money to build sixty-five thousand flats. All within a decade, all after the empire had been lost, with a crumbling economy and inflation running high. They had it all figured out, using cheap land and delivering all the construction materials via the public transport system. When finished, the flats were given to those workers who needed them most—at no cost and with an affordable rent.

My mother, who is now in her eighties, remembers the day her family moved into their new flat. She still cries when she talks about it. Before, they had shared a room and a kitchen with no toilet or running water. Then, boom, overnight they had gotten three sunny rooms with a toilet and running water inside. Poor people didn't think of having their own baths or even showers, and there was no need since there were plenty of public baths.

Our neighbors were always arguing about which bath they preferred. I liked Theresienbad and Amalienbad best. We had to use streetcars to go to both of them, and I was never sure what I liked better, the tram ride or those hours in the sauna. There I could splash in as much water as I wanted, and relax in the company of hundreds of sweating and chatting women.

These are the kind of things I should tell all these people who come and use the Hundertwasser toilets. Send them off to take a look at those remaining Zinskasernen, rent barracks, now peopled by the guest workers. Why don't they build something nice for them? No, they prefer to let Hundertwasser build, so that the tourists will come.

If things had gone a bit different in my life, and I hadn't fallen for this drunkard I married, I might be a well-known politician. After all, I grew up in a staunch socialist family, and we had the best connections. They have always needed women who know how to talk, and I was one of their top candidates until that bastard came along and ruined it all. No need to even think about him—I buried him years ago, and I only have occasional nightmares about his possible return. I'm definitely not planning to spend eternity with him, even though he threatened me with that during our last awful year. I was a fool to stay with him, but I thought I had to do it for my kids' sake. Now my kids are gone, and he is dead, and he had better stay in his grave forever and all by himself.

Even if I have to work like a horse for the rest of my life, I do not want to be buried right next to him. If he had stopped drinking when the doctors told him, I might consider it, but he drank until his very last day, and I'm sure that the grave reeks with the smell of that horrible cheap wine he used to drink. I think the worms must really like all that liquor in his body; there always seem to be so many more worms on that grave than on all the surrounding ones combined. I have to save enough money to buy another plot. My kids don't care, but they are still young; once they reach my age, they'll also start thinking about afterlife. It's not that I'm religious, but I do want to have certain eternal comforts.

Once I have all the money I need, I'll quit my job. Even though I've started liking it, and the tips are really great. People have to pay five schillings to go potty, but they are so ecstatic because of this ugly house, they often leave much more money. They like it when I tell them about all the people who have used the can before them, and they are honored because they have been sitting on the same toilet seat as some princess. Those are the easy stories, for the foreigners. For the Viennese I have to come up with something else. That's business.

Since I grew up in Vienna, it isn't all that difficult to come up with a different story for each customer. I know what's going on without having to read the newspapers. Ever since the Nazis I don't trust them anyway. I never believed a word that was written then, and after the war I never got back into the habit of reading them, even though I like to leaf through them while sitting in a café.

But I am not like this friend of mine, who sits in the same cafés day in day out, devouring all the papers. He only stops reading when I come to talk to him, or when we have our card games going. He has even given up going on vacations because he can't be any place where there are no cafés. He only comes along when we go to Budapest or Prague, because there the cafés are just like the ones here in Vienna, but he refuses to go to Munich or Zurich.

Foreigners always complain to me because the coffee in the cafés is too expensive. To the ones I don't like, I don't say anything, but to the ones who look like they might understand, I say that coffee is only expensive if they drink it and leave the place. But if they stay for several hours, talk with their friends, read newspapers, and relax, the coffee is dirt cheap.

I know it's odd for someone working in a public toilet to have an estranged relationship to newspapers. After all, most of us— I'm speaking of the older generation—have fond memories of those days when we used to wipe our asses with various assortments of newspapers, often reading them again before they were used and thrown away. But I do like things in print. Books, for example. I've read Freud twice. The first time was when I was quite young and had just started working. I had this bureaucratic job then. I couldn't face looking into all these files piled up on my desk, and I decided to take Freud to the office instead. I had a great time, but in the end, I lost my job because of Freud. I've never regretted it, though. My boss got too many complaints about files which hadn't been dealt with, and unfortunately they were all found on my desk.

I was a bit dumbfounded; after all, I was working in the city agency dealing with graveyards, and I had never imagined that the dead would come back to complain about their files. According to Freud, I was denying the obvious. In Vienna, that means denying the fact that the dead are more important than the living. My niece says that we practice ancestor worship like in China, but I don't think she knows anything about the Chinese. I know that we only take people seriously once they are under the earth and can't interfere with our daily business. We praise people who are long gone, such as Mozart or the Kaiser, and many of my women friends do the same with their dead husbands.

I'm talking too much about psychology, and that's not fashionable in this city. We are happy and grouchy in our ways, and nobody wants to let his or her soul take a look in a mirror. We claim that there are other things that need to be dealt with and that they are more important than our psyches. Currently we are all talking about protecting the environment. Somehow my job seems to be connected to all this. People who use public toilets want to get rid of all kinds of shit. Not just shit in the true sense of the word. After cleaning out their bowels, they want to clean out their pockets and bags. And they think that they can leave it all with me.

I had this big garbage container, and often it was filled to the rim by late morning. In a city that is proud because it is so umweltfreundlich, environment-friendly, I had to ask the city to bring in different containers. One for paper, one for glass, one for aluminum cans, one for metal and one for yoghurt cups. I didn't understand why they hadn't put containers in the toilets, since they were already on every street corner.

My generation never had problems sorting out garbage. There wasn't that much garbage when I was a kid, and during the war we had to separate everything; then we even had compost heaps. Some people take it a bit too far; they can never part with anything and their apartments turn into private dump sites. Maybe all people are born with an environmental reflex, and they only lose it because they are not trained to keep it?

Some customers think that garbage stinks. They are usually the same who don't want to wipe their asses because they are afraid that their hands might get dirty. There are always people who refuse to accept new rules. And after having used the toilet, people often behave strangely. Some are happy and they don't want to hear anything which might put them into a foul mood. Others are melancholy and think that this was their last shit. I have to find the right tone to keep the happy ones content, and to make the sad ones smile. I have to instill hope. At the end of this century many people, including me, are worried about nature, and I have to make them believe that together we'll be able to change things.

I often argue with my old friends from the socialist party. They believe what's written on the billboards: "Wien ist anders, Vienna is different." I try to tell them that every city in the world stinks. Not only because of my current job. It's just that some stink better than others.

"But think about our culture. It's unique," they say.

"What's unique about it?" I ask.

"The opera. Theaters. Music everywhere."

"It's all the culture of the dead. They perform music composed by someone who's dead. Most of the plays were written by people who are now dead, and while they lived nobody cared much for them. Vienna is just a big museum. Who cares about museums? Who would notice if they disappeared? And it's easy to replace a museum."

"But how are you going to replace everything typically Viennese?" they ask with shrill voices, close to a breakdown.

"I won't," I reply dryly. "Nature will take care of it." After many years of political activities and being convinced of this or that, I've ended up believing in nature. I still like politics, but political parties and politicians are no longer my cup of tea. Those who get somewhere in politics are only the little Waldheims.

The foreigners who come to piss want to know the truth about Waldheim.

I always tell them: "There is no such thing as a truth about Waldheim. The man is just a lie."

Then they laugh.

But the Viennese don't want to discuss him. Now everyone claims that they didn't vote for any of the candidates, and I'm left wondering how Waldheim got his majority. But then, it was the same with Hitler; nobody had voted for him. . .

The Viennese just can't face the fact that they have made mistakes. But then when it comes to defending or explaining themselves, they are too lazy to do it. Maybe that's what's so unique about this city—as soon as people are at home here, they lose their ambitions. They spend their days in cafés, waiting for the time to go by and hoping that their funerals will be a success. What a contrast to other cities where people are excited and hectic. A true Viennese doesn't want to be moved. Needless to say, a true Viennese ends up sitting twice as long on the john as anyone else. Well, there are no official statistics to prove this, but I've made my own observations over the years.

My friends tell me that my profession is dying out. To a certain degree they are right. But then everything in this museum is dying out, including its people. More than half of the population is over fifty. I'm not sure if they'll be able to replace us old ones fast enough. Someone much younger should be working in that toilet; after all, it's a new building. But the modern market needs us old people to give a certain respectability to these new things. I know that I'll die one day, but will my job die with me? Maybe I'll get an honorary grave on Zentralfriedhof, the main cemetery, and many tourists will come and visit my gravesite. And then they'll have to open a public toilet there, and they'll have to hire a woman like me to take care of it.

# About the Editor

Ines Rieder was born in Vienna in 1954. She has studied political science, anthropology, and social work, and works as a freelance writer and translator. Active in the international women's movement since the 1970s, she has worked with the Oakland-based People's Translation Service, publisher of *Newsfront International*. She was a member of the collective which produced *Second Class, Working Class*, an international feminist reader, and was one of the founders of *Connexions*, an international women's quarterly. Truly an international woman, Ines Rieder divides her time between Vienna, São Paulo and Oakland, California. She is best known for *AIDS: The Women* (Cleis Press), the award-winning collection of experiences of women whose lives have been touched by AIDS.

# Books from Cleis Press

*Cosmopolis: Urban Stories by Women* edited by Ines Rieder. ISBN: 0-939416-36-0 24.95 cloth; ISBN: 0-939416-37-9 9.95 paper.

*Beyond the Border: A New Age in Latin American Women's Fiction* edited by Nora Erro-Peralta and Caridad Silva-Núñez. ISBN: 0-939416-42-5 24.95 cloth; ISBN: 0-939416-43-3 10.95 paper.

*Night Train To Mother* by Ronit Lentin. ISBN: 0-939416-29-8 24.95 cloth; ISBN: 0-939416-28-X 9.95 paper.

*Women and Honor: Some Notes on Lying* by Adrienne Rich. ISBN: 0-939416-44-1 3.95 paper.

*With a Fly's Eye, Whale's Wit and Woman's Heart: Relationships Between Animals and Women* edited by Theresa Corrigan and Stephanie T. Hoppe. ISBN: 0-939416-24-7 24.95 cloth; ISBN: 0-939416-25-5 9.95 paper.

*And a Deer's Ear, Eagle's Song and Bear's Grace: Relationships Between Animals and Women* edited by Theresa Corrigan and Stephanie T. Hoppe. ISBN: 0-939416-38-7 24.95 cloth; ISBN: 0-939416-39-5 9.95 paper.

*Peggy Deery: An Irish Family at War* by Nell McCafferty. ISBN: 0-939416-38-7 24.95 cloth; ISBN: 0-939416-39-5 9.95 paper.

*You Can't Drown the Fire: Latin American Women Writing in Exile* edited by Alicia Partnoy. ISBN: 0-939416-16-6 24.95 cloth; ISBN: 0-939416-17-4 9.95 paper.

*The Little School: Tales of Disappearance and Survival in Argentina* by Alicia Partnoy. ISBN: 0-939416-08-5 21.95 cloth; ISBN: 0-939416-07-7 8.95 paper.

*The One You Call Sister: New Women's Fiction* edited by Paula Martinac. ISBN: 0-939416-30-1 24.95 cloth; ISBN: 0-939416031-X 9.95 paper.

*Unholy Alliances: New Women's Fiction* edited by Louise Rafkin. ISBN: 0-939416-14-X 21.95 cloth; ISBN: 0-939416-15-8 9.95 paper.

*AIDS: The Women* edited by Ines Rieder and Patricia Ruppelt. ISBN: 0-939416-20-4 24.95 cloth; ISBN: 0-939416-21-2 9.95 paper

*Sex Work: Writings by Women in the Sex Industry* edited by Frédérique Delacoste and Priscilla Alexander. ISBN: 0-939416-10-7 24.95 cloth; ISBN: 0-939416-11-5 10.95 paper.

*Susie Sexpert's Lesbian Sex World* by Susie Bright. ISBN: 0-939416-34-4 21.95 cloth; ISBN: 0-939416-35-2 9.95 paper.

*A Lesbian Love Advisor* by Celeste West. ISBN: 0-939416-27-1 24.95 cloth; ISBN: 0-939416-26-3 9.95 paper.

*Long Way Home: The Odyssey of a Lesbian Mother and Her Children* by Jeanne Jullion. ISBN: 0-939416-05-0 8.95 paper.

*Different Daughters: A Book by Mothers of Lesbians* edited by Louise Rafkin. ISBN: 0-939416-12-3 21.95 cloth; ISBN: 0-939416-13-1 8.95 paper.

*Different Mothers: Sons & Daughters of Lesbians Talk About Their Lives* edited by Louise Rafkin. ISBN: 0-939416-40-9 24.95 cloth; ISBN: 0-939416-41-7 9.95 paper.

*The Shape of Red: Insider/Outsider Reflections* by Ruth Hubbard and Margaret Randall. ISBN: 0-939416-19-0 24.95 cloth; ISBN: 0-939416-18-2 9.95 paper.

*Voices in the Night: Women Speaking About Incest* edited by Toni A.H. McNaron and Yarrow Morgan. ISBN: 0-939416-02-6 9.95 paper.

*Don't: A Woman's Word* by Elly Danica. ISBN: 0-939416-23-9 21.95 cloth; ISBN: 0-939416-22-0 8.95 paper

*With the Power of Each Breath: A Disabled Women's Anthology* edited by Susan Browne, Debra Connors and Nanci Stern. ISBN: 0-939416-09-3 24.95 cloth; ISBN: 0-939416-06-9 10.95 paper.

*Woman-Centered Pregnancy and Birth* by the Federation of Feminist Women's Health Centers. ISBN: 0-939416-03-4 11.95 paper.

*Fight Back! Feminist Resistance to Male Violence* edited by Frédérique Delacoste and Felice Newman. ISBN: 0-939416-01-8 13.95 paper.

*The Absence of the Dead Is Their Way of Appearing* by Mary Winfrey Trautmann. ISBN: 0-939416-04-2 8.95 paper.

*On Women Artists: Poems 1975-1980* by Alexandra Grilikhes. ISBN: 0-939416-00-X 4.95 paper.

Since 1980, Cleis Press has published progressive books by women. We welcome your order and will ship your books as quickly as possible. Order from: Cleis Press, PO Box 8933, Pittsburgh PA 15221. Individual orders must be prepaid. Please add 15% shipping. PA residents add sales tax. MasterCard and Visa orders welcome; $25 minimum—include account number, exp. date, and signature. Payment in US dollars only.